DAMNATION ROAD

MAX McCOY

PINNACLE BOOKS
Kensington Publishing Corp.
www.kensingtonbooks.com

PINNACLE BOOKS are published by

Kensington Publishing Corp.
119 West 40th Street
New York, NY 10018

All Kensington titles, imprints, and distributed lines are available at special quantity discounts for bulk purchases for sales promotions, premiums, fund-raising, educational, or institutional use. Special book excerpts or customized printings can also be created to fit specific needs. For details, write or phone the office of the Kensington special sales manager: Kensington Publishing Corp., 119 West 40th Street, New York, NY 10018, attn: Special Sales Department; phone 1-800-221-2647.

ISBN-13: 978-0-7860-2121-5
ISBN-10: 0-7860-2121-7

First printing: September 2010

10 9 8 7 6 5 4 3 2 1

Printed in the United States of America

For Karl Gregory

But you know yourself an outlaw, stubborn,
vengeful, just, Bill Doolin cornered, a Dalton
cut to pieces, a Younger hell-bent for home.

—Kim Horner, "Regression"

1898

ONE

Jacob Gamble limped into Farquharson and Morris Hardware, favoring his right leg, glancing behind him at dust-blown Oklahoma Avenue. His right boot was filled with blood and the red stuff oozed from the seams with every other step, leaving a sinuous trail on the freshly polished oak floor.

"Show you something?"

The clerk was a boy of seventeen and until a few moments before had been enthralled by a ruddy account in the *Police Gazette* of a Chicago meatpacker who had tired of his wife and disposed of her body in one of the sausage vats. The cover of the *Gazette* was a full-page illustration of three swarthy Spanish agents searching a disrobed and comely young American woman in her berth on a steamer in Havana Harbor.

"Cartridges."

Gamble slapped a revolver on the top of the display case so hard the boy was afraid the glass would crack. It was an old gun with a brass frame, an open top, and an octagonal barrel. It was filthy with residue and the rotten egg stench of recently discharged black powder radiated from the gun.

The boy whistled as he tossed the *Gazette* aside. "Navy Colt."

The gun wasn't a Colt, it was an old cap-and-ball Manhattan converted to .38-caliber rimfire cartridges, and the boy hadn't even noticed that the loading gate and ejector rod had been placed opposite normal, making it a *left-handed* gun, but Gamble didn't have the will to correct him. Gamble was light-headed, there were splotches of white crowding his vision, and his legs were weak. He gripped the display case with his dirty hands to keep himself upright.

"Carry this at Gettysburg, Granddad?" the boy asked as he picked up the Manhattan. "Damn, it's warm. You been target practicing?"

Gamble clenched his jaw and concentrated on forcing the whiteness back.

"You all right, mister? You look a might peaked."

"Cartridges," Gamble managed. "Thirty-eight rimfire."

"Don't got 'em," the boy said, rummaging among the boxes of ammo on the shelf behind the counter. "Had a box or two, a few months ago, maybe longer. Sold 'em. Have a couple of boxes of .38 Colt center fire—that's what most conversions use nowadays. Got plenty of 38-40 Winchester. Everybody wants to shoot the same round in their rifles as their pistols."

"I'm not everybody," Gamble said. He took a couple of deep breaths and concentrated on forcing the whiteness back to the edges of his vision. "Show me something new."

"Absolutely," the boy said. "Probably time you replaced that ancient iron with something modern, if you ask me. Forty-five is the most popular caliber."

Leaning over the display case, Gamble caught the ghost of his reflection: a jaw bristling with salt-and-pepper whiskers, a shock of long hair turning gray at the temples, a black leather patch over his right eye. His black coat was powdered with road dust and smeared at the elbows and cuffs with red clay.

"For my money, the best handgun is the .44 Russian," the boy continued. "Top break, fast loading. Accuracy and power combined. A real manstopper."

"What do you know about stopping a man, son?" Gamble took a deep breath, then exhaled slowly. "The Russian is what Bob Ford used to shoot Jesse James in the back of the head while Jesse stood on a chair dusting a picture. I'm predisposed against it."

Gamble glanced over the row of Peacemakers, a couple of Bisleys, a variety of Smith & Wessons—including a Russian—a half a dozen other brand names, many trash guns, and a vest pocket pistol of uncertain manufacture. Damn, he needed something . . . *bigger*. He glanced up at the rack of long guns, mostly lever-action rifles and shotgun doubles, Winchesters and Marlins and Stevens.

"Hand me that Winchester."

Gamble turned to glance through the front window to the street, and when he turned back the boy was holding out a heavy shotgun with a single barrel. Gamble was about to say he meant the lever-action carbine instead, but the big shotgun reminded him of a shoulder-mounted canon.

"Model 97," the boy said. "Twelve gauge. Only been for sale a few months. Improvement over the slide gun of a few years back. Smokeless. Shoots the new Nitro shells."

The gun was heavy. The boy said it was eight pounds and some change. Gamble put his right hand on the ribbed forestock and studied the tubular magazine slung beneath the barrel.

"Where's the lever?"

"You ain't seen one of these before, have you?" the boy asked smugly. "There's no lever. It's a slide action. You just pump it back and then forward again, and it puts a new shell in the chamber and you're still on target. Be careful, though, because if you hold down the trigger when you drive a shell home, it's going to fire."

"Dandy."

"You can stuff five rounds in the magazine, through the slot beneath the receiver, and keep one in the chamber. So, she's good for six shots, as fast as you can work that pump."

Gamble found the release and pulled back the pump, which set the action into motion. The slide shot backward out of the top of the receiver, cocking the exposed hammer and grazing the top of his thumb. Then he drove the pump home, and the bolt. Together, the actions produced a metallic *ch-chink!* that presaged mayhem.

"Helluva sound," Gamble said.

"Imagine hearing that in a dark alley. I'd fill my pants."

"I'm sure you would." Gamble was sighting down the barrel, lining up the grooves on the top of the receiver that served as the rear sight with the bead at the far end of the thirty-inch barrel.

"What d'ya think?"

"It will do."

"Knew you had a good eye." If the boy realized he'd made a bad joke, he didn't show it.

"A box of shells."

"What size shot?"

"Double buck."

The clerk took a carton of Robin Hood Smokeless Powder Company shotgun shells from a shelf behind him and slid them across the top of the display case.

"What else?"

"Ammonia."

While the boy went to retrieve the bottle from the shelf of cleaning supplies, Gamble ripped the top from one of the boxes. The shells weren't all brass, like Gamble was used to seeing, but had only a half-inch ring of brass at the base, with the rest being paper that was slick with wax.

"I'll be damned," Gamble said.

"Can't shoot the Nitros in the old guns," the boy said, placing the bottle on the top of the display case. "They're so hot they'll blow the bolt right back in your face. That's why they make 'em red, I guess."

Gamble shoved the shell into the bottom of the shotgun's receiver.

"You'll have to wait to do that," the boy said, and all the while Gamble was stuffing more shells into the gun. "There's a law about carrying loaded guns in the city limits. Just wait and I'll write up your ticket and we'll settle up."

Gamble worked the pump, producing that bone-chilling sound again, then pushed one last shell into the bottom of the receiver.

"You want to live?"

The boy nodded.

"Then we *are* settled up."

Gamble cradled the shotgun in the crook of his right arm and used his left hand to scoop up more of the bright red shells and shove them into the pockets of his dusty black coat.

"Jesus, mister," the clerk said.

"Jesus has nothing to do with it," Gamble said.

The whiteness came in on him hard just then, and he closed his eyes. His legs were numb and he felt himself sinking toward the floor. Then he heard shouting outside, and he pulled himself upright, and roughly uncorked the brown bottle. He pulled the bandanna from his neck, sprinkled some ammonia over it, then brought it toward his nose. The fumes seared his nostrils and brought the world back, fast and hard.

"You'd better get down, because it's going to be raining lead in about thirty seconds," Gamble said.

"You the law?"

"Not by a damned sight."

"Then you're . . ."

"An outlaw."

"A wicked man," the boy said, grinning.

Some would say that, Gamble thought.

"How many men have you killed?"

TWO

Gamble hadn't kept count of how many men he had killed. But they all had it coming, he reckoned, one way or another. Among the last was an opium peddler by the name of Lester Burns in Sumner County, Kansas. The killing had earned Gamble a price on his head from the district court there, and he'd been dogged from the state line by a quartet of bounty-hunting German cousins. For six weeks, they had chased him south along Hell's Fringe—the jagged border between the Indian nations and Oklahoma Territory—in an episodic gun battle that zigzagged across the winter landscape.

Along Cottonwood Creek, in Logan County, Oklahoma Territory, within sight of the wooden Santa Fe trestle, they had shot Gamble's chestnut mare out from under him. The rifle slug had struck the horse behind the shoulder and the horse had fallen hard, unable to roll back up. Gamble had extricated himself from saddle and stirrups—losing a spur in the process—and after seeing the bloody froth spewing from the animal's muzzle, had drawn the Manhattan, pressed the barrel between her eyes, and fired.

Then he had sought refuge in a cornfield that was hard against the creek, but the cousins methodically rode down the stalks and drove him out the far side. Gamble had burst from the field and made for the creek, ducking a fusillade from the murderous cousins.

The Santa Fe railway ran along the creek, and he dashed over the tracks and then jumped over the edge of the creek bank and tumbled down the red clay bank. As he scrambled for the cover of the trunk of a fallen walnut tree, he shot blind twice behind him. This was answered with a shot that passed through his right thigh and continued on to skip across the surface of the creek beyond. Gamble scarcely felt it, thinking the bullet had simply puckered the fabric of his trousers. He attempted to vault over the trunk, but caught his remaining spur on a dead branch and hung for a moment, suspended like a target in a shooting gallery, half his body exposed. Another shot zinged past, then another thudded dully on the opposite side of the trunk. Then the strap on the spur broke and Gamble fell to the moist clay. He spun around and pressed his back against the walnut trunk, the Manhattan held tightly in his left hand, trying to think of a next move that wouldn't result in the cousins shooting him to death where he lay.

"Hey, Dutch!" Gamble shouted.

There was no answer, but he could hear the cousins up on top of the bank, speaking softly to each other in German, trying no doubt to find some path down the bank that wouldn't expose them to fire.

"What do you want?" This, with a touch of an accent.

"To talk."

"We are talking. Have you many *blaue bohnen* left?"

"Speak English!"

"Bullets," the man said. "These are called blue beans in German, because they look like little lead beans stuffed into the wheel of your gun, no?"

"Only if you're looking down the wrong end."

"You must be running low on these deadly beans," Jaeger said. "We have traded shots many times since leaving Kansas, and there are four of us and only one of you."

"Odds sound about right."

"You are a fool, Jakob Gamble."

"What say we avoid the bloodletting and come up with an arrangement that will satisfy everybody?"

There was dark laughter from above.

"And what would such an arrangement be, Herr Gamble?"

"You could let me go."

"Why should we do that?"

"Because if you do, I'll tell you where there's a fortune in buried gold. It's one helluva lot more money than whatever reward is being offered for my hide. And if you kill me, you'll never find it."

There was a long pause. Gamble flicked open the loading gate of the Manhattan and turned the cylinder—he had only three rounds left.

"You're lying."

"Maybe, Dutch—there are nine chances out of ten that I am making up a whopper just to save my skin. But are you willing to throw away the not inconsiderable chance that I'm telling the truth? Think about what you could do with a strongbox filled with gold. And here's the beauty part—it costs you nothing to find out, except to hold off on killing me."

There was more whispering in German, then things fell silent.

Gamble listened to the sound of the creek and the breeze in the branches of a willow tree hanging low over the water a few yards downstream. Then he became aware of a pain in his right leg, and he looked down to discover blood dripping to the ground from where the bullet had passed through his thigh.

"Well?" Gamble called. "I don't got all day."

"We are going to kill you."

"Now, Dutch, that ain't right."

"The reward will be paid, dead or alive."

"Yeah, but you only get half if you bring me in dead," Gamble called. "Why don't you take me alive and double your money?"

"It's easier for us if you are dead—at least you won't be talking."

"But the gold, Dutch. Think of the gold."

"Stop lying. If you had that kind of treasure, you wouldn't be living a scarecrow life."

"A scarecrow life? That's mean, Dutch."

"Don't call me that. It is not my name."

"Well, Dutch, that's just too goddamned bad. It's the West, and every German is nicknamed Dutch, whether you like it or not."

Gamble was eyeing the thirty yards of red creek bank that separated him and the cousins. They would have to cross it, because the creek was not frozen over and was too broad for them to try to cross and come at him from that way, but even if he made every shot count—which was in itself so unlikely as to constitute a miracle—he would have three dead bounty hunters and a fourth one still very much alive, well armed, and filled with revenge.

Then Gamble heard sand shift and pebbles skitter down the bank, and he knew the cousins had crossed the railway tracks and were coming down the bank together, guns at the ready. Gamble pressed his shoulder against the trunk, rocking the fallen tree, and the cousins reflexively let go with a volley, splinters flying from the top of the trunk.

Gamble cursed floridly.

Then he heard the familiar rumble of a locomotive. He dared a look above the trunk and saw a Santa Fe stock train clamoring across the bridge a half-mile upstream. He also saw that the cousins had reached the bottom of the creek bank. Then he glanced behind him, and saw a cut in the bank where a flood had stacked some barrel-sized boulders near the water.

He stood, cocked the revolver, took careful aim at the fattest of the cousins, and squeezed the trigger. The bullet took the cousin in the chest and he went down heavy on his back, his arms outflung.

Then Gamble ran limping for the cut, with bullets ripping the air around him and the blood pumping in his ears. He fired once behind him as he ran, then dove for the cover of the boulder pile.

The train was getting closer—and picking up speed.

Gamble clawed his way up the cut, climbing over

rocks and roots, trying to reach the top ahead of the locomotive before the cousins came close enough for a clean shot. If he was tardy, then he would be trapped between the train and the bounty hunters, instead of trapping them on the creek side.

Near the top, he felt the strength fade in his right leg, replaced not by pain but by a peculiar numb feeling. His pant leg was bright with blood. Then a bullet splattered in the clay beside him, and this spurred him over the top. He stumbled up onto the railway bed, tripped, and landed on his knees between the rails—and in the path of the rushing Santa Fe locomotive. He could count every bolt on the front of the frying pan-colored boiler, see the glow beneath the belly of the locomotive from the fire grate, feel the ground tremble as the locomotive bore down.

The brass whistle atop the locomotive shrieked.

Gamble flung himself over the other rail to safety only a second before the wheels of the locomotive would have sliced him into oblivion. He lay on his back for a moment, gulping air, the Manhattan still in his left hand. He laughed and threw his hat in the air. When he lifted his head, the engineer was leaning out of the cab, looking back at him, and Gamble gave him a wave to show he was all right.

The engineer pulled off his glove and returned the universal salute of displeasure. Then he ducked back into the cab and pushed the throttle forward, and the locomotive belched smoke and fire from the stack as the train struggled to pick up speed.

Gamble laughed.

Then he looked the other way and could see the

end of the train approaching. It consisted of only twenty or so cars, probably moving local stock, and there was no caboose.

Gamble rolled over, stuffed the gun in his pocket, and got to his feet. He picked up his hat from the ground and jammed it on his head. Through the gaps between the trucks as the train rushed past, he could see the three cousins stooped down, guns in hand, searching.

Gamble limped toward the moving cars. Between the slats of the stock cars, he could see frightened cow eyes and matted hair and filthy hide. The stench from the cattle hit him like a wave, and the scrape and screech of iron was deafening. He knew the cousins were shooting at him from beneath the train, because he could see the bullets sparking on the ballast and rails, but he couldn't hear the shots.

The train picked up more speed.

Gamble broke into an uneven run and lunged for the grab iron on the corner of the next to last stock car. His hand closed around the rust-stained metal and it felt like his arm was going to come out of its socket as he was jerked off his feet. His boots skittered along the stones and ties for a moment. He got his other hand around a grab iron and he pulled himself up, then planted his left foot on the iron rung.

Gamble hooked an arm through the grab iron and looked behind to see two of the cousins standing on the tracks, watching the freight as it receded.

Where was the third?

Gamble rested his forehead against the rough wood of the stock car. He was too tired to curse. He forced himself to climb, hand over hand, the grab rails to the top of the cattle car, then pull himself up to the roof. He sat down on the flat portion that ran along the peak of the roof, facing the back of the train. He took the Manhattan out of his pocket, checked the cylinder to make sure that the last round would be under the hammer when the gun was cocked, and took a deep breath, trying to clear his mind of the pain that was beginning to telegraph up his right leg.

Soon, he saw a hand reach up to the roof of the last car, followed by a blond head. It was the youngest cousin, the athletic one, and he was trying to keep hold of the stock car with one hand while wielding a revolver in the other. He looked forward, squinting against the wind and smoke, and saw Gamble sitting forty feet away, holding his gun in both hands, taking aim. Just as the German ducked, the Manhattan barked, and the slug hit him in the upper right arm. His gun flew out of his hand as he was knocked spinning off the stock car, and he landed in a rolling heap in the reedy grass alongside the tracks.

Ten minutes later, the train slowed. A white sign with black letters slid past, proclaiming GUTHRIE. Approaching the depot, the locomotive switched to a siding to wait for a northbound express to pass.

Gamble climbed down the corner of the stock car and eased himself to the ground, then made his way toward town through the shacks that dotted the edge of the rail yard. Some of the shacks offered popskull liquor, others housed cribs where the unluckiest of whores plied their trade. A prostitute leaning in the doorway of one of the rough-hewn establishments watched through morphine-clouded eyes as Gamble limped past.

"Lover," she said. "You look worse than I do."

He touched the brim of his battered hat and kept walking, the sole of his right boot scraping the ground. Not far beyond the shanty town he found Oklahoma Avenue, a broad street paved with bricks that ran uphill to the center of town. Each side of the street was thick with lampposts and utility poles carrying a confusing array of wires. The buildings were all new or nearly so—Guthrie, the capital of Oklahoma Territory, had sprung from nothing only eight years before, during the land run of 1889. The architecture ranged from Victorian to Greek Revival to Byzantine, and the street corners had stone steps that led to an underground level of warehouses and stables.

It was a Friday morning and the street was thick with pedestrians and wagons and carriages. The people he met glanced away as soon as their eyes met, and if they were alarmed or concerned about the blood flowing from the wound in his right leg, they said nothing.

Gamble knew the cousins would be close behind, and his eyes scanned the storefronts for a hardware store. He was badly in need of—what was the expression that Dutch had used?—*blue beans*. On the northeastern corner of Oklahoma and Second Avenue, he found Farquharson and Morris Hardware.

THREE

"Never mind about how many times I've killed," Gamble said, the shotgun draped over the crook of his right arm. "I'll save answering for my sins to a somewhat higher inquisitor, which might take place directly."

"Want to pray?" the boy asked.

Gamble shook his head.

"I'm a good Methodist," the boy said. "I find it helps, sometimes."

"I'll bet you are and I bet it does," Gamble said, then laughed. "But asking God to help me kill? No thanks. I won't add hypocrite to my list of sins."

Gamble took another whiff from the ammonia-laden bandanna, then flung it down as he walked away, his boots making an unsteady rhythm on the floor planks. He kicked open the screen door and strode out into the street.

Thirty or so citizens were on the street, their hats and bonnets pulled low over their faces, tending their business.

"Clear out!" Gamble shouted.

The crowd paid him little note.

Gamble pointed the shotgun skyward and pulled the trigger. The gun was louder than he expected and the report echoed sharply from the storefronts. The bystanders, frozen in their steps, stared at the thin one-eyed man in the black coat holding a new shotgun.

"Run!" Gamble shouted as he pumped a fresh shell into the chamber. "Find cover, or trouble will find you."

The citizenry scrambled away, leaving three men standing in the middle of the hard-packed street, thirty yards away from Gamble. Each held a weapon. All of them were blond. The youngest of them had his right arm in a linen sling draped around his neck. Their horses were hitched at the mercantile across the street.

"There he is!" the tallest of them called, swinging his pistol around.

Gamble shouldered the shotgun and pulled the trigger. The gun boomed and the stock bucked reassuringly against his left shoulder.

The buckshot struck the tall man on the right side of his chest and spun him around, making his legs cross at an unnatural angle. The gun remained in his right hand, unfired.

Gamble jerked the slide back and the spent shell was kicked spinning out of the top of the receiver, and he kept the trigger held tight as he threw the pump forward. The barrel, which had drifted upward, now settled back on target. The gun spoke again the moment the action locked, and this time the buckshot snapped the tall man's wrist and the gun fell barrel-down in the street. The hammer fell and the gun discharged, bursting the sand-clogged barrel in a puff of white smoke and sending shards of metal singing through the air.

The tall man was now on the ground, bloody and unmoving.

Jaeger, who was nearest the dead man, laughed. Then he touched a bloody spot on his cheek where a sliver of the ruined revolver barrel had embedded itself.

"*Hurensohn*," Jaeger said, looking at his bloody fingertips.

Held loosely in his other hand was a strange-looking gun. At first Gamble thought it was a Bisley, but the cylinder was too big and the hammer had a curious flowing S-shape.

The cousin with his arm in a sling was walking forward, a Colt in his left hand. He stepped over the body of the dead man without taking his eyes off Gamble.

"Two shots," he said. "His shotgun is empty, no?"

Gamble pumped another round into the chamber and put the front bead on the chest of the man who had laughed. He was the oldest of the cousins, he was more heavily muscled, and his hard eyes told Gamble that he was in charge.

"I'm not so sure, Fritz," Jaeger said. He held his revolver loosely at his side. "It is a new type of gun, I think. Like the lever-action Winchester shotgun of a few years ago, but with an improved action."

"I should kill him now?"

"You level that peashooter at me and I'll excavate

a hole in Dutch's chest where his heart should be," Gamble said.

Fritz thumbed the hammer back on the Colt, but Jaeger raised the hand with the bloodstained fingertips.

"Wait, Fritz."

"Good thinking, Dutch."

"Don't call me Dutch. My name is Max Jaeger and I have a writ to deliver you to the district court at Wichita to stand trial for the murder of Lester Burns."

"What about poor Werther?" Fritz asked. "And Adolphus, lying dead on the creek bank? This bastard has murdered two of us, and you want him to live?"

Jaeger spoke to him sternly in German.

"We are not in the wilderness now," Jaeger said. "There are witnesses. We will return Jakob Gamble to Kansas, and we will collect the full reward, and he will hang there. Dead is dead, no?"

Gamble let the barrel of the shotgun drop a bit.

"Why are you doing this? There can't be much in this for you. What does the court pay for the serving of a warrant? Two dollars? A few cents a mile in travel? Seems you have already paid pretty dear, in chasing me to hell and back and losing your relation."

Jaeger smiled.

"Is that what you think? That we are working for *pfennigs*?"

He pulled a paper from his coat pocket.

"There is a reward offered by the governor of Kansas, John Leedy. It guarantees five hundred and fifty dollars in cash for your capture and return to

Kansas to stand trial for the murder of one Lester Burns."

"The bastard deserved it."

"The bastard was Leedy's brother-in-law," Jaeger said.

"I think we should kill him now," Fritz said. "Then we cut off his head and take it to Wichita"— the word came out as *Vichita*—"and leave the rest of him to rot here in the territory."

"Five hundred fifty?" Gamble asked.

"Yes."

"That's all?"

"That's it."

"I thought it would be more."

"You've robbed no banks or trains."

"I have a rule against that."

"You fear the Pinkertons."

"Who doesn't?"

"I admire them," Jaeger said. "I would like to one day be a Pinkerton operative. I believe I have what is called the necessary qualification."

"You never sleep?"

"I am a *hurensohn*," Jaeger said. "A ruthless sonuvabitch."

"I believe you," Gamble said from behind the shotgun barrel.

"What is all of this talking?" Fritz asked. "Let us kill him. With cousin Adolphus and brother Werther dead, the reward is split only two ways—that's two hundred and seventy-five dollars each."

"No, Fritz. With him dead, we split only one hundred thirty-seven dollars and fifty cents."

"But you said we were going to kill him at the creek—"

"It was a trick, Fritz," Jaeger said. "To intimidate him."

"You were *lying*?" Gamble fumed, jabbing the shotgun forward.

"This outrage, from the king of liars?" Jaeger asked.

"Let us kill him."

"Go ahead," Gamble said over the shotgun, which was still trained on Jaeger. "Maybe you'll get lucky—a head shot, perhaps. But even then, I think my reflex will be to pull this trigger and blow Dutch's heart and lungs through his back. Let's give it a whirl."

Jaeger sighed.

"Put your gun down, Fritz."

"Vot?"

"You heard me. Lower your gun. You want revenge because he shot you in the arm, but the truth is that you were careless. You and your idiot brother Werther have been worse than useless to me, and I am sorry now that I brought the both of you. If you do not lower your pistol, this man with the rather large shotgun will kill me."

"You do not grieve for poor Werther?"

"I grieve for Adolphus," Jaeger said. "He was the best of you all. I wish the criminal had killed you instead."

"Then to hell with you," Fritz said.

Jaeger lifted his strange pistol and fired. The bullet struck Fritz in the forehead and he fell dead next to Werther. Then Jaeger spread his arms and let the Colt dangle from his trigger finger.

"That was cold," Gamble said.

"It was necessary."

"Drop the iron."

Jaeger let the gun fall to the ground.

"What kind of gun is that?"

"German military issue. A Reichsrevolver."

Gamble lowered the shotgun, walked forward, and nudged the revolver with the toe of his boot.

"Nasty little thing."

"I think the design is quite bold."

"Shut up and put your hands behind your head."

Jaeger did. Then he smiled.

"You haven't killed me yet. You lack the necessary qualification."

"You think so?"

Gamble stepped forward and drove the walnut butt of the shotgun against the side of Jaeger's head. It made a hollow-sounding thump. Jaeger went down heavy.

Gamble put the butt of the shotgun on the ground and knelt, then went through Jaeger's pockets. He found a wad of paper money and coins and slipped these into his own vest pocket. Then he retrieved the Kansas warrant from a back pocket and studied it for a moment, and then the reward poster. It was a bad likeness. He tore both papers to shreds and threw the pieces into the air.

"I won't stand trial in Guthrie," Gamble told the unconscious man, "but you will, when you wake up, for killing your cousin Fritz. I'm sorry I won't be here to see you hang."

A crowd was beginning to cluster around Gamble and the two dead men. He noticed that the knuckle of his left thumb was barked and bleeding, from the slide shooting backward out of the receiver every time he chambered a round. Gamble stood up, cradling the shotgun in the crook of his left arm, and walked through the crowd back toward the hardware store. He tugged the brim of his battered black hat to every wide-eyed citizen he met. He could feel the whiteness creeping in again at the edge of his vision.

The boy was still behind the counter, and he raised his hands above his head when he saw Gamble approach.

"Put your paws down," Gamble said.

Gamble threw a twenty-dollar gold piece and a ten-dollar bill on the top of the glass display case.

"Now we're square."

A bell mounted on a curious wooden box on the wall behind the counter rang twice, the clapper vibrating like an alarm clock. It stopped for a moment, then rang twice again.

"What's that racket?"

"That's our number—twenty-two."

Gamble paused.

"It's a telephone," the clerk said. "You talk into it . . ."

"I know what the hell a telephone is. Just never seen one before."

"What do you want me to do?"

"Tend to it."

The clerk nodded. He picked up the ear set from

the side of the box. He listened for a moment, then nodded and turned to Gamble.

"It's for you."

"Of course it is."

Gamble was losing the feeling now in both legs. He slumped toward the floor, but found a wooden crate and sat down on it. He rested the butt of the shotgun on the floor between his feet and allowed his chin to fall to his chest.

"It's the marshal," the clerk said.

"Tell him to hold his water."

Gamble stared at the floor. Beside his right boot was a growing puddle of blood.

"That's going to make a helluva stain."

Then Gamble lifted his head and pulled a pipe from the pocket of his vest and carefully filled it with tobacco from a leather pouch. Then he struck a match on the side of the crate and brought the flame over the bowl and sucked the fire into the tobacco.

There was a stack of photo postcards next to the cash register on the counter. Gamble motioned for one, and the boy handed it over. The photo was of the outlaw Bill Doolin, dead as Hamlet's ghost, propped up on an undertaker's board, a couple of dozen buckshot wounds across his bare chest, his hair wild and his beard scruffy, his eyes open and one brow arched, as if in surprise. Gamble studied the intricately woven wicker board on which Doolin's punctured and emaciated frame lay.

"He was killed near Lawson in an ambush led by a federal marshal named Heck Thomas," the boy said. "They hauled his body to Guthrie and propped him up so that Dougherty the photographer could make the picture, then they planted him in Summit View Cemetery, east of town. Doolin's wife, Edith, had 'em printed up to sell for twenty-five cents each to pay for his funeral."

Gamble took a quarter dollar from his pocket and tossed it to the boy.

"There's a poem on the back."

Gamble tucked the postcard into his vest.

The boy surveyed the blood on the floor.

"Do you require a dressing?"

"Ask me later."

"There will be more shooting?"

"Almost certainly."

Gamble closed his eyes. He was tired.

There was squawking from the listening piece the clerk held.

"What should I tell the marshal?"

"Bid him good-bye," Gamble said.

The boy nodded and replaced the ear piece on its hook.

"You may do me one kindness," Gamble said. "Keep the old revolver for me. I will be back for it, if I am able. If not—well, it's yours."

The shotgun began to lean, and Gamble had to concentrate to correct the angle. The pipe hung limply from the corner of his mouth.

"Have you always been an outlaw?"

For nearly as long as he could remember, Gamble thought. He had carried the old Manhattan for a good part of the war. He was twelve years old when it first filled his hand, shortly after he saw his father dead at a Yankee prison in Missouri. At thirteen, he saw his mother dead at a guerrilla winter camp in

Texas—while giving birth to his bastard baby
brother. Twenty years later he held that brother's
hand while he died in Arizona Territory. And he had
watched his wife and newborn baby butchered by a
doctor near Kansas City.

"I blew that doctor's fucking head off."

"What?" the boy asked.

"Never mind," Gamble said. "What's your
name?"

"Andrew Farquharson," he said, pronouncing it
far-kwer-sun.

"So that's how you pronounce it," Gamble said.

"It's Scottish."

"Your father owns the store."

"Half of it, anyway. He's the mayor and he's pre-
siding over a city council meeting this morning."

"And his partner?"

"Granville Morris is away on business, at Kingfisher."

Gamble stared at the door of the hardware store.
He saw a skeletal figure standing in the doorway, a
figure with a crutch under one arm. He was dressed
in rags and was missing his right leg from the knee
down.

"That man in the doorway—"

"Nobody's there."

"Right there," Gamble said. "Don't you see him?"

"I'm sorry, there is no man."

Gamble shook his head.

"Andrew, I am bleeding to death. It has made me
unreliable."

"Shall I fetch Doc Smith?"

"No doctors," Gamble said. "Let me die without the added pain and humiliation of medical treatment."

The skeleton's crooked jaw was moving in phantom speech, the right arm was outstretched, and bone-white fingers beckoned.

Gamble looked away.

"He has come to lead me to the undiscovered country."

"Mexico?"

"Death, Andrew."

Gamble summoned a last bit of strength and took a shotgun shell from his coat pocket and tried to stuff it into the receiver of the Model 97. But his fingers were clumsy, as if he were wearing thick gloves, and the round fell from his grasp to the floor.

He watched as it rolled away.

Gamble could no longer move his arms or legs. His body felt as if it were being magnetically attracted to the floor. He slid from the crate, the pipe scattered dead embers and ashes, and the shotgun clattered on the oak.

The whiteness enveloped him.

FOUR

The territorial prison was a two-story, red limestone fortress on the northeast corner of Second and Noble, and the entrance was up a metal stairway that led to an iron cage on the second-story landing. But all Jacob Gamble could see, when the sound of boots on the iron rungs roused him, was the cold February sky. A rough blanket was tucked beneath his chin. He tried to move his hands, but discovered his wrists were bound at each side to the litter on which he was carried. His fingertips felt wicker.

"Stay still," the man beside him said.

"Am I dead?"

"The dead rarely speak," the man said.

"The undertaker's board."

"Borrowed. How else were we going to get you up these steps?"

The board tilted and now Gamble could see the face of the man who spoke. He had on a dark suit and wore wire-frame glasses and there was a cigar in the corner of his mouth.

"Who are you?"

"Smith," the man said. "Now, hush up. You lost a lot of blood. Get yourself all riled up and you're likely to undo all of my good work. The bullet passed cleanly through your leg, but it clipped a vessel on the way. I managed to tie it off, but not without some difficulty."

"I said no doctors."

"You said a great many things while you were lying on the table yesterday," Smith said. "You would be dead had anyone paid any mind. But I am curious—who is the man with the missing leg?"

"Long dead."

"Wraiths usually are. Oh, I could form quite a mental picture from your babbling. And I didn't ask what he was, I asked who. A family member, perhaps, or one of your victims. No elaboration? Ah, perhaps you will tell me later."

They had paused on the landing within the iron cage. Gamble could see flat iron bars above him. Then he heard the closing of the iron grate behind, the jangling of keys, the turning of a lock, and then the swinging of a door.

"What will happen to me?"

"You'll recover, after some weeks," Smith said. "Then you will stand trial. You might be extradited back to Kansas for the killing of Lester Burns, but it is more likely they will keep you here for the murders of the Jaeger cousins. You might hang. The authorities take a dim view of wild west shootouts on the peaceful and modern streets of the territorial capital."

"You could have saved them the trouble."

"What, let you die?" Smith asked. "Sorry, took an

oath against that. Also, it would have disappointed young Farquharson—he has inquired about your health so often and so regular that you could set a clock by him."

They passed into the jail, and the steel door slammed shut behind. They carried Gamble through an office area, where there was a desk and a couple of chairs, past a stairway that led to the basement kitchen, and to a grated door that led to the bullpen. The receiving area was separated from the bullpen and cells by iron bars that ran from the floor to the ceiling, and while a guard fumbled with a combination lock in a steel box near the door, forty barefoot men crowded forward and peered through the bars at the new arrival.

"Hello, Doc, who have you got there?" asked a wild-haired boy of twenty, jostling others out of the way to get a better look. "Is this him that killed the bounty hunters?"

"Never mind who he is," Smith said. "Just back up and leave him be."

"Oh, it is!" the boy exclaimed knowingly. "Mister Jacob Gamble, the fiddling outlaw, of whom you have read extensively in any of our English-language newspapers published here in Guthrie, wanted in Kansas for the killing of the brother-in-law of the populist governor, and for various other crimes and misdemeanors from Missouri to Arizona Territory. Did you bring your fiddle with you?"

"Forget the fiddle," another inmate said. "Does he have any tobacco?"

"He has neither violin nor tobacco," Smith said. "Now, watch your toes while the door swings open."

As the guards carried Gamble into the bullpen, the wild-haired boy padded alongside.

"Reckon you and I are the two most famous guests of this institution," he said with enthusiasm. "I'm Mickey Dray, and I'm sure you've heard of me, what with being the best horse thief in the territory. I was born out in the black jacks, and I can tell you I am one tough hombre, and they wouldn't have caught me at all if I hadn't slept too long one morning."

"Back away, Mickey," Smith said. "He's too weak to talk."

They took Gamble to a steel cage at the front of the bullpen, unbound him, lifted him onto the metal bunk. The guards left, but Smith remained, and pulled up a wooden stool. He took Gamble's wrist and checked his pulse, then pulled back the blanket and examined the leg wound.

"It's not so bad here," Smith said. "There is steam heat and the temperature is regulated at seventy-six degrees. There is a hot water bath in the basement, and dinner is boiled beef, beans, and cornbread. It is probably better fare than you are used to, judging from your overall state of health. You'll get the Methodists on Friday and the Salvation Army on Saturdays, if you are of a religious bent. Jailer Comley is a fair man and brooks no sadism from his employees, but will employ solitary confinement in a dark cell in the basement, when necessary, for hard cases. As jails go, it is not unpleasant."

"Still a jail," Gamble said weakly.

"Better to reign in hell than serve in heaven, eh?"

"Milton wasn't what I had in mind," Gamble said. "It has something more to do with freedom."

"You picked a peculiar occupation, then."

"I didn't pick it," Gamble said. "It picked me."

Smith smiled.

"Well, you have a rest from it," he said. "Take your ease. I'll be back to check on you every few days, to make sure you are mending."

"So as not to cheat the hangman," Gamble said.

The next afternoon, the horse thief came slinking over and sat down with his back against the bars of Gamble's cell.

"Fiddler," he said. "It's me, Mickey Dray."

"What?" Gamble asked tiredly.

"You and me are going to bust out of here."

"How do you reckon that?"

"Because we're the only two with dash enough to try it," the boy said. "From what I read about you in the papers, you are the original blue-eyed demon from Missouri, the genuine article, the real deal."

"Yeah, that's me all right. Just to figure the odds, has anybody ever broken out of here?"

"You bet," Dray said. "Bill Doolin did it."

"I have a picture postcard of what became of him after. He looked well ventilated."

"Shame about Bill all right," Dray said. "But he was just too nice of a guy. Do you know he never actually *killed* anybody in all his robbing and thieving? Actually took pride in that fact. What kind of an outlaw is that?"

"And how many men have you killed, Mickey Dray?"

"I told you, I'm a horse thief," he said. "You're the

man killer. That's why we make such a great team. Hell, most of the humanity locked up with us are in for charges that require not an ounce of courage—bringing liquor into the nations, for instance, or forgery and counterfeiting. How much guts does it take to pass a forged check?"

Dray lowered his voice.

"And there's this other thing," he said. "Horse stealing and killing bounty hunters carry the same penalty in Oklahoma Territory. It comes at the end of a rope."

"Then why steal horses?"

"Hell, fiddler. It's the only thing I'm good at."

Gamble took a deep breath.

"All right. How did Doolin bust out?"

"I wasn't here then, but I've studied enough about it to be an authority, I reckon," he said. "You see, there is one jailer—that is Comley, whom you've already heard about—and he is on duty from six in the morning to six at night. He has four guards, two on the day shift and two at night.

"It was a Sunday evening in July, and the guards on duty were Joe Miller and J. T. Tull. It was along about nine o'clock and the inmates were getting cups of water for the night from the bucket over there by the door. There was this one inmate called George Lane, half Cherokee and half black, and he reached through like he was going to cut himself a cup of water, but instead he grabbed one of the jailers, Tull, and pinned him against the bars.

"The other guard, Joe Miller, was unarmed and inside the bullpen, keys in hand, attending to some business or other. When he saw that Tull was in trouble, he made a dash for the open door of the bull pen—but Doolin beat him to the door and slammed it in his face. Then he got Miller's gun, a pearl-handled .45 Colt, from the box in receiving and trained it on Tull and made him work the combination locks in the boxes, opening all the cell block doors."

"All of the cells can be unlocked by removing the combination locks in the steel boxes?"

"Right," Dray said. "And Doolin had the key to the big front doors from Miller. The only problem Doolin encountered was a trustee by the name of Dean sitting at the desk in the receiving area. Dean moved to help Miller, but Doolin rapped him on the head with the barrel of the gun and threw him down the stairs to the basement."

Gamble laughed.

"There were about fifty prisoners in the jail that night," Dray said, "but most of 'em wouldn't leave, even though the doors were standing wide open. Doolin and thirteen others ran barefoot down the big iron steps to the street below. One of the inmates even used the telephone in the office to call for help from the marshal's office downtown."

"I've encountered the machine in action," Gamble said.

"Doolin commandeered a horse and buggy from a gent named Alvador Koontz, who had rented the rig for a date with Winnifred Warner. Doolin made good his escape, taking Dynamite Dick Clifton and Little Dick West with him. The rest of the escapees walked north along the railroad tracks for about half a mile, and then split up. Later, Doolin's mother-in-law brought the pearl-handled Colt back to Guthrie, and left it with Granville Morris at the hardware store, to return to Miller. Doolin sent along his compliments to Miller and thanked him for the loan of the revolver."

Gamble smiled.

"When was Doolin killed?"

"About six weeks later. Near the end of August. You know the story of the ambush? The eight-gauge shotgun? Shot to hell one night near Lawton while leading the bay mare that he had stolen here, trying to get his wife Edith and their infant out of the territory to begin a new life way out West. The undertaker, Rhodes, put Doolin's body on display in the front windows of the Gray Brothers Building at the corner of Oklahoma and Division. Thousands came to see."

"Not that it mattered to Doolin by then."

"But it must have been some comfort to his wife."

"What? To see strangers leering at the corpse of her recently dispatched husband, strapped to a wicker board, dead eyes staring into eternity?"

"It would be reassuring for her to know how widely regarded Bill was," Dray said. "At least, I think it would be for my wife—if I had a wife, that is. Are you married, Jake?"

"I was. Don't inquire again. And you don't know me well enough to call me Jake."

"All right, fiddler. Whatever you say."

"Were all of the escapees caught?"

"No," Dray said. "Four of them got away clean— Arkansas Tom, Crittenden the counterfeiter, E. V. Nix, and Kid Phillips. It's been a year and a half now since the break, so I'd say they are safe and sound."

"Or dead and forgotten," Gamble said.

"Nope," Dray said. "I'm sure they made it. Kid Phillips was a friend of mine—in fact, he taught me how to steal horses. I'm sure he is in the desert territories or maybe old Mexico by now, having made a fortune stealing horse flesh, sitting on the veranda of a big hacienda, and drinking whiskey while he pats the nice round bottom of a pretty señorita."

FIVE

A week later, Jacob Gamble was well enough to sit up on his bunk and play checkers through the bars with Mickey Dray. Gamble did not particularly like checkers, considering it a child's game, but there was precious else to pass the time.

"Damn it," Dray said after the third time that Gamble had beaten him. "You are hardly paying attention and you've beat me every time. This is supposed to be pleasure, and so far it's just been shameful."

"I've thirty years on you in terms of experience. It counts for something. You reach an age, you know how to do things—negotiate a fair price for a horse, divine who in the room is likely to make trouble, how to play checkers."

"Just how old are you, fiddler?"

"Forty-eight come October."

Dray laughed.

"You're older than my father."

"I expect so."

"Let's play another," Dray said, setting up the pieces.

"Later," Gamble said. "Maybe your luck will change."

"Sure," Dray said, feigning cheerfulness. "Fiddler, have you put some thought into how we're going to bust out of here?"

"I'm thinking you ought to lower your voice," Gamble said.

Dray got up and stretched dramatically.

"I've got a notion or two," Dray said. "Problem is, they all involve a stick of dynamite, two good shovels, and a loaded shotgun. We seem to be in short supply on all accounts. Maybe we could request those things from the jailers next Christmas. And oysters. Have I told you how much I love fresh oysters? I hear that rich old Arthur Stillwell has them shipped in a special tank car up from Port Arthur to Kansas City. Can you imagine? Fresh oysters in Kansas City!"

Gamble shook his head.

"Thief," Gamble said. "If you could just concentrate on one thing at a time instead of chain firing all of your thoughts at once, you might go further in life. Now, do you think you could find me a newspaper that hasn't been torn to pieces for use in the necessary and which is not more than a month old? I am curious for news about the war with Spain."

There was the rattle of the combination locks in the boxes, and then the guard, Joe Miller, swung open the door to the bullpen. A man in a Prince Albert coat and an impossibly white vest stepped inside and paused. He was in his late thirties, stood six feet tall, had clear gray eyes, and his dark and perfectly combed hair cascaded to his shoulders.

"Good afternoon, gentlemen," the man said as he walked into the bullpen and stepped among a group of inmates who were sprawled on the floor, a Bible open to Genesis in front of them. "Please, don't get up."

"Counselor," an inmate said, rolling over on an elbow. "The Methodists gave us this Bible to study, and we're only on the first book, but we've hit a snag—this story about Lot and his daughters is a horrible example for such as us, of weak character."

"Better skip toward the back and take up the story with Matthew," the man said. "Nobody can attempt to find justice in the Old Testament and keep his reason intact. Just stick to the words in red letters and you'll be fine."

The man came over to the cage where Gamble sat on his bunk.

"I see they have you in special accommodations."

"He called you counselor," Gamble said. "Just what kind of lawyer are you? If you're a prosecutor, you can just keep on walking, because I don't want none of what you're pushing."

"I was once or twice a prosecutor," the man said. "But now I'm a defense attorney. I am in town on some legal business here at the territorial capitol and my friend, Doc Smith, says you might be in need of my services."

"What's your name?"

"Aw, you don't know who that is?" Dray asked. "That's Temple Houston, youngest son of Texan hero Sam Houston, and the most famous lawyer from the Indian Nations to the Rio Grande."

"Shut up, thief. I want to hear it from him."

Houston smiled.

"The boy has correctly stated my name," he said. "As to my reputation, I leave that determination to others."

"And he's a fast draw and a dead shot," Dray enthused. "Why, let me tell you that he and his buddy Jack Love are unbeatable! A few years ago, when I was just a kid, I was playing roulette at this dive over on Harrison Avenue and getting taken pretty bad by a rigged wheel when Mister Houston and his friend came in for a beer. Mister Houston shot the place to hell with his Colt and then threw the owner in the street and whipped him like a redheaded stepchild."

"That true?" Gamble asked.

"Substantially."

"Damned shame the kid didn't learn anything," Gamble said. "Thief, let us be for a spell. It seems me and the defense attorney have some things to talk over."

Houston called for a stool, and one was provided. Then the door to the cell unlatched when a lever was pulled by the guard in the receiving area, and Temple pushed the door open and sat on the stool next to Gamble's bunk.

"How're you feeling?"

"I'm feeling, so it beats the alternative."

"They tell me you were damned close to dying from loss of blood."

Gamble shrugged.

"All right, let's get down to business," Houston said. "Do you have any money?"

"Now I believe you're a lawyer."

"Doesn't matter if you don't. Your case intrigues me and I'll defend you anyway. But my family has to eat just like anybody else's, so it's always better when I get paid. But to make this proper, you need to give me something of value."

"I don't have a dime."

"It doesn't have to be money."

Gamble hesitated. "There are only two objects of any real value in this world," he said. "One is my father's fiddle, and it is in a pawnshop in Caldwell, Kansas. The other is an old Manhattan revolver which is being held in safekeeping for me by the boy Andrew Farquharson at the hardware store on Oklahoma Avenue. I could send word that it should be given to you as collateral on my debt."

"I would not ask you for anything of such sentimental value," Houston said. "Besides, I have many fine revolvers, and am in no need of a curiosity from the war. It can be anything of value, even little value, so that I can duly report that you have retained my services."

"I have this," he said, and pulled the picture post-card of Doolin from his shirt pocket. "I paid twenty-five cents for it. It is smudged now with my own blood and is worth somewhat less, I would think."

"That will do," Houston said. He took the card and examined it briefly before slipping it into the inside pocket of his black coat. "It is, also, I should say, a fitting reminder of what is at stake."

"Take the pawn ticket as well," Gamble said. "For safekeeping, if nothing else."

"All right," Houston said. "If you insist."

"I've never had a defense attorney before," Gamble

said. "Never got close enough to a jail or a court-room to have a trial. How is this supposed to work?"

"You are going to tell me what happened and I am going to defend you to the best of my ability, within the confines of the truth."

"What is there to tell?" Gamble asked. "I killed two of the bounty-hunting cousins—one up on Cotton-wood Creek and the other in the middle of Okla-homa Avenue. They seemed determined to kill me."

"They had that right, because you were a fleeing felon and they had a writ for your arrest," Houston said. "In 1872, the United States Supreme Court gave bounty hunters the power to cross state lines, to kick open the door of your house without a war-rant, to make arrests on Sunday, and to kill felons if necessary in order to bring them back."

"Splendid."

"You knew the cousins were attempting to serve a writ?"

"Of course," Gamble said. "Why else would I run?"

"You were outnumbered four to one," Houston said. "If there was some misunderstanding, then we could argue that you feared for your life from un-known menacing parties."

"But that would be a lie," Gamble said.

"I understand. So, there is no defense."

"Am I going to swing from the end of a rope in the capital of Oklahoma Territory? I don't even *like* Oklahoma. I didn't think there was a state worse than Kansas, but I was wrong."

"The odds of your execution in Guthrie are rather long," Houston said. "This isn't the old days of Hanging Judge Parker's court in Fort Smith, where capital punishment was a form of mass entertainment. These are modern times, Mister Gamble, and there is much populist feeling. There has never been an execution at this prison. I doubt that you will be the first. Life in prison is a more likely sentence."

"I would rather be hanged."

Temple brushed his hair back from his forehead and looked at Gamble quizzically.

"There's every chance that you'll be extradited to Kansas to stand trial for the murder of Lester Burns. Kansas has the death penalty, but nobody's been hanged for twenty-eight years. Under law, the governor must sign off on the execution, and since 1870 no governor has. But the man you killed was the governor's brother-in-law. He might make an exception. If not, then you'll be returned to Oklahoma Territory for the murders of the German cousins."

"Sounds tiring."

"Why did you kill Lester Burns?"

"Because the bastard deserved it."

"Tell me about the events that led up to the killing. Did you know this man Burns?"

"Not until a month ago. After hocking the fiddle, I found myself on the prairie near Caldwell, at a tent city of dope peddlers, whores, and gamblers. Anywhere cards are dealt, whiskey flows, and love is for sale, there's money to be had. I aimed to have a little."

Six

The tent city where Jacob Gamble had met Lester Burns was on the side of a red limestone bluff called Lookout Mount. In the halcyon days of the Chisholm Trail it was where the girls from the brothels in the wide-open cow town Caldwell would sit and watch for the next group of Texans coming north. Now that the proliferation of railroads had shut down the cattle drives and ended the era of the cowboy, Lookout Mount had become a crossroads, a watering hole for the lowest elements of two worlds, a shadowy place where a man, white or red, could get a drop of whiskey or buck the tiger or know something strange before crossing into the Nations or heading back to the States.

The townsfolk called it Hell's Front Porch.

Gamble arrived on foot late one afternoon on the next to last day of 1897, a carpet of snow on the ground, his hands shoved deep in the pockets of his black coat, a north wind stinging the backs of his ears. The fingers of his left hand were touching the few silver dollars he had gotten from the fiddle.

From a distance, the Porch looked like every other gamblers' hell that Gamble had known during his thirty-five years in the West, a cluster of tents and shacks thrown up from whatever had been scavenged from abandoned cabins and barns nearby. But as he neared, he could see what appeared to be an old-fashioned round circus tent in yellow and black, with a rainbow of silk ribbons whipping from the apex. As he got closer, however, he could see that the cone-shaped structure wasn't a circus tent at all, but a large old Plains Indian lodge.

The lodge was a tilted cone that must have been forty feet in circumference at the base, and narrowed to a point at the smoke-darkened top some fifty feet above the ground, from which lodge poles bristled. Bits of bright colored cloth and rags were tied to the poles. A long slit down one side of the top was the smoke hole, with the smoke flaps opened like wings on either side. Smoke flowed from the top, and the upper two-thirds of the lodge glowed like a Chinese lantern from the firelight within.

The black-and-yellow bands covered half of the lodge, the half facing town, while the other half—facing the Indian Nations—was covered in paintings depicting dozens of historical events in the history of whoever had owned the lodge. Gamble walked around the lodge in wonder, looking at primitive depictions of many battles with other tribes and with the blue-coated soldiers, sacred birds and animals, and stars falling to earth. There were holes in the story, however, because in places the buffalo hide was ripped, or chunks had rotted away, and these offenses had been patched with whatever had been at hand—canvas, burlap, blankets, and even portions of a quilt or two.

On the far side of the lodge were several horses, picketed. It was a sorry lot of animals, except for one chestnut mare. Her dark eyes followed Gamble as he made his way past.

When Gamble had trudged all the way around again to the east-facing entrance of the lodge, he encountered a thin white man in a full-length elk robe. He was bald, and an earring dangled from the lobe of his left ear. When he smiled, a gold front tooth caught the light of the winter sun.

"Welcome, friend."

"Welcome to what?" Gamble asked.

"Whatever you want it to be," the stranger said. "My name is Burns and this is my place. Something, ain't it? Used to belong to an old Kiowa warrior by the name of Laughing Bear. Now it's mine."

"Laughing Bear?"

"The old fool never accepted the terms of the Medicine Lodge Treaty or defeat after the Red River Wars," Burns said. "For thirty years they have tried to keep him on the reservation down at Fort Sill, and for thirty years he kept jumping the reservation, coming up here to this old buffalo hunting ground he knew as a boy. But come on in out of the cold wind, friend, where we can talk and warm our old bones by the fire."

Burns held the shieldlike buffalo skin door aside and Gamble ducked in, then fastened the door after him. Gamble parted the tattered *ozan*, an inner partition that helped keep out the cold and prevented

incautious shadows from being cast on the outer
lodgeskin.

The lodge fire was well-banked. On the stones
around the fire were pots and pans, cups, and food—
beans and bacon, sugar and salt, a can of Arbuckles
coffee, canned peaches. On the other side of the fire
was a line of wooden crates turned on their sides and
stacked to make shelves, and the shelves were filled
with whiskey bottles. On top of the crates were three
or four lacquered trays which held opium pipes,
bowls, and other paraphernalia. The bowls were ce-
ramic, and were about the size and shape of door-
knobs; most were decorated with dragons, lotuses, or
Chinese characters.

At the edge of the firelight, near the *ozan*, were a
half-dozen flickering opium lamps. Beside each
lamp was a shadowy and furtive figure, humped beneath blankets or reclining with their pipes cradled
in their arms. Most were asleep. Two of them stirred
as if in a dream, fidgeting with their pipes.

One of the opium smokers was a woman of indeterminate age, with pallid skin and a tangle of chestnut hair. Around her waist was something that looked
like a snakeskin. Her dull eyes lingered on Gamble,
then she skewered a ball of opium with the tip of a
steel needle and thrust it over the chimney of her
lamp. Once the pill was heated to an orange glow,
she transferred it to the bowl of her pipe and then
wrapped her lips around the stem, sucking the vapor-
ized opium into her lungs. Her eyelids quivered in
the kind of ecstasy that Gamble had only seen before
when a woman achieved sexual gratification.

He forced himself to look away, and followed Burns.

Sitting beside the fire, absentmindedly tending it with a hickory branch, was an Indian girl of thirteen. She was wearing a Chinese robe in vivid red silk and a Mandarin hat of the same color was perched on her head. Her legs were drawn up beneath her, revealing a pair of slender feet with bright pink soles.

"What's with the getup?" Gamble asked.

The girl's dark eyes flashed.

"Couldn't find a real Celestial outside Denver or Oklahoma City," Burns said.

Gamble glanced cautiously around before taking the wicker chair that Burns indicated. He kept his coat on, even though it was warm by the fire, to hide the Manhattan in its holster on his left hip.

Burns shrugged out of the elk robe, threw it on the ground, and settled into an identical chair beside Gamble. The girl picked up the robe, smoothed it, and hung it from a deer antler tied to one of the lodgepoles.

"Warmer than any damned tent I've ever slept in," Burns said. "I feel sorry for those other fellows out there, freezing their butts off in the middle of a Kansas winter. Now, how about some whiskey?"

"Or dope?"

"I provide it as a public service," Burns said. "Since they outlawed it in Caldwell, I had to set up here on the prairie so these fiends could get their heads dosed. They'd go to pieces without it. And friend, I didn't offer you dope because you don't look the type."

"You're right," Gamble said, removing his hat and

placing it upside-down on the deer hide between them. "I'd prefer some coffee now. Whiskey later. And I can pay for the whiskey up front, if you like." Gamble took a silver dollar from his pocket and tossed it into his hat.

"No offense, friend, but whiskey would warm you quicker than Arbuckles," Burns said. "But you can get whatever you want here, that's what I always say."

He spoke a few words to the Indian girl, and she threw some grounds and water in a gallon-sized tin can. As she leaned over to place the can on a hot stone just inside the fire circle, Gamble watched the flames reflected in her eyes.

"What are the games of chance at the Porch?"

"Old Buell runs a crooked poker game in the shack across the way," Burns said. "Faro, some-times, but it's the old-timers who mostly want to buck that tiger. The young ones want poker, and are freer with their money. Me, I prefer craps. Do you play the bones, friend?"

"Sometimes," Gamble said, still watching the girl, who had the affect of someone much older and infi-nitely sad. "You were going to tell me the story about Laughing Bear."

At the sound of the name, the girl looked up. She held Gamble's gaze for a moment, then turned back to the fire.

"Indeed," Burns said. "He was so old he claimed to remember a time before the Spanish came, but that's absurd. He would have had to be more than four hundred years old. But that's how Indians are—they tell themselves the damndest stories and be-lieve them."

"Perhaps he meant Jedediah Smith. Some of the old ones make no distinction among Spanish, Texans, and other whites."

"Could be. Jed Smith was killed out here someplace on the Kansas plains, but they never found his body. Hell, it was the Kiowa that might have killed him. That would put Laughing Bear in his eighties, which would be about right."

"So why did Laughing Bear come back here?"

"Damned if I know," Burns said. "The last time a buffalo was seen in Sumner County was 1884. They can't even have the Sun Dance anymore because they can't get the buffalo head to hang up on the altar. He did the Ghost Dance back in 1890 to drive the whites away and bring the buffalo back, and he took the peyote, and he believed everything old Wovoka said about if you just danced hard enough, the earth would swallow up the whites. But then the soldiers from Fort Sill busted the movement all up and ending up shooting the old bastard in the chest."

"So Laughing Bear is dead?"

"As old as death and twice as ugly," Burn said. "But no, not dead. Survived the bullet. Claimed his ghost shirt saved him, just like Wovoka promised. He's asleep over there, out of his mind on opium and alcohol. Now that he can't get his fix of peyote from the Rio Grande valley anymore, he had to find some substitute to enter the dreamworld where he can talk to his ancestors. I was happy to oblige."

"And the government?"

"Leaves him alone now. The agency at Fort Sill reckons it would be a wasted trip if they sent the soldiers after him—figure he'd be dead of old age before they got here. But, it's going on six months now, and the old bastard is still breathing. He keeps his medicine bundle always within reach and won't let me see inside, guarding it like it's his tribe's Ark of the Covenant."

"How'd you get the lodge?"

The girl looked up at this, and Gamble thought she might say something, but she bit her lip instead.

"Traded for it, fair and square," Burns said. "You see, Laughing Bear has found a new messiah, a blind old charlatan by the name of Afraid-of-Bears. He's a peyote-gobbling, war-dancing troublemaker who claims that the second coming of Jesus Christ will take place at noon on Friday, July 15, 1904, at Saddle Mountain on the Kiowa Reservation."

"That's a peculiar prophecy for a Kiowa medicine man."

"Well, it kind of makes sense when you take into account that Afraid-of-Bears says that Christ will be accompanied by all of the buffalo the whites have killed, and that the old way of life will be restored. Like a lot of heathens, the Kiowa aren't particular about where their power comes from—Jesus has been good medicine for the whites, so why not the Kiowa? Power is power."

The coffee had boiled and the girl used a pair of pliers to grasp the side of the gallon can and fill two blue enamel cups.

"I'd like to hear what the old man has to say," Gamble said, taking the hot cup from the girl and nodding his thanks. "In the morning, when he wakes up."

"If he wakes up," Burn said, taking the coffee without looking at the girl. "Anyway, he doesn't speak a word of English. You have to ask his granddaughter here to translate, and the little squaw bitch is as notorious a liar as he is."

Gamble held the cup in both hands and blew across it.

"What's her name?"

"Something unpronounceable," Burns said.

"Tsat-Mah," the girl said.

"See? Gibberish."

Gamble swirled the coffee in the enameled cup.

"What's it mean?"

The girl made an opening gesture with her hands.

"Little Door Woman," she said.

"When the old man dies," Burns said, "the girl will be mine. Poor child, she will have no one else to care for her in this world. Lucky she has me, because many in this camp would force their affections upon her—or worse."

Gamble drank the weak coffee and sat staring at the fire, and the warmth made him sleepy. When he felt he could no longer keep his eyes open, he placed the cup on one of the flat stones near the fire and slipped his hand beneath his coat to rest on the brass and walnut grip of the loaded Manhattan.

Gamble woke with a jerk, his eyes snapping open. Sunlight was streaming in through the smoke hole above him, and he could see wisps of clouds in the winter sky. The fingers of his left hand were still touching the revolver.

He glanced over at his hat. The silver dollar was gone.

Little Door Woman was kneeling beside the fire, frying bacon in a cast-iron skillet. The interior of the lodge was hazy with smoke, and most of the sleepers from the night before were still huddled beneath their blankets, snoring.

"Where's Burns?"

"Making water," the girl said. "Or, making logs."

There was a rustling sound in the back of the lodge, and the girl called something in Kiowa. Her grandfather came forward, a blue blanket draping his naked shoulders, and he sat cross-legged a yard or so away from Gamble.

The girl placed a tin plate with a slab of bacon and a few hunks of fried cornmeal in front of the old man, and he grunted his thanks, but did not touch the food. Then she brought a plate for Gamble, who held it on his lap and used his pocketknife to cut the bacon. It smelled faintly rancid, but Gamble ate it because he was so hungry his stomach ached.

The girl sat down between the men. She and the grandfather exchanged a few words. Then the old man slowly turned his head to look at Gamble, and as he did the sunlight from above caught him full in the face. His eyes were clouded with cataracts, his beaklike nose was bulbous and scarred, and his cheeks and forehead and chin were a mass of fissures.

"Grandfather says you are the one-eyed white man from his dreams."

"He probably remembers me from last night."

"He says he has been dreaming of you since the Winter When Horses Ate Ashes. That was when the snow was so deep that the horses could not get to the grass and were so hungry they ate the ashes from the campfires."

"How long ago was that?"

She shrugged.

"Years, I think."

"How many years?"

"Time is not like that for us," she said. "Our time doesn't pass in a straight line, as if shot from the barrel of a gun. Instead, time is a wheel. We keep a winter count, and each year is named for something that happened. Grandfather wanders now among the winter counts. Last night, he was in the Winter the Stars Fell and fighting the Osage Takers of Heads. Tonight, he may go back to When Horses Ate Ashes, so it is difficult to say whether that winter is in the past or whether it has not yet happened again."

"All right," Gamble said. "Ask him, then, what happened in the white man's world When Horses Ate Ashes."

She spoke to her grandfather in a tone that was apologetic and amused. The old man thought for a moment, then began speaking and held up a gnarled hand and with his thumb and forefinger made the universal sign for a pistol. The girl asked another question, then nodded.

"He says it was during the time the whites made the great war with each other," she said. "Also, it was the winter you took up the gun. He saw you, in his dreams. You were a boy, but before a giant put out your eye with a rock. It is the same gun you carry beneath your coat now."

That was thirty-six years ago, Gamble thought. The old Indian must have heard the story. Gamble had gone West after the war and many people knew the story of his fight with the guerrilla chieftain Alf Bolin in Taney County, Missouri.

He speared a chunk of bacon with his knife.

"How old is your grandfather?"

"Old," she said. "He was born when the Kiowa still lived in the mountains, before we came down to the flat land and we became a horse people. He has outlived forty-three wives and all of his children."

"That's impossible. Nobody is four hundred years old."

The girl shrugged.

"And yet there he sits," she said. "His *daughw-daughw* will die with him, and he will have no one to pass the medicine bundle to because he has no favorite living son. I am the last of his kin—a lowly girl."

"What is this power he has?"

"*Daughw-daughw* is the power of the universe and all things have it," she said, "but some things and some people have more of it than others. The sun has more than an eagle, the eagle more than a rabbit, and the whirlwind more than a summer breeze. A warrior gathers *daughw-daughw* through many battles won. Have you killed men? Then you now have their power as your own."

Gamble sighed.

"The only thing killing has got me was trouble."

"You're alive, aren't you?" she asked, reacting to his condescending tone. "I'm sure you think all of this is just superstition, a bunch of fairy tales, that we Kiowa are just like the rest of the poor ignorant red children. But we see how the world works clearer than any of you whites, whose eyes are clouded by so many of your own lies that you can no longer see the sun in the sky or the moon at night."

"Hold your fire," Gamble said. "My bastard brother was raised by the Chiricahua, and he believed in this power you speak of. My inconstant mother thought she could divine the future in a deck of cards. Me, I'm fairly ecumenical—white or red, I think it is all hokum."

"Which road are you on?"

"You mean, which way am I headed? West."

"No, which *path.*"

"West, always west."

"The medicine wheel has seven directions and seven colors. We are here in the middle, on the earth, which is green. Up above, which is where Grandfather will soon be headed, is yellow. Some folks go down below, which is brown."

"Yes, I've put a few down there myself."

"Spirits can also go in the four other directions. North is blue, sadness and defeat, and winter, a time of waiting. East is red, the spring, and victory. South is white, the summer, a time of plenty and happiness. That's the best place to go. Grandfather will probably go there after going up and shaking hands with Jesus."

"And my road?"

"West," Little Door Woman said. "The black road. Autumn. The place where the souls of your enemies and the great black spirit dwells. The black spirit wants to tear out a man's soul and carry it away to the west, to put it into a black box buried deep in the black mud, and to place a black serpent coiled upon it."

Alarmed, she glanced at him with hard eyes.

"West. You're sure?"

"I've been heading west since the day I was born," Gamble said. "Too late to change now."

"Does the white man have a name for the black path?"

"Damnation Road," Gamble said.

The old man grumbled, then pushed his plate away.

"What's the matter?"

"He says he is ready to die and will not eat the food because it would be a waste," she said, then began picking at the bacon and putting it in her mouth. "But he says that every morning. He will only eat after I have taken a little."

The old man smiled and reached out a hoary hand and touched the girl's cheek. Then he turned to Gamble and began speaking quickly.

"He says there are many people in the land of the dead who are anxious to talk with you."

"They may not have long to wait," he said. "I am damn near fifty years old myself."

"Yes, you are old," the girl said. "And ugly, as are all whites. But grandfather says you still have many winters left before you are reunited with your mother and your half-brother."

"That's who wants to talk to me?"

"No, Grandfather says, it is the ghost of your father who grows impatient—he is no longer content to stay in the land of the dead, but wishes to cross over."

"Why?"

The girl looked thoughtful as she put the plate back on her grandfather's lap.

"This is very bad medicine," she said. "We do not speak of our own ancestors in this way, or even speak their names, for fear of inviting them over from the dreamworld. But Grandfather says that it is proper to speak to you of these things, because you are white and things for you are like looking in a mirror—that is, they are reversed."

Gamble rubbed his forehead with his left hand.

"See?" she said, pointing.

"Little Door Woman, not that I believe any of this—but ask your grandfather if he knows what the ghost of my father seeks."

She turned to the old man and asked.

"How could he know?" she asked. "My grandfather doesn't speak your language. He says that you will have to cross into the land of the dead and ask him yourself."

"With dope and whiskey? No."

"Grandfather uses the poison because he is too old to sleep deeply enough to enter the land of the dead," she said. "But there are other ways, all of which bring you close to death. Starvation. Sickness, especially fever. Sunstroke. Freezing. Loss of much blood."

Gamble sighed and put the plate down beside him.

"Whiskey and opium don't sound so bad."

The girl brushed the hair from her eyes.

"They are poisons and lead to death as well," she said. "Like smallpox and guns, they are gifts from across the water. The horse is the only good thing the white man ever brought. Well, that and bees. I like honey."

"You seem remarkably well informed," Gamble said.

"For a little squaw, you mean?"

"Is that what I said? No, you are uncommonly bright for a person your age, no matter what the shade of your skin. As for gender, I'd expect you to be smarter than a boy your age—girl heads ripen quicker."

She attempted to suppress a smile, but could not.

"It's the Methodists," she said. "They are well meaning, but terribly confused. They have built a church on the reservation at Mount Scott and are teaching us to read and write American and to wear civilized clothes and to take Christian names, but it is making us a nation of broken people. Someday soon I will be forced to return, I suppose. But for now, my grandfather needs me."

"When your grandfather dies," Gamble said, "you had better light out quick. The way Burns looks at you makes my stomach feel like I ate something rotten."

"It's probably the bacon."

SEVEN

Gamble grabbed his hat, made sure the Manhattan was secure in its holster, and stepped outside the lodge to relieve himself in the snow far on the other side of where the horses were tied. The chestnut mare was still staked where she had been the night before, and as he walked back she nickered and tossed her head.

"Sorry, girl," Gamble said, touching her muzzle. "Don't have a thing for you. I can barely feed myself. But maybe I can find you an apple or something later."

There was a dirty strip of snow between the rows of shacks and tents. Wood smoke seeped from the stovepipes poking through the wood and canvas, and the sound of hard laughter rang in the cold air. He looked at the sun, still low in the sky, and judged that it was eight or eight-thirty in the morning.

Gamble trudged through the mottled snow toward the biggest tent. It had a wooden door that creaked badly when it was opened. The floor was made of dirt and there was a crackling stove toward the back, a bar made out of an oak plank set across two whiskey barrels along the east wall, and a few empty round card tables on the opposite side. But in the middle of the one-room tent was an ornate craps table with carved legs and a green baize surface. Hanging from the pole that supported the peaked roof overhead was a brass lantern with six arms that held flickering kerosene flames.

Five men were clustered intently around the craps table. Some of them were already, or were still, drunk. The woman he had seen smoking opium the night before was leaning against the shooter, an arm around his waist.

Gamble walked over to the bar and ordered a shot of whiskey from a gaunt man who had an unruly salt-and-pepper beard that spread over his chest like a bib. He tossed the quarter dollars down as if he didn't care what the drink cost, picked up the shot glass in one hand, and leaned back and put an elbow on the oak plank.

"You Buell?"

"What's it to you?"

Gamble sipped the whiskey. It tasted like something that would come in a bottle of horse liniment.

"Lester Burns said you run an honest poker game here," he said. "Wouldn't mind trying my luck."

"Sure thing," the bearded man said. "But right now, the game is craps. You could throw the bones until we get some cowboys interested in cards."

"Not my game," Gamble said. "Maybe I could get up my own table."

Buell's eyelids flickered.

"Rent on the tables is five dollars an hour," he said.

"That's only fair," Gamble said, even though he had less than four dollars left from hocking the fiddle.

"And the house gets a taste of your winnings."

"How much?"

Buell paused.

"Ten percent," he said, finally.

"Now, that's something we should negotiate," Gamble said, and took another sip of the bad whiskey. "Fair would be paying a cut or an hourly rate, but not both. My preference is the hourly rate."

"No."

"All right," Gamble said. "The house percentage, then. But three percent, not ten."

"I have overhead," Buell said. "This tent, wood for the stove, the tables and chairs. Seven percent."

"You're right," Gamble said, and drained the shot glass. He turned it upside down and put it on the plank. "I'm imposing on your goodwill. Forgive me." He tipped his hat and walked toward the entrance.

"Hold on," Buell said, but Gamble did not. Then, in a lower voice: "Five percent."

Gamble stopped. He turned and walked back. He leaned over the plank.

"Deal," he said. "But just so you know, I play an honest game."

"Then how the hell do you plan to make any money?"

"I plan to win," Gamble said. "Now, reach into some of that overhead of yours and give me a deck of cards."

Gamble took the deck and walked over to the cleanest of the round tables, the one in the back toward the stove, and sat down with his back to the corner. He shuffled the deck, cut it, then fanned the cards out on the table, facedown. He folded his hands across his stomach and waited.

"Craps!"

The shooter shoved the woman away from him, and she stumbled and fell against one of the tables, nearly upending it. Her shawl slipped from one shoulder, revealing a bruised breast overlapping a wine-colored corset. Around her waist was a wide belt made of rattlesnake skin.

"Settle down there," Buell called.

"I told her to give me elbow room," the cowboy said, pushing his hat back, spilling a sheaf of straight blond hair over his forehead. In a fancy tooled holster on his right hip was a nickel-plated Peacemaker with a bone grip. "The bitch cost me a month's pay on that last throw. She's the one what should pay."

His drunken friends laughed.

Still on the floor, the woman tucked her breast back into the corset. She turned her face away from the men, but not from Gamble. Her eyes locked on his, defiant.

"Yeah," one of them said and slapped him on the back. "Blame your bad luck on the whore, Timothy. What was your excuse in Pawhuska?"

"Go to hell," the shooter said. "And don't call me Timothy."

The men at the table laughed harder, and the shooter became red-faced. He pushed away from the table like a spring uncoiling, grabbed the woman's wrist, and jerked her to her feet.

"You owe me twenty-five dollars, you filthy cunny," he shouted.

"Go to hell," the woman said. "You rolled those bones, I didn't."

"Yeah, but I would have done a better job if you hadn't been ahold of my johnson."

"Is that what it was?" the woman said. "Thought maybe you had a pencil in your pocket. A really short one."

The cowboy bent her hand back over her wrist. The woman cried out in pain and leaned back, trying to ease the pain.

"That's enough," Gamble said, his hands still folded across his stomach.

"Did you say something, pops?" the cowboy asked.

"You heard me," Gamble said. "Take your hands off the woman."

The cowboy twisted her hand back with a final sadistic flourish, then suddenly released it. She fell in a heap on the floor, clutching her hand.

"There," the cowboy said, walking wildly in a circle "Are you happy, pappy? You'd better watch your step with me, old man, or you just might get all busted up."

He lunged at Gamble with a feigned punch, but Gamble did not flinch.

"You think you're tough," Gamble said, "but you're not. You're just drunk. You work on one of the big spreads in the Nations, probably the Miller brothers, and maybe you impress the girls in town, but you're not a real cowboy. You wouldn't have held a candle to any of the men that came up the Chisholm Trail twenty-five or thirty years ago."

"How the hell do you know?"

"I was there," Gamble said. "For a season or two, anyway. I was about your age and so full of shit that my eye damned near turned brown. But that's one of the advantages of a long life—you get over that."

"You're as old and washed up and as full of it as my Pa."

"Maybe. But that doesn't change the fact that you aren't as tough as you think. You wouldn't have been good enough to ride the river with any of the men I knew back then."

The cowboy grinned drunkenly and looked over at his friends, but Gamble was keeping an eye on his right hand. His fingers were hanging too loose and too close to the bone-handled Colt.

"Thing is, I don't have to be as tough as those old boys," he said. "I just have to be tougher than *you*."

The cowboy whirled around while trying to pull the gun out of the fancy holster. The front sight caught on a loop of leather stitching, the half-cocked hammer fell, and the gun discharged. The cowboy fell to the floor, a .45-caliber slug in his thigh.

"Sonuvabitch," he said in a matter-of-fact tone. "I think my leg is broken."

Gamble was half out of his chair, the Manhattan in his left hand, the hammer drawn. The cowboy's friends were standing around the craps table, motionless.

"I should kill you," Gamble said, then gently lowered the hammer on the Manhattan and placed it on the table. "But I won't. I want you to live to be fifty or sixty years old and have some punk come try you and see how it feels to be called old and washed-up when you know that you are one cold and sober second away from having to splatter that kid's brains all over the floor. You will remember that, won't you?"

"Yes, sir," the cowboy said. He had wrapped his hands over the wound and was watching the blood spurt from between his fingers. "I'll remember, I promise."

"What are you waiting for?" Gamble asked. "Get him out of here. Find a doctor or a vet or a dentist, I don't care which."

His friends grabbed the cowboy by his boots and under his arms and carried him toward the door.

"Take the gun," Gamble said.

One of them scrambled back, snatched the bone-handled Colt from the floor, and ran out. The door slammed behind him with a clap.

It was suddenly silent in the tent. The pit man, a scruffy-looking character with wire-rimmed glasses and a bowler hat, used the stick to scratch his head.

"Christ," Buell said, uncorking a bottle of rye and pouring himself a shot. "You sure know how to break up a game of craps. Them boys was good customers. I should have stuck to the five dollars an hour."

The woman walked slowly over to Gamble and placed a hand on his arm.

"Thanks," she said.

"Don't thank me."

"Oh, but I must."

She wet her lips, then leaned down to whisper in his ear.

"How about a poke?"

"Pass," Gamble said.

"A blowjob, then. You can't turn that down."

"Watch me."

She stroked his cheek.

"Do you prefer boys?"

"That's revolting," Buell called from behind the bar, then downed the rye. He made a face and poured himself another. "For Christsake, Penny, leave the man alone. Go away for a while and come back when it's time for your show."

The woman frowned, then turned back to Gamble.

"Don't I know you?"

"No."

"You sure look familiar."

"Everybody says so."

"Why are you so cold?" she asked, drawing one of the cards from the middle of the fanned deck with her forefinger. But instead of flipping it over, she kept her forefinger on it.

"Now you."

Gamble hesitated.

"I don't play except for money."

"How about a sawbuck?"

"Show me coin or paper."

"I don't have it now, but I will, after the show."

"What kind of show is it?"

"Oh," she said, slyly, "You'll just have to see it to believe it. Ten bucks. What do you say?"

"Ten dollars, on credit? I don't think so."

"I'm good for it. In fact, Old Buell will advance me the money, right?"

Buell waved.

"All right," Gamble said.

He pulled a card from the left side of the deck and turned it over, not looking at it until the motion was complete. It was the one-eyed Jack of Spades.

The woman turned over her card.

The four of clubs.

"Damn," she said. "I am the unluckiest woman in the world. Double or nothing?"

"No," Gamble said. "Buell?"

Buell poured another shot of rye. Then he took an eagle from his pocket and gave it a toss. Gamble caught the gold coin and closed his fist tight around it.

"Thanks for playing," he said.

The woman turned and walked out.

Buell walked over to the table with the bottle of rye and two shot glasses in his hand. He placed the cleaner one in front of Gamble, filled it, then re-filled his own glass.

Gamble took a silver dollar from his pocket and slid it toward Buell.

"Your cut," he said. "Tell me about that woman."

"Penny Dreadful?" Buell asked. "She's the highest-priced whore on the Porch, a dope fiend, and a woman who is in the prolonged act of suicide. Don't know her real name, but I hear tell she came here from Denver, where she was married to a big shot banker and bore him a baby boy. But the child was colicky and cried all the time, which upset the husband, and Penny was frantic to find a way to restore wedded bliss. So to quiet the baby, she began giving it a patent medicine to put it to sleep. Problem was, the medicine was ten parts sugar and water and one part alcohol and morphine. After a week, she finally gave the baby just enough so that it never woke up at all."

Gamble sipped the rye.

"The husband accused her of poisoning the child and the prosecutor tried her for murder, but the jury leaned for accidental," Buell said. "But they might as well have locked her up, because her husband divorced her and drove her to the streets. Nobody in Denver would have anything to do with her. So, she is making money the old-fashioned way."

"What's this show tonight?"

Buell grinned.

"Penny doesn't just want to kill herself, she wants to debase herself in the worst ways first. That's a powerful hate she has for herself, but it's powerful lucky for me. Along about midnight, when the boys are gambled out, we'll throw a tarpaulin over the craps table and turn the lamps up real bright. Then Penny will climb up there and take all comers. Those that can't pay to do will pay to watch."

"Christ," Gamble said.

"I'm sure there'll be a special show tonight, seeing as how it is New Year's Eve."

"And you allow her do this."

"Allow her?" Buell asked. "I *encourage* her. You understand that I am a pimp and a whiskey peddler and run an illegal gambling establishment out of a tent on the line between the States and the territories? How long do you reckon it's going to be before the authorities ride in and close me and everybody else in the Porch down? I'll serve hard time when they catch me. But before that day happens, I'm out to make as much money as possible, and it seems that my clientele likes to witness intimate acts. And Penny Dreadful does things they don't even have names for yet."

Gamble finished the rye, then held his hand over the glass when Buell tried to refill it.

"Does anything separate us from the beasts?" he asked. "Wait, I slander the beasts, because they cannot conceive of such depravity. Their cruelty is dictated by survival. Ours is for amusement."

"You talk strange sometimes," Buell said.

"You have me pegged," Gamble said. "Look, I'll be out of here and settled up by the time the show starts. I'm as curious as the next man, but knowing her story has tarnished the attraction."

"Suit yourself," Buell said. "But you'll miss an eyeful. You know, if Lester Burns would sell me that cute little Kiowa gal he has over there—now, wouldn't *that* make a show."

The door screeched open and a man with graying hair and wire-rimmed glasses stepped inside, rubbing his hands to warm them.

"You fellows open?"

"Hell," Buell said, rising and taking the shot glasses and the bottle of rye with him.

"What're you looking for?" Gamble asked.

The man walked over to the table and removed his overcoat, revealing a Montgomery Ward suit. He eyed the deck of cards, pushed his glasses up on the bridge of his nose, and gave Gamble a toothy smile.

"Poker," he said.

EIGHT

Gamble left the tent shortly after ten o'clock with forty-eight dollars in paper and coin tucked into the pocket of his vest. He had won steadily, beginning with the clerk in the mail-order suit, and continuing with a pair of bachelor farmers, the city prosecutor from Caldwell, some hired hands on their way back to Kingfisher, and a widower who played and lost a couple of five-dollar hands while waiting for Penny Dreadful's show to start.

It was snowing again, but there was no wind, so the big flakes drifted down from the black sky as if somebody were sprinkling powdered sugar on a cake. It didn't make the Porch look any prettier, he thought.

If it hadn't been the middle of the night in winter, he would have walked back to Caldwell, redeemed his fiddle from the pawnshop, even if he had to roust the owner from home. Then he would buy a ticket on the next southbound Santa Fe at the depot. But he was tired, the path to town was covered in a fresh blanket of snow, and his joints ached. He didn't relish the thought of sleeping outside the depot, if it was locked. It was New Year's Day, and Gamble was uncertain of what kind of schedule the station master in the sleepy cow town of Caldwell would keep on a holiday.

He glanced over to the lodge that housed the opium den. It was glowing warmly.

"Damn, I hate winter," he muttered. "Almost as much as winter hates me."

He started trudging for the lodge. He would give Burns a dollar or two to sleep there again, have a bite or two of whatever Little Door Woman might be cooking, and set off early in the morning. The Porch gave him an uneasy feeling, and the sooner he left, the better.

Gamble ducked into the lodge. Opium lanterns glowed in the dark corners.

"Happy New Year," Burns called from his chair near the fire. "It's 1898. Seems a strange number, doesn't it? You know, we might not have that many years left—some say that 1900 is going to be the end of the world."

"Predictions are risky. Ask the Millerites."

"Come, sit by the fire," Burns said. "I understand you've been speculating on pasteboard at Buell's. Any luck?"

"Enough," Gamble said, lowering himself into the chair. Little Door Woman brought him an enamel cup of coffee. She still wore the Chinese costume. Gamble murmured his thanks, and she smiled at him.

"You left before Penny Dreadful's show."

"That's right."

"A moralist," Burns said, then laughed. "You

would change your mind if you saw what she can do with a billiard ball."

"I will sleep here for the night, if it's square with you," Gamble said. "Just let me know what I owe in the morning, counting breakfast."

"Didn't think you were here for the dope," Burns said. "Let us greet the new year together. Girl, bring us some whiskey—make it bourbon, not the awful stuff the lotus eaters drink."

"All right," Gamble said. "I'll take some in my coffee."

Little Door Woman brought over a bottle of Old Crow and poured some in Gamble's coffee. Burns took the bottle from the girl, then held it up in a toast.

"To the twentieth century," Burns said, touching the bottle to the rim of Gamble's cup. "Who would have thought we'd live to see it?"

"We haven't, not yet."

Gamble woke shortly after sunrise. He was still in the chair, but someone had placed a blanket over him in the night. Little Door Woman was already up, throwing some meat into the skillet. The coffee was boiling beside the fire. She had on the silk robe, but not the hat.

"Breakfast soon," she said.

"Bacon?" Gamble asked, wary.

"No," she said, allowing herself a smile. "Fresh ham. And eggs. He who is still asleep brought it back from town last night. Grandfather, wake up. It's time for you to refuse to eat."

Gamble glanced over at the old man. He was still motionless beneath his robe.

"He used to be up long before dawn, every day," the girl said. "But now because of the dope he sleeps later and later, lingering among the winter counts."

Gamble rose, pulled on his boots, and stepped outside for a necessary trip to the other side of the horses. The sun was rising in a splash of copper and red, the sky was blue and nearly cloudless, and the prairie was a gently scooped white blanket. It would be a pleasant walk to town.

He patted the chestnut mare on his way back.

After seating himself in the wicker chair, Little Door Woman handed him a plate of ham and eggs. He placed it carefully on his lap, took up the fork, and began to eat.

"Thank you," he said.

The girl placed a hand on Burns's shoulder and shook him.

"Wake up, smelly drunk," she said. "Your breakfast is ready. You too, grandfather."

Neither man stirred.

Gamble took twenty dollars in coins and held them out.

"What's that for?" the girl asked.

"Traveling money," Gamble said.

"I cannot take it."

"You can," Gamble said. "Light out at the first chance you get. Go back to Fort Sill and live among your people. Grow up in peace."

"But my grandfather needs me," she said. "Put your money away."

Gamble reluctantly returned the coins to his pocket.

"Grandfather!" the girl said. "Get up. Breakfast."

The old man rolled over and brushed a tangle of gray hair from his face.

"Granddaughter, I had a dream," he said, staring up at the blue sky beyond the smoke hole of the tipi. "White Buffalo Woman came to me—oh, how beautiful she was!—and she showed me all of the winter counts that you will paint before you die."

"But grandfather, I cannot keep the winter count."

"But you will!" he said. "White Buffalo Woman has decreed it, for in your lifetime you will see things beyond belief—the entire world will shake twice with war, the fire gourd will fall from the sky and burn everything it touches, an eagle will fly around the moon and back, thoughts will be sent around the earth, connecting the dreams of all people. And in the end, many years from now when you are an old woman, older than I am now, the Kiowa will be free."

"Was Jesus in your dream?" the girl asked. "Did he bring the buffalo back?"

"No," Laughing Bear said, puzzled. "He was not. But White Buffalo Woman said you must keep track of all of these things to come so that you can tell those of our people who sleep through them, and then are awakened."

The old man sat up, sloughing the robe off.

"Grandfather," she said, placing his breakfast before him. She picked up the robe and put it over his shoulders. "The dope even brings dreams to the whites."

"No food," the old man said. "It will be wasted. You eat it."

"Grandfather . . ."

"It is time for me to die. Thank you for being kind to your grandfather. Remember what I have told you about White Buffalo Woman and the winter counts to come."

Then the old man closed his eyes. His chin fell to his chest and his breathing stopped.

"Grandfather?"

She touched his shoulder. The old man slumped to the floor.

"Grandfather!" the girl screamed, shaking the body.

"Goddamnit," Burns said, sitting forward in the chair and blinking hard against the light. "What it is?"

"The old man died," Gamble said.

"For sure or just threatening?"

"Oh, this time it's for sure."

The girl threw herself over the body, shaking with tears.

"All right, then," Burns said, yawning. "Little what's her name has now become my property. God knows I've waited long enough. But I promised her grandfather that as long as he was alive, she would not be whored out. That's changed."

The blanket around one of the sleeping opium smokers rustled, and then was flung away. Penny Dreadful propped her head on her hand and asked what the hell was going on.

Gamble told her.

The woman blinked, absorbing the information. The she wiped the drool from her mouth and sat up, hugging her knees.

"You're not actually going to sell her to old Buell, are you?"

"What's it to you?" Burns asked. "Afraid of the competition, I reckon. She'll put you plum out of business, billiard balls or no."

"What I do is one thing," she said slowly. "My choice. Nobody has to understand it but me. But this little girl doesn't have any choice."

"Nobody has a choice in this life," Burns raged, standing. "Do you think I wanted to be the proprietor of a third-rate opium den on the fucking Kansas prairie? What child dreams of that? Christ, my brother-in-law is *governor* of this flat, godforsaken excuse for a state. But I did the best with the hand I was dealt. This little bitch will just have to do the same."

The other opium addicts were awake now, and they began scurrying for the entrance. In a moment, they were gone.

"If I was you, honey," Penny Dreadful told the girl, "I'd run."

The girl made for the entrance, but Burns grabbed the hem of her silk robe and pulled her back. She turned around, clawing and kicking, while Burns bunched the silk in his hands. But then the fabric tore and the robe came away, and she was suddenly naked—and free.

She began to run, but Burns lunged and grabbed an ankle with his right hand, and she fell. When he had dragged her back to him, he wrapped his left arm around her narrow shoulders and, with his right hand, took a straight razor out of his pocket. He flicked it open.

"Is this what you want?" he asked. "I'll slit your throat before letting you go, you little bitch."

Penny Dreadful gave a cry and then covered her mouth.

"Her name is Little Door Woman," Gamble said. He was standing and was holding the Manhattan easy in his left hand. "You'd best close that razor and let go of her."

"Or what, moralist?" Burns asked. "You going to shoot me?"

"That's the size of it."

"Ha!" Burns said. He put the razor against the girl's neck and began backing toward the entrance, dragging the girl behind him. Her feet were kicking out wildly, and as they passed the crates on which the whiskey sat, one of her pink heels struck the bottle of Old Crow a glancing blow. It teetered for a moment, then fell and shattered on the bottles beneath.

"Oh, that's coming out of your hide," Burns said.

Gamble cocked the Manhattan and advanced, trying to get a clear shot that wouldn't endanger the writhing girl.

A puddle of whiskey had formed beneath the broken bottles, and as it grew it began sending rivulets downhill toward the fire in the stone circle.

Gamble cursed.

The whiskey ran between the stones. Suddenly, blue flame was zipping uphill toward the bottles of liquor.

"Get out of here," Gamble shouted to Penny Dreadful.

"No," she said.

The liquor ignited with a *whump* as Gamble followed Burns and the girl outside. The razor had drawn a smear of blood where it touched her neck.

"Let her go."

The lodge was brilliant with the glow of the alcohol fire and flames were shooting from the smoke hole.

"After I trade her off," Burns said, "I swear I'm going to come back and show you—"

He didn't get the last of it out, because the girl had sunk her teeth into the hand that held the razor. The muscles in her jaws stood out as she bit down, and there was the sound of teeth grinding on bone. The razor fell from his hand into the snow, and Burns cried out.

With his other hand, he made a fist and struck the girl in the temple. She fell backward, a strip of his skin still between her teeth. Blood welled on the back of his hand and fell in splatters upon the ground.

"Run," Gamble said.

Burns reached out and grabbed a handful of the girl's long black hair, jerking her back. Gamble took his shot, shattering the man's wrist apart with a .38-caliber slug.

Now free, the naked girl ran.

"What the hell is going on out here?" Buell asked, standing in the snow twenty yards away. He was wearing only his union underwear and a pair of unlaced boots. His stick man and other motley residents of the Porch were arrayed behind him.

Burns held up the hand which dangled from the ruined wrist.

"Goddamn you," he said.

"I'm sure he will," Gamble said.

Then he fired a round into the left side of Burns's chest. The man staggered backward, his face gone blank with surprise. Then he steadied himself and, as realization came, he fixed Gamble with a wicked stare. He knelt, used his left hand to pick up the razor, then rose. He took a couple of steps toward Gamble, his face glowing with rage.

Gamble fired two quick shots, the slugs hitting just inches from the first wound. Burns fell over dead in the snow, the razor still in his hand.

The report from the last gunshot echoed from the side of Lookout Mount, then it became very still. The fresh blood steamed in the snow.

"That was murder," Buell said.

"It was self-defense," Gamble said, the Manhattan still in his hand. He ejected the three spent shells and replaced them with fresh cartridges from his pocket.

Gamble glanced around for the girl, but did not see her.

Then Gamble ran back to the burning lodge and threw the door covering aside. The heat made him shield his face with his arm. He shouted for Penny Dreadful, but there was no response—only the strangely sweet smell of burning flesh.

He holstered the gun and walked around to the horses. The animals were shuffling and stamping their hooves, trying to move away from the fire. Gamble took his pocket knife and methodically cut the leads that tied each of them to the picket line, starting with the buckskin.

He saved the chestnut mare for last, leading her

far away from the burning lodge. He dropped her lead in the snow, and she stayed there. He retrieved the blanket and saddle and tack from beneath the tarp and then took his time about rigging her up, speaking gently to her as he did.

"Mister."

It was Little Door Woman. She was still naked, her body shivering, but was determinedly pulling the buckskin by the lead rope through the snow. Her neck and chest were splattered with blood.

"Are you hurt?"

"Not my blood."

Gamble found another blanket beneath the tarp and threw it around her shoulders, then used a piece of rope to cinch it around her waist. Then he lifted her up onto the buckskin's back.

"You can't walk in the snow in bare feet," he said. "You'll lose some toes."

"My feet are all right."

"I don't see how. Tear some strips from the blanket and wrap them up. You'll have to ride him bareback, and guide him with the lead. Can you handle it?"

"I'm Kiowa," she said. "Can I come with you?"

"No," Gamble said. "I'm going to have people coming after me, and it wouldn't be safe. You're responsible for the winter count now, so you have to be careful."

"But I want to come with you," she said.

"Don't be foolish," Gamble said. "I'm an old man."

Gamble took a handful of coins from his vest pocket, wrapped the money in a bandanna, and handed it to her.

"Take this money now," he said. "No arguments.

Nobody should travel without money. And I've done it often enough to know."

"I thought you liked me."

"I do," Gamble said. "In the way that kinfolks like each other, you know? If I had, say, a girl child, I'd want her to have your kind of—what was that word for power?"

"Daughw-daughw."

"Yeah, that's it. Your kind of *daughw-daughw.* You'll do all right, daughter."

She smiled.

"You know which way to town?"

She pointed to the north.

"Go find the Methodist Church. They'll feed you and clothe you and take you back to Fort Sill. You don't have to pay them. Just tell them you love Jesus and everything will be square."

She nodded.

"Do you think an eagle will really fly around the moon?"

"Nothing would surprise me," he said.

"Me neither.'

She rode off, not looking back.

Gamble took his time in saddling the mare, to make sure that none of the denizens of the porch went after Little Door Woman. When he was sure she had gotten away, he knelt down and tightened the cinch strap again. Then he put his left boot into the stirrup and swung up into the saddle.

"Good girl," Gamble said.

Then he glanced over the Porch one last time.

The lodge poles had collapsed and the tipi was just a glowing pile of embers, burning away to nothing. A pillar of black smoke streaked the winter sky. The body of Lester Burns was still facedown in the snow. Buell and the others were milling about on the far side of the burned tipi, watching him.

"I knew you was bad news the moment I saw you," the old man called. "You'll have to answer to the law. Lester Burns was a wicked bastard, but he was one of us."

Gamble swung up onto the back of the mare.

"If you're so damned law abiding," he called, "why don't one of you get a gun and try to stop me?"

Nobody spoke or moved.

"I can wait."

Still nothing.

"That's what I thought."

"How far do you think you'll get in fresh snow?" Buell called.

"Don't know," Gamble said. "But I aim to find out."

He touched the brim of his hat.

"Happy New Year."

Gamble turned the mare, then put his heels to her sides. She shot forward, toward Oklahoma Territory.

NINE

Temple Houston tipped back the wooden chair and crossed his booted ankles on the top of the wooden desk. Folded and tucked into the pocket of his Prince Albert was the morning's paper.

"Mind if I see that?"

Jacob Gamble was on the other side of the desk, his feet flat on the floor, his hands bound by a pair of heavy iron cuffs. He was wearing the same clothes, now cleaned and patched, that he had been arrested in—a white shirt with no collar, a black vest, and dark coat. He took the paper, unfolded it, and put it on his side of the desktop. The headline screamed in seven-two-point type across all five columns at the top of the front page:

OKLAHOMA ANSWERS CALL FOR VOLUNTEERS!

Then, below:

Troops Being Organized for 1st Volunteer Cavalry Regiment across Oklahoma and Indian Territories—Recruiting Stations at Guthrie, Fort Sill, Muskogee

And in much smaller type:

New Mexico, Texas, Also Helping Recruiting Effort.

"Thinking about joining up?" Houston asked.

"Why not? I fought the Yankees thirty-five years ago," Gamble said. "Reckon I could bring myself to kill a Spaniard or two."

Houston laughed.

"Hell, even Fightin' Joe Wheeler has volunteered for this one, and the old rebel is sixty-two. You're a young man compared to him."

It had been a month after he had related the story of the killing of Lester Burns and being chased along Hell's Fringe by the German cousins, using up his money and his ammunition in the process. They were in a second-story office down the hall from the federal courtroom in the Herriot Building on the corner of Division and Harrison, where Gamble had been transported by Jailer Joe Miller for an extradition hearing. Miller was waiting outside the closed door while Houston conferred with his client.

A frenzied version of "Yankee Doodle," muted by the window glass, was drifting up from the street below, where a war rally was nearing its climax.

"It's going to be tough to explain to a territorial jury why you stole a pump-action shotgun from the hardware store and shot it out in the middle of the street instead of surrendering peaceably and going back to Kansas to plead your case," Houston said.

"You can try."

"Not even I am that good."

"You think I should waive extradition to Kansas?"

"No," Houston said. "You don't have a single witness to testify on your behalf, and from what you tell me, several who are eager to bear false witness against you. Truth is only useful if you can prove it."

"Then it's hard time for me."

"Yes, if Leedy doesn't stretch your neck first."

Temple slid open the middle door of the desk and began idly rummaging through the contents. He examined a few ink-encrusted nibs and a broken pencil, then threw them back.

"We've got to walk into that courtroom in about ten minutes and tell the judge what we're going to do," Temple said. "You know, I once represented a horse thief in your position, and he asked me for my best advice. I opened a window and left the room."

"We're on the second floor."

"Yes, that is unfortunate," Houston said, turning to glance out the window. On the street below, the band had taken up "The Battle Hymn of the Republic" encouraged by a crowd that went from curb to curb.

"I'm afraid letting another prisoner go like that will land me in the federal prison. The courts don't have as much of a sense of humor as they used to."

"It is a graceless age."

"I can't encourage you to escape," Houston said, "but I can point out that you have certain advantages that neither Bill Doolin nor Jesse James had. No wife and child to worry about, no other kin to keep you nearby, no gang members to betray you."

"No bullet while I stand on a chair to straighten a picture."

"The thing that does in most outlaws is that they can't leave their identities behind," Houston said. "Used to be, a man could escape to the frontier and become somebody new. Nobody ever asked what your name was in the States. But now, the frontier is gone. Oh, there's little patches here and there—Arizona, for example, and parts of New Mexico—but to truly escape I think you'd have to leave the country."

"Not that fond of it."

"How about the Pinkertons?" Houston asked. "They've been known to follow somebody overseas and haul them back. Ever had the Pinkertons on your tail?"

"Never."

"So, no Pinkerton file card with your particulars carefully recorded—height, weight, hair and eye color. The Bertillon measurements—the distance from your nose to the tip of the index finger of your outstretched hand, for example. And no mug shots."

"Never been photographed at all," Gamble said. "But what about this?" he asked, pointing a thumb to the eyepatch. "That's fairly distinctive."

"Eyewitness testimony is notoriously unreliable," Houston said. "I'll bet nobody around Caldwell, Kansas, can remember for sure whether that patch is over your left eye or your right."

"I forget myself, sometimes. It confuses me every time I look into a mirror."

"The idea is to go and sin no more," Houston said.

"That might be difficult, given my temperament," Gamble said. He was testing the handcuffs, folding his hands and trying to draw them though the manacles.

"Billy the Kid could slip his hands out of the cuffs when he wanted to, but his wrists were thick and his hands small," Gamble said. "I can't do it."

"Pray for a miracle," Houston said.

There was a knock at the door.

"What is it?" Houston called.

"There's a visitor to see the prisoner," Miller called. Houston shot Gamble a questioning look.

Gamble shrugged.

"Who is it?"

"It's his daughter. A breed."

"All right," Houston said, and he put his boots on the floor and smoothed his coat. "Let her in."

The door opened and there stood a thirteen-year-old girl in a blue print dress and her dark hair pulled back with a pink ribbon. In her hands she carried a wicker basket.

"Daughter," Gamble said.

"Hello," Little Door Woman said. "Mother refused to come, but I thought it my duty as a good Methodist to comfort you in your hour of need. After all, no matter what you have done, I simply can't disown you—I pray for your wicked soul every day."

"Perhaps I should leave you two alone," Houston said.

"That would be a kindness," Gamble said.

"Yes, that's all right," Miller said. "I checked the basket—sandwiches and some fruit. But remember, you only have a few minutes before you have to go before the judge."

"I understand," the girl said, stepping into the room after Houston had stepped out. "This won't take long."

"If you need anything, I'll be right here," Miller said. "All you have to do is shout."

"Of course. Thank you, sir."

Miller pulled the door closed.

"Surprised?"

"You could knock me over with a feather," Gamble said in a low voice. "How'd you find me?"

"I can read," she said, placing the basket on the desk. "It's been in all the newspapers about your hearing today, and about the shootout with the bounty hunters. So, I took my Jesus clothes and slipped away from the reservation. Oh, don't worry, I'll go back, but I figured it was best if nobody knew where I was."

"Why?"

"Because of this," she said, hitching up her skirt to reveal a wicked-looking skinning knife in a beaded sheath she had strapped to her thigh with rawhide.

"Sorry it's not a gun," she said, untying it. "Tried to get one, but they're expensive, and then I tried to steal one, and nearly got caught. So it's this old knife."

"I'll make it work," Gamble said, taking the knife and sheath into his manacled hands and tucking them into his shirt front. "Now, you had better get out of here, because things are going to happen right quick. You'll have a lot of explaining to do if they catch you."

"They won't," she said, taking the basket. "All Indians look the same to them. Oh, don't forget—there really is food in here."

"I don't know how to thank you, Little Door Woman."

"Seems to me you already have."

Gamble reached in and took one of the sandwiches.

"For later," he said. "Now, take off. Walk easy

until you hit the street, and then you run—and don't stop until you're back on the reservation."

"They'll hunt you."

"It's what they do," Gamble said. "Now, go."

She nodded.

"Sir!" she called.

After a moment's pause, Miller swung open the door.

"Thank you," she said, clutching the basket with one hand and wiping a tear away with the other. "This was difficult, but it was the right thing to do."

"Certainly," Miller said.

"God bless you," she said, and walked past him into the hall, then turned smartly and walked toward the stairs.

"Where's Houston?"

"Already in the courtroom, waiting," Miller said, motioning for Gamble to come out. "I hope you have seen what effect your actions have had on that sweet little girl."

"Oh, I have," Gamble said.

"Finish that before we get into the courtroom."

Gamble took a bite out of the corner of the sandwich. It was sourdough and cheese, with a sweet pickle that crunched satisfactorily in the middle.

Miller locked the door to the office, and then motioned for Gamble to lead the way down the hall to the big double doors that entered into the courtroom. Gamble started down the hall at a leisurely pace. He brought both hands up for another bite, but the sandwich slipped out of his fingers just before he could get it to his mouth.

"Sonuvabitch."

"Leave it," Miller said.

"Can't leave it in the hall in front of the courtroom," Gamble said. "Somebody's going to slip on it."

"You pick it up then."

Gamble held up his cuffed hands.

"I'm a mite challenged here, or I wouldn't have dropped it in the first place."

"Oh, all right," Miller said, getting his handkerchief out of his pocket. He bent down to retrieve the sandwich. Suddenly, Gamble threw his arms around his neck. In his left hand was the old skinning knife with its gleaming curved edge.

"Damn it, not again."

"Keep your voice down," Gamble said, pressing the knife against his throat. "You reach for your gun and I'm going to slit you from ear to ear. Yeah, you can feel how sharp that is, can't you?"

"Yes," Miller said, his eyes blinking.

"No, keep your head down," Gamble said. "Real quiet, you're going to get your key and unlock these cuffs. Got the key? Okay, bring it up and use both hands, real slow. No shouting for help or other nonsense. You know what I'm going to do if you try anything heroic, right?"

"Yes," Miller said.

He found the key in his pocket and brought it up.

"I can't see the lock," he said.

"Feel your way around for it."

Miller turned the key around in his hand and moved it over the thick part of the cuff, but fumbled. The key fell to the floor with a sharp sound.

"Pick it up," Gamble said.

Miller lifted the key from the floor.

"Deep breath," Gamble said. "Try again."

This time, the key slipped into the keyhole on the first try. Then Miller turned the key, and the cuffs went suddenly slack. Gamble held the cuffs and the knife in one hand and took Miller's pearl-handled Colt .45 Peacemaker from his holster.

"Put them on."

As Miller clamped the cuffs around his own wrists, Gamble sheathed the knife and stuck it in his pocket. Then he walked Miller back down the hall, toward the stairs.

"Are you going to shoot me?"

"Keep going. No, put your hands down. It looks suspicious."

"And a gun in my back doesn't?"

"Shut up."

They started down the stairs.

"Can I ask you a favor?"

"You can ask."

"Well, if you're not going to shoot me, could you at least rough me up a little? I mean, this is the second time for this. It will look bad if it doesn't look like I put up a fight."

"You're crazy," Gamble said as they reached the bottom of the stairs. The bottom floor was a dry goods store, but it was empty because the employees were on the sidewalk, watching the rally.

"All right," Gamble said, switching the gun to his right hand. "Close your eyes."

Miller did, and Gamble drove his fist into his right cheekbone. The jailer staggered and fell against the stairs, shaking his head. A trickle of blood was running from a nostril.

"Thanks," Miller said.

"Don't mention it."

Gamble tucked the .45 into his waistband, buttoned his coat over it, and stepped into the multitude around the recruiting stations on Harrison Avenue. Gamble pressed his way into the crowd while "The Stars and Stripes Forever" blasted from the bandstand, which was covered in red, white, and blue bunting.

The fools don't know what war is about, Gamble told himself while smiling and making small apologies as he threaded his way toward the opposite corner; this generation had never fought a war, so they had no idea, but they'd find out soon enough.

Once clear of the crowd, he hurried, but did not run, down Harrison to First, and then went north on First to Oklahoma Avenue. If there was any commotion behind him, he could not hear it above the sound of the band and the cheering crowd. On Oklahoma, he turned left and within a block was at Farquharson and Morris Hardware, where he went directly to the gun counter.

"What can I show you?" the fat old man behind the counter asked.

"Where's Andrew?"

"At the rally, I imagine."

"You his father?"

"No, I'm Morris. You a friend of the family?"

"Just of Andrew," Gamble said. "He showed me a Model 97 Winchester some time back, and I've taken a fancy to it. Would like to take it home with me today."

The old man turned and studied the rack of long guns.

"It's the one on the end."

"Oh, yeah," Morris said. He carefully placed the gun on the counter.

"Box of nitros, too. Double buck."

Morris turned, took a box of Petersens from the shelf, and placed them next to the shotgun.

"Not those, please," Gamble said. "I prefer the Robin Hood brand. Had good luck with them last time out."

"Of course," Morris said. He replaced the shells.

"Fine," Gamble said. "Now, I think Andrew was holding a gun for me."

"Really? He didn't say anything to me about it."

"It's an old one, a converted .36. Look under the counter, maybe."

The old man rummaged in the shelves beneath.

"There's only this old piece down here."

Morris came up from beneath the counter with the Manhattan.

"This can't be it, though, because that's the gun that what's-his-name left here just before the shoot-out with the bounty hunters," Morris said.

"That's it," Gamble said, drawing the pearl-handled Colt from his waistband. "I'm what's-his-name."

Morris rolled his eyes.

"Keep your hands where I can see them," Gamble said, examining the Manhattan. "Hands up higher, that's right. Back up a bit."

"You're going to end up as dead as Doolin."

"We all do, someday," Gamble said.

"Did you ever get any .38 rimfire cartridges in stock?"

"No call for them," Morris said.

"In that case, this won't do me much good," Gamble said, putting the Manhattan back on the counter. "Ask Andrew to keep it safe for me. Send it over to the gunsmith and have it chambered for some round you do stock—a .38 Colt center fire, perhaps. I'll be back for it, sooner or later."

He picked up the shotgun, turned it upside down, and shoved five shells into the magazine. Then he pumped the slide, driving a round into the chamber with the *ch-chink* he remembered from before. Then he cradled the shotgun in the crook of his right arm while he took the pearl-handled Colt, opened the gate, and worked the ejector until all of the cartridges were on the floor.

"Return Miller's gun to him, with my compliments," Gamble said. "Tell him he put up one helluva fight, and that I was lucky to get away. Got that?"

Then Gamble walked out the door and turned west on Oklahoma Avenue and proceeded at a steady pace, the shotgun under his arm. He was sure that Morris was watching him, and would soon be telephoning the authorities that Gamble was making for the depot. But at First Street, Gamble turned south, and walked unhurriedly down the block, exchanging pleasant greetings with those who passed. He took a right on Harrison, sure that Morris was still watching, and as soon as he cleared the corner, he ducked down the stone steps into the labyrinth of warehouses and stables beneath the streets of Guthrie.

Jacob Gamble found an unused and relatively

clean stall in a far corner of the underground livery.
He settled in the straw with the shotgun across his
lap and waited for nightfall. It was so peaceful in the
livery, with the distant and monotonous sound of
commerce coming from near the entrance, that he
fell asleep. When he awoke, the livery was quiet.

In the tack room, he found a broad piece of leather
and fashioned a sling for the Model 97. In a wooden
box where the lost-and-found items were thrown he
found a battered old Stetson, gray, that fit him rea-
sonable well, and a full-length sheepskin coat.

"It will do," he said.

Then he put a bit and bridle on a bay dun and led
it from its stall. He put a blanket on the horse's back,
then followed that with the best saddle he could
find. When he was done, he went to the mechanic's
toolbox and found a heavy pair of bolt cutters,
which he used to sever the chain from which the
padlock dangled on the other side of the gate. He
swung the gate inward, allowing access to the broad
ramp that led to street level. He slung the shotgun
across his back, mounted the horse, and rode up the
ramp to Second Street.

Guthrie was dark. The dun's hooves clattered on
the brick streets as he rode through the center of
town. A clock that hung out over the sidewalk from
the corner of the Capitol National Bank said it was
a few minutes after midnight.

When he reached Noble Avenue, he turned the
dun to the east to Indian Territory. It would take
him five days, traveling mostly at night, to reach
Muskogee.

TEN

The Muskogee recruiting station was a wooden desk on the street in front of the Mitchell House. On the desk were an open ledger book and an inkstand. Behind the desk was a corporal in a blue wool blouse and trousers of a lighter shade, not so patiently taking information in turn from each of the hundred or so would-be recruits who had queued up in front of the desk.

The hopefuls were a cross section of Indian Territory manhood: cowboys, Indians, gray-headed veterans of the Civil War, blacksmiths, clerks, farmhands, adolescents who had not yet had their first shave, lawyers, accountants, secondary school teachers, and criminals.

Jacob Gamble was standing in the front third of the line, the battered Stetson pulled low, the Model 97 slung over his shoulder. He had reached Muskogee shortly after dawn. On the way into town, he had passed a dairy farmer driving a flatbed wagon filled with cans of milk. As he passed, he saw the old farmer admiring the bay. He stopped, called to the man, and with an economy of words explained he was on his way to join the volunteers to free Cuba and might be interested in selling the horse, saddle and all. He walked the rest of the way to the Mitchell House, two hundred and fifty dollars tucked into his vest.

When it was Gamble's turn to step up to the desk, the young man in blue wool glanced at him through a pair of wire-rimmed glasses and put down the pen.

"Sorry," the corporal said in a vaguely eastern, college-educated accent. "No offense, but you're too old."

"How old is too old?"

"You have to be in good physical shape," the clerk said. "And you have only one eye. Next."

"Now, just hold on," Gamble said. "I want to kill me some Spaniards. I'll be damned if they're going to sink our battleships and strip-search our women. The papers say this outfit is looking for men who can ride and shoot, true frontiersmen, and that all comers are welcome to apply, as long as they are patriotic."

The corporal removed his glasses, closed his eyes, and rubbed the bridge of his nose.

"There are currently twenty volunteers for every man actually taken as a recruit," he said. "There are boys of fifteen swearing they are twenty. There are men of sixty swearing they are thirty-five or forty years old. So, just how old are you?"

"Why, I'm thirty-five," Gamble said.

"Thirty-five. You're sure?"

"My mother never lied to me."

"You don't look thirty-five."

"I've lived an outdoor life," Gamble said. "Folks tell me I look rugged, but not old. Look, I've come all the way from the Choctaw Nation to do my patriotic duty."

The men behind Gamble began to grumble.

"Come on," a black cowboy behind Gamble protested. "We've been standing here all morning. We're afraid we're going to miss the war."

"You've wasted your time," the corporal said. "You need to find a regular colored regiment."

"Hold it right there," the cowboy behind said. "I know this man. He's half Cherokee. I know you're taking Indians, because you've passed three while I've been watching."

"He's colored," the corporal said.

"He's Cherokee," the cowboy said. "He's plenty good enough to ride the river with, so he's plenty good enough to fight for our country. And you let this fellow pass as well—hell, you can't tell nothin' by looks. He just might be thirty-five."

"All right," the corporal said. "Settle down. I'll let the old man pass. But I'm sure he'll flunk the physical." He picked up the pen and dipped it in the inkwell.

"What's your name?"

"Jacob Dunbar."

"Age?"

"Told you, thirty-five."

"Right. Place of birth?"

"Southwest City, Missouri."

"Current residence and occupation?"

"Durant, Choctaw Nation. Payroll guard."

"All right," the clerk said, giving Gamble a tri-folded slip of paper with *Dunbar, J.* written in ink on it. "Take this inside, give it to the person inside wearing a uniform like mine, and wait for your name to be called."

Gamble took the slip of paper and walked up the steps to the hotel. He handed the paper to another young man, who showed him a seat on a long wooden bench next to a closed office door. He took a seat next to a man in city clothes who was at least twenty years younger and a head taller than Gamble. The man in the suit was nervous, and he leaned forward, resting his elbows on his knees, glancing anxiously at the door. He rubbed his hand briskly together and looked at Gamble.

"How're you this morning?"

"I'm fair," Gamble said, stretching his legs and crossing his ankles. "You?"

The man in the suit nodded vigorously.

"Ready to fight."

"Oh?" Gamble exclaimed. "How many fights have you been in?"

"Plenty," the first said. "There was this time at the Blue Duck Saloon back home when I took three men on at once. By the time I was done, my knuckles were—"

"Hold on," Gamble said. "You mean, you've been in fistfights."

"Well, yeah."

"Ever shoot anybody?"

"No, never had to."

"Had anybody shoot at you?"

"Never."

"Imagine those two things happening simultaneously."

The man in the suit nodded his head.

"You been shot at much?"

"Some," Gamble said.

"What's it like?"

"It's not so bad. Mostly, you're concentrating on staying alive and getting the other guy, or at least you should—if you don't, you're going to lose your nerve and end up dead right quick."

"I can see that."

"It helps to breathe."

"What do you mean?"

"Just what I say. You should remind yourself to keep breathing. Ever had buck fever? You held your breath, right? That's the natural reaction. But you have to fight the urge, breathe, and think coldly. It works just the same as when you gamble. You have to develop an attitude that is, well, dispassionate. It gets easier with practice."

The pair of cowboys that were behind Gamble at the desk came in, handed their papers over, and sat down on the bench, their hats in their hands.

The door to the office opened and a young man walked out, his shirt over his arm, his face clouded with disappointment.

"No luck, huh?" the anxious man asked.

"No luck at all," the dejected man said. "The doc says I'm too fat to ride a horse in the volunteer cavalry."

"Why, you don't look fat at all."

"Five pounds over."

The physician came to the door and called for the next man.

"Here I go," the anxious man said. "Wish me luck."

"Luck," Gamble said. Then, under his breath: "But probably not the kind of luck you want."

"Hey, you look familiar," the black cowboy said to Gamble. "Where're you from?"

"Just about everywhere," Gamble said. "Missouri—originally. You?"

"Lived in the Cherokee Nation all my life," the man said, extending his hand. "Name's Zeke. My father was from Missouri—a runaway slave. He came here and fell in love with my mother, a Cherokee girl."

Gamble turned to study his face.

"Your father wasn't from northeastern Missouri, was he?"

"Shelby County."

"Met a runaway slave there, when I was a boy during the war," Gamble said. "Seemed like a nice fellow. Had a fine voice. Hid him out in the loft of the barn and brought him some food, and he sang me some songs in return. Was determined to get west, which was odd—it made sense for runaways to go the other way, toward Illinois. But he reckoned true freedom was in the West."

"What was his name?"

"Don't know," Gamble said. "But wouldn't that be a strange coincidence, if that man were your father?"

"Mister, that couldn't be," the black cowboy said. "You're just thirty-five—you wouldn't even have been born yet."

The cowboys laughed, slapping their knees and throwing their heads back. Gamble allowed himself a smile.

"You got me there."

The door to the office slammed open and the anxious young man strode out, his face as crimson as if he had been sunburned.

"No luck?" Gamble asked.

"None," the man said. "I'm four inches too tall to be in the cavalry. He told me I'd have to wait and join an *infantry* regiment. Infantry, can you believe it?"

The cowboys winced.

"All right," the physician said. "Next."

Gamble rose.

"See you in Cuba," he told the cowboys.

He walked into the room and the doctor closed the door behind him. He was a man of about sixty, with gray hair and a paunch that extended from his unbuttoned black vest. His shirtsleeves were rolled up and there was a hand-rolled cigarette hanging from the corner of his mouth.

Gamble threw the old coat on the examining table and turned toward the doctor, leaning against the table and crossing his arms.

"Hell," the physician said, fumbling in his vest pocket for his glasses. "I can't even see yet and I can tell you're too damned old for this. What are you, forty-five? Fifty, maybe? And, you only got one eye."

The man found the glasses and hooked them over his ears.

"What's it going to take?" Gamble asked.

"What do you mean?"

Gamble reached into his pants pocket and brought out a handful of greenbacks.

"What's the going rate?" he asked, then counted out five twenty dollar bills onto the table.

Without comment, the physician puffed on his cigarette.

"You sign that paper, and I'm on my way to the Caribbean, right?"

The man nodded.

"If I sign it."

Gamble counted out another sixty dollars.

"That's eight months pay for a working man."

The doctor stared at the money, squinting against the cigarette smoke.

"You must be desperate, to make such a vulgar gesture," the doctor said, squinting against the cigarette smoke. "What kind of a doctor do you think I am?"

Gamble shrugged.

"Thought you might be a hundred and sixty dollar doctor," he said, picking up his coat. "Appears I was wrong."

Gamble picked up the money.

"Hold on." The physician threw the cigarette on the floor and ground it out with heel. "Make that a year's worth of wages and I'll swear you're not a day over thirty and that you had both your eyes when I examined you."

Gamble counted out two hundred and forty dollars.

"Welcome to the Rough Riders," the doctor said.

1899

ELEVEN

It was only eight o'clock in the morning, but the wind was already growling like an animal. It came from beyond the southwestern horizon, picking up sand and dirt along the way, and scouring the land raw.

Jacob Gamble sat in a galvanized washtub, his pink arms and legs dangling over the sides, his left hand gripping a brown bottle of beer, the brim of a battered brown campaign hat pulled low to keep the dust out of his eyes. The hat was misshapen, stained with sweat, torn at the crown, and had the crossed sabers cavalry insignia pinned to the front.

Gamble took a swig of warm beer.

"God, but this is an awful country."

The woman kneeling behind blew a strand of dark hair from her eyes and she used both hands to wring soap from a sponge. She was wearing only a man's flannel shirt, unbuttoned, and with the sleeves rolled to her elbows. Her bare forearms gleamed with bathwater.

"It's not so bad," she said, dragging the sponge languidly across his shoulders. "It's peaceful, at least when the wind dies down just before dark. There's nobody around to pester you. That's why you came here, wasn't it? So nobody would pester you?"

"That's what I said, so nobody would pester me. But I didn't count on this damned blowing grit getting into everything. It even gets in the food. Hell, I think all my teeth are worn flat because of it."

She leaned down and kissed his shoulder.

"Your teeth," she said, "are still plenty sharp."

Gamble grunted and took another swig of beer.

Driven by the wind, a tumbleweed rolled across the ground, not a dozen yards beyond the tub.

"I hate those damned things," Gamble said. "You never saw any in the old days. Then, about twenty years ago, you'd see one here and there—hung up in a fence, usually. Now, they're everywhere."

"They seem normal to me."

"That's because you grew up with them. But I grew up before Russian thistle won the West."

She scrubbed his lower back.

"It's going to be hotter than a two-dollar pistol today," he said.

"But it's not now," she said. "You promised to tell me about the war. When will you?"

"What do you want to know? Like most wars, it began in April," Gamble said. "It lasted about one hundred days, and when it was over, folks were dead. There were widows and orphans. We liberated Cuba and sunk the Spanish fleet in the Philippines and got Puerto Rico and some islands in the Pacific as spoils of war. We knocked over the Spaniard imperialists and have now become world-class imperialists ourselves."

"No," the girl said. "Tell me about your part."

"I killed Spaniards," he said. "Spaniards tried to kill me."

"Are you always this difficult?" the girl asked.

"What's your name, girl?"

"Agnes," she said. "You know my name."

"Ah, Agnes, forgive me," Gamble said. "But yes, you will always find me at least this difficult, sometimes more. Ask anybody."

She frowned.

"Did you have another nightmare?" she asked. "About your father?"

"Ghost," Gamble said. "No nightmare. Big difference."

"Well, I haven't seen him."

"I would count that as a blessing."

He finished the beer.

"Fetch me something to write with."

She dried her hands on the tail of the shirt, stood, and walked barelegged through the open door of the sod house behind them. She came back with a pencil, a pocketknife, and a ledger book.

"Who are you writing?" Agnes asked.

"The governor of New York."

"You are so full of jokes," Agnes said.

"Yes, I am a fellow of infinite jest," Gamble said, sharpening the pencil with the pocket knife. "I am about to write a Republican for a favor, and isn't that a hoot."

Gamble opened the ledger book to a blank page, moistened the pencil lead with his tongue, and began to write.

Colonel, Sir,
   Perhaps you remember me, Jacob Dunbar.
I was with Company L of the Rough Riders in
Cuba, from Las Guasimas to the end of the
campaign . . .

Gamble paused.

Thinking of Cuba gave Gamble an odd feeling. It was as far from the war he had experienced as a boy in Missouri as anything he could imagine. It was equal parts carnival, theater, and abattoir. The night after the landing, on a tropical beach, scoured by the blindingly white searchlights from the warships, they had built scores of campfires on the sand to dry their wet clothes and to cook up an early breakfast of bacon and coffee. Platoons of nude men were running into the surf, laughing and joking.

While the Rough Riders had drilled with their newly issued .30-caliber Krag-Jørgensen bolt-action carbines, none had yet fired them—the ammunition for the rifles did not arrive until they had reached Cuba. Some had been allowed to keep trusted personal weapons, especially the .30-40 Winchester which would fire the government rounds. Also on the beach sat a weird-looking contraption called a "dynamite gun" which had a narrow fourteen-foot barrel with an air cylinder slung beneath it; it used compressed air to lob a five-pound package of high explosives less than 900 yards—a shorter distance than the Krags could propel their bullets. Meanwhile, thousands of other troops were being off-loaded from the transports, including regular and colored regiments, and there was a shortage of small boats—and the surf was running high. One boatload

of colored soldiers capsized, and two of them—
laden down with their gear—had drowned. For the
Rough Riders, the landing was the crowning chaos
that had followed weeks of chaos, from hasty training at San Antonio to a confused boarding of troop
ships at Tampa. Because of the lack of adequate
transport, the regiment's mounts had been left
behind and the Rough Riders had arrived in Cuba
without their horses.

Before arriving in Texas, Gamble had removed
the eye patch and begun wearing smoke-colored
glasses in wire frames that looped behind the ears,
making it difficult for others to spot the milky and
blind right eye. When asked, he said the colored
glasses had been prescribed by a doctor for an eye
condition—granulated eyelids. Wasn't that what
Jesse James was said to have suffered? At San Antonio, because of his ability to persuade the rowdier
elements with the territorial company to accept a
modicum of army discipline, he had been made sergeant by the company commander. The commander, Captain Allyn Capron Jr., a fifth-generation
career soldier whose grandfather had been killed
during the war with Mexico, was blond, blue-eyed,
and square cut, and worried that the war would be
over before the territorial volunteers would have a
chance to fight. Capron left behind a wife at Fort
Sill, and his father—who was an artillery officer in
the regular army—was also bound for Cuba.

During training, Capron had suspended the tra-
dition of saber practice and instead made the volunteers prove their riding and shooting skills. Capron
had allowed Gamble to keep his Winchester Model

1897 shotgun, after witnessing Gamble turning a succession of watermelons to pink mist with it from the back of a horse. Although Gamble was a competent rider, with deadly aim, he did not relish the exercise as much as the other volunteers; he considered horses a thousand pounds of unpredictable, and when the horses were delayed and did not make the transport ship at Tampa, he was secretly relieved.

He had always done his best fighting on foot.

The day after the landing near Daquiri, the Rough Riders were marched through to Siboney, where they made camp in heavy rain. In the morning, they were ordered to join with regular troops and Cuban rebels to advance inland and engage the Spanish, who were retreating from the shelling from the white-sided American warships. The jungle was thick and the men were forced to move single file down the path, with Company L near the front. Four miles north, at a fork in the trail called Las Guasimas, the column found the Spanish.

The Spanish were about to abandon their entrenched position and fall back to Santiago, but the appearance of Cuban insurgents and the Americans made them dig in. They opened up from the jungle with their Mausers, which fired a 7mm smokeless round, making it impossible to spot the location of the Spanish gunmen. Many of the regular Army soldiers carried the old trapdoor Springfields, which shot black powder, creating a puff of white smoke that immediately gave away their position.

Gamble was near the front of the line when the bullets began rippling the jungle around him. He clutched the Model 97 and threw himself in the foliage beside the trail. Ahead, a Cuban scout and a Rough Rider sergeant named Hamilton Fish lay dead. Capron came running up from behind, a revolver in his hand.

"Captain!" Gamble shouted. "Get down!"

Capron appeared not to hear him. Running, he fired three shots from his revolver into the jungle hillside ahead, then he paused and turned.

"Let's go, men!" Capron shouted. "This is the moment we have been waiting for!"

Just then a bullet struck Capron in the thigh, and he dropped to the ground. He struggled to get up, and then another bullet struck him in the chest. The captain fell on his side on the path, his revolver beside him.

"Damn it to hell," Gamble said.

He threw off his bedroll and haversack, slung the shotgun over his back, and ran forward in a crouch. He grasped the back of Capron's collar and dragged him off the trail, to the protection of a boulder.

Gamble ripped open Capron's tunic, sending buttons flying. There was a dark hole in his left chest, oozing blood. He clamped his right hand over the wound.

"Surgeon!" Gamble shouted.

"It's nothing," Capron said, a pink froth staining his blond mustache.

"Be still," Gamble said. "You're hit right good. Surgeon!"

The firing became more intense, and Gamble unlimbered the shotgun and held it at the ready.

"Advance," the captain croaked. "We've got the Spaniards on the run. We must press our advantage."

"The Spanish occupy the high ground and they

have us pinned down," Gamble said, pressing his kerchief against the wound.

"Are you refusing an order?" Capron rasped.

"Damn right I am," Gamble said. "Sir."

There was a flash of color on the trail ahead, and Gamble saw for a moment the distinctive blue and white striped *rayadillo* fabric of a Spanish uniform. He took up the Model 97, thrust its barrel over the rock, and fired. If the buckshot hit anything, there was no sign.

"Surgeon!" Gamble called again.

"What's happening?" Capron asked.

"Nothing good," Gamble said. There were moans from both sides of the trail from wounded Rough Riders.

A lieutenant came rushing up the trail and dropped in beside Gamble and Capron.

"Thomas," Capron said, smiling.

"We've got to get you back to the dressing station, sir."

"I want to see it out," Capron said. "I want to see it all."

"You will," Thomas said.

"The sergeant rushed forward and pulled me from the line of fire," Capron said. "He deserves a commendation. Remind me later to put that in my report."

"I will," Thomas said.

The heat and humidity were oppressive. Sweat ran down Gamble's chest, and he stripped off his shirt and threw it aside, but kept his canteen and his cartridge belt.

"Orders?" he asked.

"The colonel believes the Spanish are holed up in an old distillery up ahead," Thomas said. "A ruined rock building. We must advance along this path and take it."

"Advance?" Gamble asked. "They're likely to cut us to pieces."

"That's right," Thomas said. "Advance. Gather some men."

"Yes, sir," Gamble said.

Again he set off down the trail, but this time the rattle of the Mausers seemed farther away. As he went forward, he motioned for others to follow, and bare-chested soldiers emerged cautiously from the jungle. Fifty yards down the path, they came upon a Rough Rider, dead, flung on his back beside the path, his head shattered, a pool of dark blood soaking the rocks and leaves, his Krag rifle beside him. Crawling over his chest and face were a undulating cluster of land crabs, their legs and pincers in constant motion, their purple-red bodies shockingly obscene against the young man's white flesh.

One of the soldiers began brushing the crabs away with the butt of his rifle, but Gamble put a hand on his shoulder.

"There's no helping him now," Gamble said. "Come on, we don't want to give the Spanish a chance to make any more of us into crab food."

They pressed on, steadily trading shots with the enemy, who always seemed just ahead. Other troops came up, and after an hour and a half they came to a series of shallow breastworks and an old stone building, all deserted, but littered with piles of 7mm shell casings. The Spanish had been falling back toward the village of Santiago from the moment the Rough Riders had set foot upon the path. Even though the U.S. forces suffered seventy dead and wounded (including Lieutenant Thomas and a correspondent for *The New York Journal*), compared to less than a dozen for the Spanish, the engagement was declared an American success.

The next morning, a man in his middle fifties wearing an artillery officer's uniform sought Gamble out. He found him napping, with his back against a stone wall.

"I'm Captain Capron," he said. "Allyn Capron Sr., actually. I am told that you were with my son yesterday when he . . . well, when he died."

Gamble pulled on the smoke-colored glasses.

"I was with him when he was hit," Gamble said. "Not later, sir."

"Tell me about the boy's death," the man said, sitting down next to Gamble. "I've heard nothing definite. How many times was he shot?"

"Twice. Once in the thigh, and the second time in the chest."

"He kept on, didn't he?"

"Yes," Gamble said.

"He didn't quit?"

"No," Gamble said. "He made light of the wound and urged his men to advance."

"That's good," Capron said. "I knew he'd die right."

Gamble nodded.

"Well, I suppose it will be my turn next," the man said. "It will make the third of us. His grandfather was killed in Mexico. I hope I get off five good rounds at the bloody Spaniards, and I hope that when it is my turn to go, I die right as well."

"Your son was a fine soldier," Gamble said. "The colonels say he was the finest soldier in the outfit, and I guess they should know."

The man smiled and put his hand on Gamble's knee.

"You don't know what a comfort you have been," he said. "Thank you, Sergeant. Now, is there anything I can do for you?"

Gamble studied the man and decided to trust him.

"Confidential?"

The man nodded.

"I was in some trouble in the territory," he said. "Think you could put a word in for me with the authorities?"

Allyn Capron Sr. contracted typhoid a few days later and returned to Florida, where he died.

You see, Colonel, my real name isn't Dunbar, it's Jacob Gamble. I had to change it after I got into some trouble at Guthrie, O.T., and it seemed proper that I used my mother's maiden name. The thing is, Captain Capron Sr. had promised to help me ask for a pardon for my crimes from President McKinley, but of course there was no time to do that during the fighting in Cuba— and no point after. What I was hoping, Colonel, is that you might be able to pick up the promise the Captain had made me in Cuba. You can reach me in care of my friend and attorney, Temple Houston, Woodward, Oklahoma Territory.

Gamble stared at what he had written, and then leaned his head back against the rim of the tub. The water had become warm. He pushed the hat back on his head and looked at the sky. High above, a turkey buzzard was wheeling.

Since being mustered out at Guthrie last year, Gamble had been hiding out in No Man's Land, that narrow strip between Texas and Kansas where there was no law and damned little of anything else.

He looked at the sheet of paper again and, in a fit of anger, crumpled it into a ball and threw it. The wind caught it and carried it along the ground, like it was a tumbleweed. Agnes stepped out of the sod house and put her foot on it.

"Why'd you do that?" she asked, picking the paper up from the ground. She unfolded it and read what Gamble had written.

"Jacob, you must mail this," she said.

"There's not a post office within thirty miles."

"The Rock Island is laying tracks south from Liberal," she said. "I'm sure they're past Sanford Switch by now, maybe even all the way to Texas line. The switch is only twenty miles from here. You can walk it."

"That's optimism," Gamble said.

"Climb out of that tub," she said. "Shave your face and comb your hair. Your clothes are washed and ironed. I'll pack your other things."

"Sounds like you're trying to get rid of me."

"You've been planning your escape for weeks," she said. "You might as well go ahead. Oh, don't give me that look. It's better to talk about it. This way, you don't have to lie to me."

"All right," Gamble said.

"You're not coming back, are you?"

"No."

"Then I just want to know one thing," Agnes said. She folded her legs beneath her, sat beside the tub, and put a hand on his forearm. "What did I do wrong?"

"Girl, you did nothing wrong," Gamble said. "But I'm damned near thirty years older than you. It would be a special kind of sin if I stayed."

"Not if I wanted you to."

"Especially if you wanted me to," Gamble said. "Find yourself a younger man, have kids or not, live a good life. Don't waste yourself on me."

She shook her head.

"Seems that should be my decision, not yours," she said.

"You've been living in that soddie since your Daddy dragged you here in the run of 1890," Gamble said. "He'll be here forever—he's buried out back. But you're still walking and talking, and you can get out. But you won't if I stick around. You'll stay here and make a kind of living by growing potatoes and selling warm beer and weak whiskey to the odd cowboy."

"Then take me with you."

"So you can watch as they hunt me down and kill me?" he asked. "You might want to ask Edith Doolin about how that feels. No, Agnes, I'll not let you play that role."

"Then don't play Bill Doolin," she said. "You really are an old fool, aren't you? Send that damned letter, get the pardon you were promised, and come back for me."

"And what if there's no pardon?"

Agnes hit the side of the tub with her fist, splashing water in Gamble's face. She stared at him with narrowed eyes, seemingly on the verge of telling him something, then changed her mind and looked away.

"Then you rob the biggest fucking bank you can find," she said, "and I'll meet you in Mexico."

TWELVE

The panhandle seemed to stretch forever in every direction that Jacob Gamble looked—except down. He walked at a steady pace, the shotgun slung over his left shoulder, a haversack riding on his right hip, the smoke-colored glasses shielding his eye from the wind and sun.

At about noon, he found a rock almost big enough to sit on, squatted down on it, and uncorked the stopper from the tin, canvas-covered canteen. The water was hot and metallic tasting. Then he unwrapped the ham sandwich that Agnes had packed him, removed half of it, and wrapped the rest back up in the brown paper and returned it to the haversack. He ate slowly, glancing idly at the dirt and scrub around him. There were clusters of buffalo bones scattered about, where twenty years before a buffalo hunter—for profit, for sport, or simply out of boredom—had pumped a few rounds into a herd. There were some scattered rocks embedded in the hard earth. One of the rocks, ten yards away, was bulbous and a dirty white color and had a jagged hole the size of a walnut on top.

Gamble realized it was not a rock, but a human skull.

He walked over to the skull and nudged it loose from the dirt with the toe of his boot. The skull rolled over to stare at him with blank eye sockets and a grin that was missing many teeth.

"Hello, old-timer," Gamble said. "Been here long?"

Then the wind quieted and he could hear the thud of hooves, the rattle of trace chains, and the squeal of wood. He turned and saw a heavy wagon pulled by a team of oxen approaching from the east. The back of the wagon was heaped with a cargo of what from a distance looked like a jumble of broken up furniture, in white.

Five minute later, the wagon rattled to a stop beside Gamble's rock. The driver was a weird-looking man with wild gray hair, a face with a low brow and a broad jaw, and limbs that seemed too long for him. On the right side of his forehead was a curious discolored patch, blue and brown, that was disturbingly ugly. His clothes were filthy and he appeared unarmed, except for an enormous knife with a brass hilt that was sheathed at his belt. He set the brake, dropped the reins, and jumped from the wagon to the ground.

"What are you after?" the bone hauler asked, his eyes threatening to pop from their sockets.

"What do you mean?" Gamble asked.

"The shotgun," the man said, snatching up a buffalo rib and tossing it in the same motion. The bone clattered on the pile already in the back of the wagon. "What are you hunting?"

Gamble turned philosophical.

"Whatever comes along, I suppose."

"Nothing will come along," the bone hauler said, picking up another rib bone and giving it a toss over his shoulder. It missed the wagon by a yard. "Everything's dead, all of it, just like the buffalo."

"Well, not everything is dead," Gamble said. "We're walking and talking."

"We're dead all right."

Then the bone hauler spotted the skull and scooped it into his freakishly long fingers. He examined it for a moment, then lobbed it like a ball into the bed of the wagon.

"What the hell?"

"Bones is bones," the man said.

"That one was human."

"Bones is getting scarce," the bone hauler said. "Used to be, I wouldn't have to go more than five or six miles outside Dodge and have a wagon full. I have no idea where the hell we are now. Do you know?"

"No Man's Land," Gamble said. "Old Cimarron Territory, the Seventh County, now Beaver County. The Panhandle. Dodge City is more than a hundred miles to the northeast."

"No, I don't think Dodge is that far," the bone hauler said, then turned his attention again to the ground. "See any more of the old fellow? Usually, there's more. Rib cage, vertebrae, long bones, fingers and toes. That noggin was pretty light—it's been out here a long time. Maybe some poor Indian that got thwacked on the head with a stone axe and left here in the Cimarron desert and a coyote carried off the head."

"More likely the rest of him—or her—is buried in the dirt."

"Right, good thinking," the bone hauler said. He dropped to his knees and began digging with the blade of his knife.

"What are you doing? The remains of humanity can't add much weight to your pile."

"Bones is bones."

The knife flashed, carving away dirt and sand.

"Aha!" he cried, picking a phalange from the hole. "A finger."

"Surely that is too small to—"

The man flung it toward the wagon. It fell far short.

"Why are you wearing that ridiculous jacket?"

Gamble self-consciously rubbed the yellow trim on his cuff. The jacket was unbuttoned over a collarless undershirt. His blue jeans were stuffed into a pair of tan cowboy boots.

"It's the only jacket I have," he said. "We didn't wear these in Cuba, we were given them just before we mustered out. In Cuba we had wool, not khaki."

The man continued gathering and throwing buffalo bones at a furious pace.

"Cuba," he said. "Cuba. Don't recall hearing of that town before. What part of Oklahoma is that?"

"It's an island," Gamble said. "About a hundred miles off the coast of Florida. There was a war there last year. Hear of it?"

"No. Who won?"

"We did," Gamble said.

The man grunted.

"You know who is president now?"

"Sure," he said. "Hayes. No, Garfield."

"You're only four or five behind," Gamble said. "It's been William McKinley for a few years now."

"Never heard of him."

Gamble looked at the dark splotch on the man's forehead.

"How long have you been doing this?"

"Since sixty-nine or seventy, maybe."

"That's a long time to make your living beneath the sun."

"I told you, we're all dead," he said. "Dead and don't know it. We're all corpses, and we just think we're eating and drinking and fucking, but it's all an illusion. The world has gone away and each and every one of us is but a shade upon the earth."

"The cancer has made you as mad as Ahab."

"Of course," the bone hauler said. "But that doesn't mean I'm wrong."

The bone hauler was on his knees, stabbing the ground savagely with the knife.

"Balls, I'll never find all of him," he said, rocking back on his heels. "Now, what am I going to do?"

"Perhaps what you were doing before."

The bone hauler's face went slack, his eyes clouded, and his chin dropped to his chest. The knife fell from his fingers. His spidery fingers went up the side of his face to his forehead to probe the cancerous mass.

He threw his head back and let out an inhuman cry.

Then he snatched up the knife by the blade and

brought it to his forehead and began scraping at the tumor. Blood flowed over his brow and into his eyes.

"Stop that," Gamble said.

The bone hauler paused, the whites of his eyes flashing through a veil of blood. He dropped his hands and the knife slipped from his fingers.

"The cancer is killing me," he said.

"But you can't get it out that way," Gamble said.

"Can't get it out any way. I've consulted with surgeons. To remove it, they wanted to hack out a chunk of my brain as well. Not much of a choice, is it?"

The bone hauler tore a strip of dirty cloth from the tail of his shirt, mopped the blood from his eyes, and wound the cloth around his head.

"Would you kill me?"

Gamble didn't answer.

"Just put that shotgun against my temple and blow my brains out," the man pleaded. "I'll fall right here, and my bones will mix with those of that old feller and make a complete set and then some."

"I wouldn't feel right about it."

"Told you, we're already dead. Where's the sin?"

"I cannot do it," Gamble said.

"Coward."

"When's the last time you've eaten?"

"I don't know."

Gamble took the other half of the sandwich from the haversack and held it up.

"Here," he said.

"I can't. The thought of it makes me sick."

The bone hauler got to his feet, picked up the knife, and returned it to its sheath. He walked over to the wagon, climbed up into the seat, and released the brake.

"Where you headed?" Gamble asked.

"Does it matter?"

The bone hauler flicked the reins and the mules surged forward. The wagon passed Gamble amid a cacophony of protesting metal, leather, and wood. He watched the tailgate as it drew farther and farther ahead, then looked up at the blazing sun high in the sky.

THIRTEEN

Jacob Gamble sat on the wooden bench outside the Sanford Switch depot, his arms crossed over his khaki uniform, the letter to Theodore Roosevelt in a breast pocket. His hat was low over his smoke-colored glasses. On the platform beside him was the haversack and the pump shotgun.

The railway agent was leaning against a post, sweating.

"You a Rough Rider?" the agent asked.

"I was," Gamble said, wishing he had another jacket.

"What was it like?" the agent asked. "Cuba, I mean."

"Hot," Gamble said.

"Hell, this is hot."

"Hotter than this," Gamble said. "And damp. With crabs."

"I thought about joining up," the agent said, his bloodshot eyes darting about. "Would have, if it had lasted a little longer."

"Sure."

"How about that ride up San Juan Hill?"

"We didn't ride," Gamble said. "We walked."

"You go in as a lieutenant?" the agent asked, looking at the insignia on the collar of the khaki jacket.

"No," Gamble said.

"Then how'd you get those bars?"

"The Spanish shot all of the company's officers."

"Wish some of my bosses would goddamned die," the agent said, nodding.

"How far do the tracks go?" Gamble asked.

"Damn near to Texas by now," the agent said. "The train goes all the way to the end of track, to drop off passengers and supply the work crew, then backs up all the way to Liberal. Helluva way to run a railroad."

The agent pulled a bag of tobacco out of his pocket and began rolling a cigarette. When he had the thing assembled to his satisfaction, he stuck it in the corner of his mouth and struck a match on the post. He took a long drag, coughed, and picked a fleck of tobacco from the tip of his tongue.

"Where're you from?"

"Indian Territory."

"What's your name?"

"Dunbar."

The agent nodded.

"Sure you don't want to leave that letter with me?" the agent asked, exhaling smoke. "I'll make sure it gets on the express car. I've already sold you the 10-cent Special Delivery stamp."

"I'll wait," Gamble said.

"Suit yourself," the agent said, taking out his

pocket watch and popping open the lid. "But you'll be sitting on that bench for more than three hours."

"I've sat places longer."

The agent shrugged and walked back inside the depot.

Gamble crossed his legs and rested his head on the back of the bench. He was nearly asleep when he heard boots on the platform. Fearing that it was the agent come back to make more small talk, he kept his eyes closed.

"I grew kind of fond of the beef and beans and cornbread at the jail in Guthrie," a familiar voice said. "How about you, fiddler?"

"Mickey Dray," Gamble said, then opened his eyes.

"In the flesh," the boy said. "Boy, howdy, look at you. All fine and military and an officer, to boot. Love the glasses. You made the folks in Guthrie hopping mad with your escape, I tell you what."

"Keep your voice down," Gamble said. "The station agent is a curious sort. How'd you get out?"

"Acquitted," Dray said. "Don't you love our American system of justice? Seems that star witness against me turned up dead along Cotton Creek, and they had no choice but to release me—after all, I was safe in jail when the poor wretch threw himself off the bridge and dashed his brains out on a rock below."

"I'm sure he had some encouragement."

"Dynamite Dick wasn't supposed to kill him," the boy lamented, shaking his head. "Just scare him enough to keep him from testifying. I feel kind of bad about it."

"So you're back to stealing horses?"

"Naw," Dray said, sitting down on the bench and brushing his long hair out of his eyes. "I've moved on to bigger things. Matter of fact, the next job I pull is going to involve a certain Rock Island payroll."

"You mean, the next job you and Dynamite Dick pull."

"No, I mean just me," Dray said. "And I'm looking for a partner."

"I don't do banks or trains," Gamble said. "It attracts the Pinkertons."

Then Gamble thought of Agnes and of living the rest of his life in peace in Mexico. What would it take? Five thousand? He turned his head and looked through the window into the depot. He could see the agent sitting at his desk, pouring a tin cup of whiskey from a bottle he had taken from the bottom drawer of his desk.

"All right, horse thief," Gamble said. "Just for chuckles you tell me what you have in mind."

The boy grinned.

"Well, you know the Rock Island is driving south to the Texas line," he said. "They're five or ten miles from the Texas line and they've got a crew of Irishmen laying rail."

"Big work crew?"

"A couple of hundred," he said. "And they get paid, in cash money, the second Friday of each month."

Gamble was doing some mental calculations. A month's wages for two hundred workers would be fifteen to twenty thousand dollars, maybe more.

"How do you know all of this about the payroll?" Gamble asked.

"Because I was down at the mick's camp at the end of last month when the payroll arrived," he said. "It was hell on wheels, let me tell you. As long as the Irish have money in their pocket, the booze will flow. And when they drink, they start running their mouths. I was playing cards with four of them and heard it all."

Gamble looked over his shoulder to make sure the agent was still at his desk. He was, refilling the tin cup with more whiskey.

"So, what's your plan?" Gamble asked. "You're going to have to get the train stopped, somehow. In the old days, they used to pile up logs or tear up the tracks. Jesse and Frank James pried up the rails at Adair, Iowa, and ended up derailing the entire damned train and killing the engineer by accident. It's a touchy business."

"You're going to love this," the boy said, then reached into his pocket and pulled out a metal device that was about the size of a deck of cards, but with four lead ribbons running from the top and bottom.

Gamble picked it up. It was unexpectedly heavy and he nearly dropped it.

"Careful," Dray said. "It'll blow your hand off."

"What is it?"

"A torpedo," Dray said. "This is what the railroad uses when they want to stop a train to warn them of danger up ahead. Three or four of these are hooked to the rail with these lead straps, and they explode—bang, bang, bang!—when the locomotive passes over. The explosions are loud enough for the engineer to hear over the noise of the train, so he brings the train to a stop double quick."

"Clever," Gamble said. "How many of these do you have?"

"Three," he said. "Stole 'em when I was in the railroad camp."

"Okay," Gamble said, handing the torpedo back. "You get the train stopped without killing anybody."

"Reckon to stop the train about halfway between here and the end of the line, where there is a whole lot of nothing. And we've got our choice of state lines to cross after—they won't know whether we slipped down into Texas, up to Kansas or Colorado, or over to New Mexico."

"All right, but you haven't told me how you're going to rob the train."

"That's the problem," Dray said. "Sure, I know the payroll will be in the safe in the express car, but I can't keep the train crew covered and open the express car all by myself. I need a partner."

"Or two," Gamble said. "There's going to be a lot happening at once. You not only have to worry about the engineer and fireman in the cab of the locomotive, but the conductor and the passengers as well. You have to get the express car door open, somehow."

"Dynamite says he has a technique for that."

"Okay, so you do have a partner. But then you have to persuade the express messenger to open up the safe, forthwith."

"What's the best form of persuasion?"

"A cocked and loaded pistol against the head," Gamble said. "If he is still reluctant, then a ball in the kneecap would be the next argument."

"That's the part I have trouble with."

"Shooting somebody?"

"Don't think I can do it."

"Then you're in the wrong line of work," Gamble said. "Why don't you get Dynamite Dick to help you with that part?"

"Afraid of him."

"Thought he was your friend."

"Keep thinking about him and me dividing the loot after," he said. "Keep imagining myself dead on the plain and him riding away with all of it."

"That would prove difficult for him," Gamble said, "if you had a partner who had some experience in killing."

The boy grinned.

"This could be done with three people," Gamble said. "One on board and two on the ground. My preference is to be the one on the train. From what you've told me, I'm sure this Dynamite Dick can handle shooting kneecaps. You would have to be sure to wear disguises."

"Sure," Dray said. "But what about you? It would be a little suspicious to wear a bandanna over your face from the time you get on the train. And after the robbery, they'd have a pretty damn good description of you."

"No, they'd have a description of Lieutenant Dunbar," Gamble said. "Frankly, I'm a little tired of the lieutenant—it's about time to become myself again."

"But what about your rule about banks and trains?"

"I'll make an exception," Gamble said, "for one last job. Then I retire to Mexico, or maybe farther south. Not even the Pinkertons could find me there."

"I like the way you think," Dray said.

"So, when were you planning to do this?" Gamble asked.

The boy grinned.

"Today is Friday, June ninth," Dray said. "It has to be now, or we wait another month. I came to the switch to ask the agent about the schedule for today."

"We've only got three hours."

"That's enough time," Dray said. "Get on that southbound train and be ready to raise hell when it stops. I'll have you a horse waiting."

Gamble leaned forward and rested his forearms on his knees.

"Why should I trust you?"

"Because we're pards," the boy said. "Because we served time in jail together. Because I think you're all out of luck and this is the very last chance you got."

They shook hands.

"Now, get out of here before somebody takes notice of you," Gamble said. He waited until he thought another twenty or thirty minutes had passed, then went inside the depot.

"How much for a ticket south?"

"What," the agent asked, slurring his words. "You have a sudden urge to see Texas?"

"Something like that."

"You'll have to take a coach at the end of the track to take you into Texas, but when you reach the tracks on the other side you can get another ticket that will take you to Amarillo."

"I understand. How much?"

"Two dollars and fifty cents," the agent said.

Gamble dug into his pockets and came out with a handful of coins. He counted out the full amount, which left him with only thirty-five cents.

The agent stamped and then handed him a ticket.

"What about that letter?" the agent asked. "I should put it in the mail bag for the train to take back on its return to Liberal."

"Think I'm going to hold onto it for a spell," Gamble said. "It's one of those sensitive things—I'd better give it some more thought before I post it. Thanks all the same."

"Sounds like a waste of a ten-cent stamp to me."

FOURTEEN

Jacob Gamble walked down the aisle, the haversack slung over his right shoulder. He had broken the shotgun down to board the train, and a few inches of barrel and the butt of the scarred walnut stock poked out of the haversack. The coach was empty except for an older man and a younger, auburn-headed woman sitting together near the middle, and Gamble touched the brim of his hat as he passed.

The man, who had a full head of white hair and a carefully manicured mustache to match, nodded and gave Gamble a warm smile, while the woman nodded. Her dress was deep blue, and snug, limning a figure that was worthy of Italian marble. Her lower face was covered by a fan, but her eyes widened as she looked at Gamble. Her gaze created an unpleasant yearning feeling deep in his stomach, as if he'd drank some rotgut whiskey but wanted more. Gamble went on and swung into an upholstered seat near the gangway that led to the next car following, the express car.

The woman leaned over and spoke briefly to her

companion, her face hidden by the quivering fan, which was black silk with a curious pattern of intertwined blue-green serpents and scarlet roses. Then the white-haired man turned in his seat to face Gamble.

"Pardon me," he said in an upper-class English accent. "This is a rather large coach, and rather lonely, and my niece was wondering if you would like to sit with us."

"Wouldn't want to be a bother."

"No bother, really," the man said. "On the contrary."

Gamble hesitated. If he insisted on staying by the doorway nearest the express car, it might look suspicious.

"Sure," Gamble said, picking up the haversack and the shotgun barrel and making his way back up the aisle. The seats were arranged so that passengers could face each other, and Gamble settled into the seat opposite the couple near the aisle. He slung the haversack on the empty seat beside him and tossed his slouch hat atop the sack. He left the dark glasses on and smoothed his hair with the palms of his hands.

"Powerful hot today," Gamble said.

"That it is," the man replied. "Forgive me, where are my manners? Introductions are in order. I am Lord Weathers."

"A lord, huh?"

"Quite. And you are—?"

"Jacob Dunbar."

"Pleased to meet you, lieutenant," Weathers said, pronouncing it *leftenant*. "Allow me to introduce my niece, Anise."

Her name rhymed with Janus.

"Anise Weathers, Lieutenant Dunbar."

The woman lowered the fan. Her chin and her lower cheeks were covered with a series of blue tattoos, imperfect lines radiating down her chin and across her cheeks, giving her face a somewhat skeletal appearance.

"Charmed," she said in an indeterminate accent, offering a gloved hand. She was twenty-seven or twenty-eight years old, Gamble judged, with auburn hair and hard blue eyes. She had high cheekbones, a clear broad forehead, and would have been considered a beauty by conventional standards, if not for the blue tattoos.

"I couldn't help but notice your uniform," she continued, "and I confided to my uncle that I hoped you would sit and tell us a bit about your experiences in fighting the Spanish."

Gamble gave her hand a brief squeeze.

"It would bore you, I'm sure."

"Come now," Weathers said. "What was your outfit?"

"The First U.S. Volunteers," Gamble said. "Company L, Indian Territory."

"The Rough Riders," Weathers said.

"Yes, but the name is a misleading," Gamble said. "We did all of our fighting dismounted."

"How exciting," Anise said. "We have seen the Vitagraphs brought back from Cuba. How strange to see moving pictures of an actual war. How do the images compare to what you actually saw?"

"I'm sorry, but I did not see them."

"Any chance you'll be called upon to go to the Philippines and fight the insurgents?" Weathers asked. "I hear they are having a hot time of it in Manila. You Americans free them from the Spanish yoke and now they are fighting annexation."

"My company has been mustered out," Gamble said. "The fighting for me is over."

"Are you indeed a cowboy?"

"No, miss," Gamble said.

"An outlaw, then," she said, her eyes sparkling. "I understand that more than one Rough Rider had a dark past he was attempting to escape from. Did you escape yours, Lieutenant Dunbar?"

"Anise," Weathers said. "Don't be so direct."

There was a lurch and the car began moving.

"That's all right," Gamble said. "To answer your question, miss, I did not. My father still haunts me. He died in Missouri during the war."

"And you were hoping to exorcise his ghost by your own martial adventure?" Weathers asked.

"Something like that."

"Where are you headed, if we may inquire?"

"Amarillo," Gamble said. "Looking for work. Whatever is available."

"So, you are a man of the world," Weathers said. "No regular job or family to tie you down?"

Gamble smiled.

"All of my kin are dead, long ago."

"Oh, I'm so sorry," Anise said.

Gamble looked out at the panhandle rolling by.

"Don't be," he said. "It won't change things."

"My closest relatives are dead as well," she said quickly. "They were killed when I—"

"Anise," Weathers said.

"No, Uncle, it is quite all right," she said, holding

up her hand. "We have pressed Lieutenant Dunbar for far more information than we had any right to, and he has been a perfect gentleman in not staring or blurting out those horrible questions we've heard so often."

"No need, miss," Gamble said. "I spent some time in Arizona Territory nearly twenty years back, and I recognize Mohave tribal tattoos when I see them. There is no shame in having been a captive."

"Your opinion is among the minority," Anise said. "Despite their fascination, both men and women seem to despise me because I lived through my ordeal. There is a general assumption that I was contaminated in some way by my captivity and that I would have been better off dead than being returned to white society. When I was rescued, in fact, I was afraid one of the white cavalry officers, an old Indian fighter, was going to put a bullet in my head for that very reason—said it would be best for all involved that I never be reunited with my family."

"What year was that?"

"Nearly thirteen years have passed," Anise said. "I was freed when General Crook accepted Geronimo's surrender at Skeleton Canyon in 1886."

"How did you wind up with the Apaches?"

"They took me as a slave the year before," she said. "My sister and I were captured by the Mohaves after the slaughter of our parents near the Rio Colorado. We were children—Olivia was the younger, by two years. We were treated in the most horrid fashion. We were made to fetch water, carry wood, and fight the camp dogs for scraps of food. The tattoos branded us as slaves, for quick identification in the

event we attempted an escape—which we did, many
times, for which we were beaten. Then we were sold
to the Apaches, and were taken far into Mexico, and
were treated no better. We were property, really,
but not considered *valuable* property. I'm sure you
can imagine the rest. Olivia did not survive the
captivity—died of pneumonia shortly before my
rescue—but sometimes I think death was the kinder
outcome."

"You have that luxury," Gamble said. "You lived."

"Of course. What a practical man you are, Lieutenant Dunbar. Well, life did go on for me, of sorts,"
Anise said. "Then, when Geronimo was waging his
last campaign against the whites, I was brought up
to Skeleton Canyon in Arizona Territory, where a
trooper noticed my blue eyes. Another child who
had been captured, a boy named Jimmy McKinn, or
Santiago as we called him, was also freed."

"I read about it," Gamble said.

"My dear uncle, my closest relative, was cabled
and came all the way from London," Anise said. "I
have lived with him since. This is my first trip back
to the American Southwest since being saved thirteen years ago."

"And you have lived in London since."

"Yes."

"Do you miss it?"

"When I am in the city I usually wear a veil over
the lower half of my face, to thwart stares and wag-
ging tongues," Anise said. "But it is too hot on the
train for that, so I rely on the fan. Frankly, I am relieved to be away from the constraints of civilized

society for at least a little while. Civilization can be so cruel, don't you think?"

Gamble did not trust the chronology that Anise gave, but did not question it; he never expected to see her or Lord Weathers again, so he had simply nodded occasionally as Anise talked.

"You must think it odd to return Anise to the scene of such painful memories," Weathers said. "But I believe it will prove therapeutic."

"If you're bound for where she was captured, then you've taken the wrong train," Gamble said. "The Santa Fe would have taken you damned near to the Colorado River."

"Oh, we're not going there," Anise said. "We're bound for the New Mexico territory."

"That's enough, Anise," Weathers said in a firm voice. "Don't burden the lieutenant with the details of our itinerary. We should maintain some decorum, you know."

"Uncle," she said. "This is the West. We're not in one of your stuffy drawing rooms and we're not even in the *States* anymore. People are frank out here, and they speak frankly. Isn't that right, lieutenant?"

"Not only frank, but downright rough."

Gamble glanced out the window. The train was moving at a steady pace, possibly forty or forty-five miles an hour, and the coach was gently rocking, and sand and scrub were whispering by.

Then there were three quick reports ahead.

"What in thunder was that?" Weathers asked, rising halfway to get a better look out the window. Then Weathers was thrown back against his seat as the air brakes engaged and the train shuddered and slowed.

Before the train had stopped, Gamble had taken the shotgun from the haversack and was fitting the barrel and tube magazine assembly onto the receiver. Once mounted, he turned the lock pin at the end of the magazine, then began stuffing shells into the bottom of the receiver.

"Do you expect trouble?" Weathers asked.

Gamble racked a shell into the chamber.

"Stay down," he said.

"But what—"

"Stay put," Gamble said firmly. "Stay away from the windows. Do not move until somebody tells you it is safe. Do you understand?"

"Yes, of course," Weathers said.

"That goes for you, too," Gamble told Anise.

"I'll do whatever you say."

"Good Lord," Weathers said, peering out the window. "There's a man trackside with a white hood over his head and a rather large sidearm. It looks like pictures I've seen of the Ku Klux Klan!"

"Keep gawking," Gamble said, "And you'll likely get your head blown off."

"Get down, Uncle," Anise said, pulling the old man to the floor with her. "Go on, Lieutenant Dunbar. I'll keep watch over my uncle."

Gamble slung the haversack over his shoulder. He walked quickly to the end of the car, through the gangway, and dropped down the metal steps to the ground.

At the express car door was a figure wearing a white cone-shaped hat with a broad flap sewn to the front that hid the face, but with two ragged eye holes. Across its chest was a white apron with rows of pockets, most of which were stuffed with fused sticks of dynamite. In its right hand was a .44 Russian revolver.

"Hello, fiddler."

The voice was low and rough and not Mickey Dray's.

"Shut up," Gamble said. "Don't call me anything. What the hell kind of getup do you have on?"

"A hood's a hood," Dynamite Dick said.

"And the bomb strapped across your chest?"

"You know they call me Dynamite Dick, right?"

"You're insane. Where's the horse thief?"

Dan pointed to the roof of the express car. Mickey Dray, wearing a hood that matched the Dick's, was kneeling on the roof of the express car. Dick took a stick of dynamite from the apron and tossed it up to Dray, who caught it and stuffed it beneath the top edge of the big sliding door.

"You haven't done this before, have you?"

"No, but I've blown a lot of other shit up," Dick said, jamming a stick of dynamite beneath the bottom of the door. "How hard could this be? You just go along and take care of the train crew." Dan took a cigar from a pocket and lifted the hood, to stick it in his mouth. Then he began searching the apron for matches. "We can handle it back here just fine."

Gamble shook his head. He turned and began running to the front of the train. He had nearly reached the tender when the locomotive groaned and the drive wheels churned with a terrible scraping sound that made Gamble's ears ache. There was a low rumble as the locomotive separated from the rest of the train and began to chug away, the fireman scrambling back over the tender to the shelter of the cab.

"Good," Gamble said. "Cowardice is a virtue in others."

He turned and began trotting back to the express car at the end of the train. Then there was a terrific explosion and the big sliding door was flung out, sailed a hundred yards from the train, then knifed downward and hit the prairie with a hollow sound. Gamble put a forearm over his face as bits of wood and metal sprinkled down. When the heavy stuff was done, he lowered his arm and saw a plume of white confetti drifting overhead, spread by the afternoon breeze.

"Now, there's a waste of postage."

Holding the shotgun at the ready, Gamble slowly approached the express car. The car was sagging a bit, the roof was peeled back, and there was a smoking hole where the door had been.

There was no sign of Dynamite Dick or Dray.

"Horse thief?" Gamble called.

There was a pistol shot from inside the car, then another.

"Damn it," Gamble said.

As he drew near the car, he threw the shotgun to his shoulder.

"Horse thief?"

There was no answer.

"Messenger, are you in there?"

Still, no answer.

He came to the door and peered inside. The floor

of the car and the side of the tracks were covered with piles of letters from the ruptured mail bags. The express safe door was standing open, and the messenger was facedown in a puddle of blood beside it, a double-barreled shotgun in his hand.

Dynamite Dick was also crumpled on the floor, a bloody blotch staining the side of the hood. Mickey Dray was kneeling beside him, a ring of keys in his hand, removing the padlock from the leather cinched top of the canvas payroll bag.

Gamble climbed up into the blackened car.

"What happened?"

"The messenger shot Dick," Dray said. "I killed the messenger."

"Damn it all," Gamble said. "This wasn't supposed to happen."

"Yeah, everybody knows about not killing the messenger."

Dray opened the bag, thrust a hand inside, and pulled out a bundle of paper money.

"There's a fortune here," he said.

Gamble knelt beside Dick.

"He's dead," Dray said. "Don't waste your time."

Gamble pulled off Dick's hood. He had been in his thirties, his hair was wild and black, and a craggy, misshapen face—one of the ugliest Gamble had ever seen. There was a bullet hole in the back of his head.

"The messenger shot him?"

"That's what I said, wasn't it?" Dray was cinching up the payroll bag.

Then Gamble went to the messenger, careful not to turn his back on Dray. He grasped a shoulder and turned the body over. There was a neat bullet wound in the messenger's temple, a mottled powder burn around it. He had been shot point-blank.

Gamble glanced over at Dray. He had pulled off the hood. The payroll bag was in his left hand, but his right hand was holding the .44 Russian beside his leg.

Gamble was holding the Model 97 at his waist.

"Let's go," Dray said.

"As soon as I move, you're going to lift that gun and try to kill me," Gamble said slowly. "But you're not sure how quick I can bring the shotgun to bear, so you're a a little scared, ain't you?"

"Fiddler, why would I do that?"

"Because I know you killed the messenger after he opened the safe, and then you put a round into Dynamite Dick's melon so that you could have an extra share and you wouldn't have to worry about anybody giving up your identity to the Pinkertons. You never were afraid of Dynamite Dick, were you? He was afraid of you."

"Yeah, I had to kill the ugly sonuvabitch," Dray said.

"Using that logic, you have to kill me, too."

"No, fiddler. We're pards."

"Then holster that piece."

Dray took a deep breath and rolled his head on his shoulders.

"Can't do that," he said.

"Well, we have to do something," Gamble said. "We can't stay here much longer, or we'll both hang for the killing of the messenger. You go first."

"Think I'll wait for—"

Before Dray could get the word *you* out, Gamble had flung himself backward. He rolled once, then came up with the shotgun at his shoulder and pulled the trigger. The buckshot hit Dray in the leg and he went down on one knee, the Russian in his outstretched hand firing. The slug went wild, punching a hole in the roof of the car.

Gamble slamfired the shotgun.

This shot struck Dray across the chest and abdomen. He was knocked back, the Russian falling from his grip, a pink mist spraying over the piles of letters behind him. He fell on the floor, an arm across his stomach, his eyes wide.

Gamble walked over, kicked the Russian away, and knelt down to pick up the payroll bag. Dray reached up with his right hand and grasped the front of Gamble's uniform.

"Fiddler," the boy said through blood-stained teeth. "Don't leave me."

"Where are the horses?"

"The soddie on the south ridge," Dray said.

Gamble put his boot on Dray's chest and pushed. Dray kept his grip on the fabric, ripping open the breast pocket as Gamble pushed him away. Spilling out, the letter fluttered to the floor.

Gamble cycled the pump, chambering a fresh shell, and aimed at Dray's chest. But he did not fire. Dray's eyes had become fixed and he was no longer breathing.

Gamble kicked the body in the side, hard enough that he heard the snap of ribs.

"You should have stuck to horses."

The car was strangely silent now.

Gamble could hear the breeze whispering over the ruined coach and his own heartbeat pounding in his temple. The Model 97 seemed strangely solid in his hands, as if he had just roused from sleep and found himself holding a dream object made real.

Then his attention narrowed on the payroll bag.

All that was left was to pick up the bag, jump to the ground, and make for the horses on the ridge. Once out of sight, he would discard the smoke-colored glasses and the khaki uniform with the yellow trim and the weirdly commanding persona of Dunbar, and stay in Oklahoma Territory only long enough to pluck Agnes from the prairie on the way to Mexico.

Gamble knelt. He cinched up the payroll bag, tossed it out the door. Then he walked over to the door and was about to jump down after it when he remembered the letter. He looked back at the paper that blanketed the floor like snow, all white, all about the same size and shape. It might take him a few minutes to sort through the pile to find the letter, and he might not have a few minutes to spare. In any event, he had the payroll—it didn't matter what became of the letter.

"To hell with you, Lieutenant Dunbar."

He jumped to the ground. He switched the shotgun to his right hand and was reaching for the bag when someone called from the vestibule of the passenger coach.

"Boy, howdy. There's the payroll."

It was the conductor, easing himself down the steps, a snub-nosed revolver held loosely in his hand. He was sixty years old, wearing a uniform with big brass buttons over his paunch, and his white mustache drooped at the ends.

Gamble cursed. To the south, he could see the soddie on the ridge less than a quarter of a mile away. The Model 97 was still in one hand, the hammer was cocked, and he knew it would be a simple matter to shoulder the piece and blow the conductor and his little gun into the next county.

Yet, Gamble hesitated.

"The messenger?" the conductor asked.

"Dead," Gamble said with resignation. He lowered the hammer on the shotgun and carefully leaned it across the payroll bag. "So are the other two."

Gamble sat down on the ground and rested his forearms on his knees. He lowered his head, thinking about how close he had come to getting away with a lifetime of security. How would he and Agnes have spent the years he had left? Sitting on the veranda of their hacienda, drinking Mexican beer, talking about nothing more important than what to have for supper. But it was all gone now because he could not bring himself to kill an old man in a blue suit—and not only was it gone, but Gamble would find himself back in jail on his way to the gallows.

Gamble laughed darkly.

The conductor crept past him and peered into the express car.

"Damn, son, you're a one-man wrecking crew."

"Is it all over?" Lord Weathers called from the door of the coach.

"It's all over," Gamble said.

Weathers came down the steps.

"The lieutenant here has saved the payroll," the

conductor said. "He killed the bandits, but not before they had killed the messenger, poor devil."

Gamble's head came up.

"No, that's not right," he said carefully.

"What do you mean, son?"

"I killed the bandit there with my shotgun, but not the one with the dynamite," Gamble said. "One bandit had already killed the other, to take all of the loot."

"No honor among thieves, huh?"

"It seems not. You'd best be careful with the carcass of the older fellow, because in the pockets of that white apron there's enough of old peace-loving Alfred Nobel's favorite toy to blow us all into the afterlife."

"You've done it," the Englishman said, slapping Gamble on the back. "I told the conductor that you sprang into action at the first sign of trouble. And you gave them a little of what you gave the Spanish in Cuba. What dash! You are indeed a Rough Rider. Splendid!"

"Not so splendid," Gamble said. "Three men are dead."

The conductor shook his head.

"Them old boys on the locomotive are going to have some answering to do," the conductor said. "I can't believe they skeedaddled like that. Say, I watched as you walked forward before they took off. What were you doing?"

Gamble coughed in his hand.

"Trying to corral them, but didn't get the chance."

Anise came slowly down the steps. She now had a veil over her face, a veil that matched her deep blue dress. She walked over, glanced at the payroll bag, then at Gamble.

"You're bleeding."

She grasped his left hand and lifted it to get a better look. His thumb knuckle had been gouged by the action on the shotgun. She lowered the scarf and brought his hand to her lips.

FIFTEEN

The tall blond man stepped down from the train and surveyed the depot at Sanford Switch with a critical eye. He was wearing a pinstriped suit and a bowler hat and strapped to his hip was an odd-looking revolver. He walked across the platform and through the open door to find the station agent hunched at his desk, working on paperwork with a pencil that was little more than a nub, a cup of whiskey at his elbow.

"You must be the Pinkerton man," the agent said, looking up.

"You're just as quick as you look," the man said, brushing the blond hair from his forehead, revealing a scar on his temple. "My name is Max Jaeger, but everybody calls me Dutch. I'm on my way to inspect the wreckage of the express car, but I'm told the bodies of the thieves were brought here. I'd like to see them, please."

"Out back," the agent said. "They're laid out on a bed of ice in the back of a wagon, so they aren't stinking too badly yet. Waiting for the train to take 'em to the furniture store in Liberal to be laid out proper."

"Tell me about yesterday before the robbery."

"Nothing to tell," the agent said. "Normal day."

"Was anybody loitering around the depot that day?" Jaeger asked. "Passengers? Any tickets sold?"

"Just one," the agent said. "Bought a special delivery stamp and put it on a letter he had with him, then decided to hang onto the letter without posting it. Bought a ticket to the end of the line. Said he wanted to see Texas."

"Seems odd."

"He was a normal enough fellow."

"What did he look like?"

Jaeger brought a pencil and notepad from his pocket.

"Normal."

"Was he short, tall—"

"Tall."

"Tall as me?"

"A little less, I think."

"Fat or thin or medium?"

"Thin."

"Hair color?"

"Dark, maybe. Gray at the temples."

"So he was older."

"Not old, exactly. Forty-five or fifty."

"Eye color?"

"Don't know. He was wearing these dark glasses."

"What kind of glasses?"

"Smoke-colored, to protect them from the sun— there was something wrong with his eyes and he couldn't stand the light. Granulated eyelids, whatever that is."

"Clothing?"

"Uniform."

"He was a soldier?"

"Rough Rider," the agent said. "A lieutenant. At least, he was wearing the uniform jacket and a slouch hat that was all beat to hell. He had on blue jeans and cowboy boots."

"So this is the man that foiled the robbery," Jaeger said. "I have a telegram about it. Ah, here it is. It describes a Lieutenant Dunbar armed with a Winchester shotgun who killed a bandit and recovered the payroll."

"He didn't tell me his name," the agent said. "But yeah, that sounds like him."

"Were there other passengers?"

"An Englishman and his niece. He was an old gent with white hair. Harmless. The girl had all of her parts in the right place, if you know what I mean, but she was wearing this thing over her face."

"A veil?"

"Yeah, that's it."

"Perhaps she was a muslima?"

"Don't know what that is."

"A follower of Allah."

"No, I don't think so. Seemed like there was something wrong with her face she was trying to hide."

Jaeger nodded and made a note.

"This letter. Did the soldier say what it was about?"

"Nope, but I remember that it was addressed to the governor of New York."

"You're sure?"

"We don't get many of those here."

Jaeger nodded and made a few notes.

"Tell me"—Jaeger said as he closed the notebook and returned it to his suit pocket—"were you drinking yesterday as well?"

"What, this?" the clerk said, tapping the cup. "It's just—"

"Yes, I know what it is." Jaeger walked over, picked up the cup, and sniffed. He replaced the cup with the same disgust as if it contained offal. "Please refrain from drinking on duty. I'm sure you will, if you want to avoid a report being sent to your superiors at the Rock Island."

Jaeger walked to the back of the depot and went to the flatbed wagon. He flipped back the tarp to reveal the blue-tinged faces of Mickey Dray and Dynamite Dick. Their blood was like black tar on the ice below them.

"Ah, if only I could bring you back to ask just one question," Jaeger said, picking up one of the hoods and looking at the bloodstain. "Were you two alone?"

Jaeger sighed and tossed the hood back.

Then he pulled a pack of postcard-sized photographs from his pocket and began shuffling through them, comparing the face on each to those of the dead men. He paused when he came to the mug shot of Mickey Dray. He flipped the photograph over. In addition to a concise physical description of Dray, there was this notation: *Arrested for horse theft January 1889, jailed Guthrie, O.T.*

Jaeger rubbed the scar on his forehead.

There was no Pinkerton photo in his stack for the other corpse.

He took a Kodak 1A folding pocket camera from his jacket, opened the bellows, checked the exposure settings, and focused on the face of the dead outlaw. He steadied the camera, held his breath, and tripped the shutter with the same care that he would have used to squeeze the trigger of a rifle. He wound the 116 film forward to the next frame, changed his angle, and took another photo.

Satisfied, he closed the camera and returned it to his coat pocket.

He threw the tarp over the corpses and walked back into the depot. The agent sat bolt upright in his chair. The cup of whiskey was gone from the desk.

"Where are the passengers now?"

"Bound for Amarillo," the agent said. "Took a coach over the section and picked up the tracks on the Texas side, if they stuck to their plan."

"Your telegraph is connected to Amarillo?"

"The tracks don't go all the way, but the wire does."

"Wire instructions that these three—the soldier, the Englishman and the girl—are to be held over until I have a chance to interrogate them."

"You want them arrested?"

"No, not yet, nothing to arouse suspicion," Jaegers said. "Put them up at railway expense at one of the better hotels. Tell them—tell them a representative of the Pinkerton Detective Agency would like to personally express his thanks."

SIXTEEN

"Lieutenant, what are your plans?"

"Simple," Gamble said, holding up his whiskey glass to catch the candlelight. "I'm going to finish this glass of bourbon, then ask for another."

Anise laughed.

"You know what my uncle meant," she said, smoothing her napkin. Their table was in the shadows in a far corner of the dining room, and she had removed her veil. "We want to know what kind of professional plans you might have for the next few weeks, if we may be so bold."

"I am between assignments at the moment."

The table was littered with the remains of their meal—plates with oyster shells, steak bones, slivers of asparagus, and half-eaten rolls. The restaurant was on the ground floor of the Texas House, the best hotel in Amarillo, where the Rock Island had insisted on putting up the trio. Gamble planned on being long gone by sunup.

"Then your services are for hire?" Weathers asked.

Gamble took another sip of whiskey. He was still

wearing the smoke-colored glasses and, since the sun had set while they were eating and no daylight was now coming in from the window, Weathers was just a shadow on the other side of the table.

"Your skill with firearms and your calm in an anxious situation recommend you for a rather unusual assignment," Weathers said.

"I'll pass," Gamble said.

"Just like that?" Anise asked. "Without a hearing?"

"No disrespect," Gamble said. "But whenever somebody talks me into something, I end up regretting it. Usually, I end up losing a little skin in the process."

"Every time?" she asked.

Gamble finished the whiskey and signaled for the waiter to bring him another. Anise, however, held up her hand and called for the man to hold the order.

"Let's try something special," she told Gamble in a conspiratorial tone. "Do you think Amarillo might be continental enough to serve absinthe? Let us find out." Then, to the waiter: "Absinthe, *s'il vous plaît?*"

"Of course," the waiter said.

"Three glasses, and make sure there is plenty of ice."

"Two glasses," her uncle said.

"Two, then."

The waiter nodded and went to the bar.

"Bourbon suits me just fine."

"Have you ever had absinthe?"

"Never felt that poetic."

"Indulge me," Anise said.

Gamble removed the smoke-colored glasses and fished the leather patch from his pants pocket, threw the strap over his head, and tugged it into place.

"Better," he said.

Anise was resting her chin on her hands.

"At least hear us out," she said.

Gamble waved her off.

The waiter brought a tray with a pair of glasses, two flat spoons, some sugar cubes, a thin dark bottle, and a pitcher of ice water.

"Would you like me to bring forth the spirit?"

"I'd prefer to do it myself, thank you," Anise said.

She placed a glass in front of Gamble, poured about an ounce of green liquid from the bottle, then put a sugar cube on the spoon and rested it on the rim of the glass.

"This is an art," Anise said as she tilted the pitcher of ice water with a steady hand, wetting the sugar cube. "The trick is to place just the right amount of water on the sugar—thus. Now, watch the *louche.*"

As the sugary water dripped from the spoon into the green liquid, opalescent pearls formed and swirled. Soon, the entire glass was a milky white.

"There," Anise said.

Gamble picked up the glass and held it to the light.

"Isn't this made with a kind of poison? Wormwood?"

"It is a plant from the Holy Lands."

"And in the Book of Revelation, a star which falls and poisons a third part of the waters," Gamble said. "Or maybe an angel. I don't remember which."

He brought the glass to his lips and sipped.

"Bitter," he said. "Like licorice."

"Of course," she said, preparing her own drink. "It's flavored with anise."

Weathers took a leather case from his jacket, flipped open the top, and offered him a cigar. Gamble took it, cut the end with his pocket knife, stuck the cigar in his teeth, then leaned forward toward the candle flame.

"Good smoke," Gamble said, puffing. He took another sip of absinthe. "All right, I'm comfortable. Talk if you want."

"This must remain strictly between us," Weathers said.

"I'm a man of discretion."

"Uncle!" Anise said. "Get on with it."

"Of course," Weathers said. He glanced around, to make sure nobody was close enough to overhear, and then leaned forward conspiratorially. "What we told you before is true—we are on our way to New Mexico Territory, but not to Skeleton Canyon. Simply put, we are on our way to recover a fortune in Confederate money that lies in the Apache treasure cave somewhere along the *Jornada del Muerte.*"

"The *Jornada?*" Gamble asked.

"You know it?"

"It's a hundred-mile stretch of hell on earth," Gamble said. "The conquistadores named it, and they named it well—'the Journey of Death.' It was the roughest part of the old royal road from Mexico City to Santa Fe, it's still so rough and so remote that it's like heading back to the middle of the seventeenth century."

"I understand the difficulties," Weathers said.

"Do you?" Gamble asked. "Have you been there?"

"No," Anise said softly. "My uncle has not. But I have."

Gamble puffed on the cigar.

"After I was sold to the Apaches," she said, "I was with Geronimo and his band of Chiricahua during the final years of the fighting, around the Southern Four Corners area—where Arizona, New Mexico, Chihuahua, and Sonora meet."

"You said as much before."

"You can see me in those famous photographs made by Fly during the surrender," Anise said. "He took pictures of the captive white boy, Santiago McKinn, standing with a group of starving Chiricahua children in front of a falling down wickiup. Then he posed me on a blanket and took a lurid close-up of my face—of the tattoos. It has been widely reproduced—on the front pages of all the Hearst papers and in the *Police Gazette*. Surely you've seen it."

"Missed it," Gamble said. "The treasure cave?"

"A month or so before the surrender, Geronimo's band raided a ranch house and made off with some household silver and a small quantity of Double Eagles the family had been saving. My sister and I were given pack mules and made, under guard, to haul the loot up the *Jornada* to about where Engle is now, and then west into the mountains to the treasure cave. Geronimo said he was born at the headwaters of the Gila River, that his Apache ancestors had come from those mountains, and the area was sacred to him."

Gamble sipped some more absinthe. Strangely, he felt both drunk and keenly awake.

"The cave was terribly frightful," Anise said. "Not only was the climb tortuous, but the narrow cave entrance was guarded by human skeletons, and in their rib cages were coiled the biggest rattlesnakes I had ever seen. One of our band, the warrior named Massai, was able to calm the snakes with a few words so that we could pass. Inside, there were the strangest objects—medicine objects. Relics, mainly. Armor from the time of the conquistadors, a Spanish bit, an old bowie knife, a mountain rifle. It was like an Apache museum and treasury, but the treasury was running low. There were little piles of gold ore and a few coins here and there, Double Eagles and old Spanish eight reales, mostly. A few bars of silver."

"And the rebel money."

"Yes, the Confederate money," she said. "It was in a strongbox against the wall, and on the side of the box it said, 'Territory of Arizona, CSA.' I asked Massai about it, and he said the Apaches had taken it during a raid on Rebel soldiers when he was a boy. He said it was worthless because the gray coats lost."

"The rebels did hold southern Arizona and New Mexico territories during 1861 and 1862," Weathers said. "It ended when Sibley tried to capture northern New Mexico—and the entry to the Colorado gold finds and the California ports—and was pushed back at Glorieta Pass. During those two years, the Apaches made constant war on the Rebels—just as they had on the Spanish, the Mexicans, and the Yankees. It is not inconceivable that these native fighters managed to capture some of the funds used to mount the New Mexico Campaign."

Gamble shook his head.

"Let's say for a moment that I believe your story," he said. "This Massai fellow was right. By the end

of the war, Confederate notes were shin plaster—
less than worthless. Their primary use was to start
the morning fire or to chink cracks in the walls. It's
not worth braving the *Jornada* for a pile of molder-
ing banknotes that amount to nothing more than a
historical curiosity."

"I didn't say they were banknotes."

"You said Confederate money."

"That's right."

"Well, paper was the only kind of Confederate
money there was. Oh, there were plans for all kinds
of coins—and Dixie had plenty of gold, early in the
war—but it was all in Yankee coins, which were
mostly melted down into ingots."

"Not all of it," Anise said.

Gamble stared at her.

"You're saying that you saw a crate of Confederate gold coins."

"I'm saying exactly that."

"I am hesitant to call a woman a liar," Gamble
said, snubbing the cigar out in a saucer. "But what
you saw fourteen or fifteen years ago could not have
been Confederate gold coins. It must have been a
dream, or some kind of waking fantasy. The
Apaches were starving by the time of the surrender,
and if Geronimo had access to any quantity of gold,
he would have used it to buy food and guns. Especially guns."

Anise smiled wickedly.

"You think I had the fantods, lieutenant?" she
asked. "You think I was delirious and imagined the
gold? You must think I invented this episode of my

life from whole cloth. Oh, I am sorry to have wasted your time. But there is one thing."

She opened a silk purse and removed a golden coin.

"How do you explain this?" she asked.

The coin gleamed in the candlelight.

"The Apaches considered the Rebel coins next to worthless—they even used a few to cast bullets for some of the older rifles. Because he considered them trash, Massai let me take this one."

"You mind if I see it?"

She placed it in his palm. It was heavy, like a Double Eagle.

Gamble turned the coin to catch the light and tried to read the inscription, but found it was too close to focus on. He held it out at nearly arm's length, but it was too far to see any detail.

"Damn it," Gamble said.

"I have the same problem with newspapers," Weathers said as he removed a magnifying glass from a coat pocket. "Here, I find this helpful."

Gamble took the magnifying glass.

On one side, the coin had an engraving of Liberty holding a shield emblazoned with the Rebel battle flag, and symbols of the southern economy around her, including stalks of corn and a bale of cotton. Arrayed around Liberty was CONFEDERATE STATES OF AMERICA, and at the bottom, 1861. The edge was fluted, just like a Double Eagle.

Gamble turned the coin over.

CSA TWENTY DOLLARS, it said in the center. Around this were thirteen stars, and around the stars was a chain with thirteen links. The links were named for the eleven seceded states and the two divided border states, Missouri and Kentucky.

"I'll be damned."

"Possibly," Anise said. "But we shan't worry about that now."

"Are you sure it's real gold?"

"For God's sake, don't bite it," she said. "Yes, we've weighed it and it's the same as one of your twenty dollar American coins."

She held out her hand. Gamble placed the coin in her palm.

"There are other tests," he said. "Specific gravity, for example. Acid."

"Yes, yes," she said, returning the coin to her purse. "We're quite satisfied. It's real gold."

Gamble studied the reflected candlelight in her eyes.

"Do we have your interest, Lieutenant?" Weathers asked.

"I'll allow that," Gamble said. "What's my role in all of this?"

"Troubleshooter," Weathers said.

"Hired gun," Anise added.

"A fortnight from now, we expect to have recovered the lost Confederate gold from the Apache treasure cave and to have returned to civilization. We will pay a thousand dollars for two weeks of work."

"I'd like that in advance."

"You'll get half now," Anise said. "The other half when we recover the gold."

"No," Gamble said. "The full thousand, no matter what, because I'm not convinced you can find that cave again. And if you do recover any gold, I want a share."

"We will not pay the full amount now," Anise said. "Half now, as I said. The other half upon reaching the cliffs below the cave by the twentieth of June, no matter if the gold is recovered or not."

"Why June twentieth?"

Anise smiled.

"Is this acceptable or no?"

"I still want a share, should this fairy tale come true."

"All right, Jacob Dunbar, you may have a share, but that thousand dollars that you've been paid for your services as a gunslinger is deducted from your share. There, you have the best of both worlds—you are paid for your time if there is no gold, and you become a partner if there is."

"How much of a partner would I be?"

"Ten percent," Anise said.

"A third," Gamble said.

"Out of the question," Weathers said.

"Twenty percent," Anise said.

"A third."

Weathers shook his head.

"Dash doesn't come cheap," Gamble said. "If I'm going to put my neck on the line in the *Jornada,* then I get a full share or I don't go."

"You seem to be forgetting that there would be no chance of recovering this hoard if I hadn't suffered years of humiliation by savages," Anise said. "If not for me, none of this would be possible. You may be a hero, Lieutenant Dunbar, but you are a greedy one."

Gamble smiled.

"We will not give you a full third and a guarantee of a thousand dollars for your services as a hired gun if our campaign fails," Anise said.

"Your campaign will fail," Gamble said. "It all sounds too good to be true, some type of classic con, although I don't understand your angle yet."

"There's no angle," Anise said. "You get rich or go bust just like us."

"I'm already bust," Gamble said, his head swimming from the bourbon and buzzing from the absinthe. "What do I have to lose?"

"Just your life," Anise said under her breath. "Or worse."

"What?"

"Nothing," Anise said.

Gamble finished his drink.

"We leave tomorrow, early," he said. "We have only ten days to get you to this mysterious place before the twentieth day of June. Do you have a map I can study?"

"Of course," Weathers said. "But what about the Pinkerton man coming to see us?"

Gamble shrugged.

"To hell with the Pinkerton," Gamble said.

Then he called for the waiter to bring him another bourbon.

SEVENTEEN

Jaeger knelt in the remains of the ruined express car and shook his head. The interior smelled of burned wood and smoke and dried blood. Flies buzzed in the stifling heat.

"Amateurs," he said.

He picked a letter from the pile, one with a heavy rust-colored smear, and glanced at the address. San Antonio. He let it fall back to the floor. The wind had spilled some of the mail outside the car, onto the side of the tracks.

"What are you looking for?" the new express messenger asked. He had come with Jaeger on the train from Liberal.

"A letter," Jaeger said. "Addressed to the governor of New York. It will have a special delivery stamp."

"That would make it United States property," the messenger said. "It's a felony to tamper with the mail."

The messenger waited a moment, then couldn't control his laughter.

"Sorry, I can't hold a poker face," he said, slapping his thigh. I'll see what I can find."

"Good," Jaeger said, annoyed.

While the messenger and his assistant started going through the bag, he took his field glasses from the leather case slung around his neck. He began to scan the landscape, and most of what he saw was sand and scrub. The glasses passed over the old soddie on the south ridge, then came back to it. He had seen something flick out from behind a ruined mud wall. He waited, and in ten seconds he saw it again, and this time he was sure that it was the swish of a horse's tail.

"Ah, that's where you hid them."

He climbed down from the car and started hiking across the prairie. Halfway to the soddie, he removed his jacket and flung it over his shoulder. When he reached the broken mud house, his shirt was heavy with sweat.

He rounded the corner of the soddie's longest wall and stared for a moment at the three horses, all saddled, and tied to a stake driven in the ground.

"Of course," Jaeger said.

They were fine horses, a dun and two sorrels, and they were undoubtedly stolen. He reached out to touch the saddle of the dun, but the horse snorted and thrust its head back, nipping Jaeger on the back of the hand.

"Schiesse," Jaeger muttered.

He drew the Reichsrevolver, shoved the barrel toward the horse's skull, and pulled the trigger. The horse staggered, but did not fall. Jaeger shot again, and this time the animal collapsed.

The sorrels cried and backed away, straining against the tether. Jaeger pointed the revolver at the closest horse and had nearly fired another round when he checked himself. He held the barrel up, the blood running from the back of his hand and staining his shirt cuff. Finally, he put the gun back in the flap holster.

He knelt, using his knife to cut away the saddle and other tack from the dead horse. He found nothing of value, not even a name on the saddle. He drew the brand on the flank of the horse in his notebook—a Rocking K—but expected it to confirm that it was a stolen animal.

Jaeger took the leads of the sorrels and led them down the hill to the train, where he handed them off to one of the train crew. He told them to unsaddle the horses so that he could inspect those rigs as well.

"What were the shots?" the messenger asked. "Rattlesnake?"

"Ja—yes, snake," Jaeger said, not wanting the messenger to know he had shot a horse for biting him. In the West, Americans took abuse of horses almost as badly as they took mistreatment of children. Germans serve horses in Sauerbraten.

"Damned rattlers are thick this year," the messenger said. "He didn't get you, did he?"

"No," Jaeger said. "Scraped my hand against the wall."

"Good," the messenger said. "These rattlers wouldn't kill you, but will make you damned sick. Now, the rattlers down in the Arizona and New Mexican territories, some of those will kill you deader than Julius Caesar. Oh, we found your letter."

Jaeger took the envelope and slit the end with his knife. He shook out the letter, sat down in the shade of the express car, and spent the next twenty minutes reading and re-reading the pages. When he was done, he folded the pages and slipped them back into the envelope, which he tapped against his knee while he pondered his options.

"Can't kill a war hero," he muttered. "That would make the agency look bad. But if I bring the bastard in to stand trial, he's likely to get acquitted or receive some kind of pardon because of his uniform."

"What's that you say?" the messenger asked.

"Not a thing," Jaeger said.

"Anything useful in that letter?"

"No, not really. Do you smoke?"

"Hell, who doesn't?"

"Then lend me a match."

Jaeger struck the match against his heel, then held it to the bottom of the envelope. He held it until the bright orange flames nipped his fingers, then flung it away.

EIGHTEEN

Jacob Gamble was quite drunk by the time he fell into bed in his room on the second floor of the Texas House. Between bolting the door and actually pitching headfirst onto the mattress, he had managed to do a kind of staggering pirouette in which he shed every stitch of clothing except his right sock. He fell instantly and deeply asleep.

In his dreams, his mother was waiting.

He was seven years old and she stood behind him, her hands clasped over his eyes, pressing his head back against her waist. Her fingers felt cool on his eyelids.

"Don't open your eyes, Jacob," she murmured. "Don't open your eyes."

"But I can't see," he protested.

"Don't open your eyes."

"Why not?" he asked.

"Don't open your eyes, Jacob."

"But how will I know what to do if I can't look?"

He reached up and grasped her wrists and pried them, one at a time, from his eyes. They were stand-

ing in their cabin of forty years ago in Missouri and
it was the depth of a summer night. The only light
came from the open window. Outside, a full moon
had turned the yard into a weird monochrome
landscape—the rail fence and the woodpile and the
maple tree were rendered in the silver tones of a tin-
type. There was a breeze from the south, and the
curtains made from flour sacks rippled inward.

On a pair of sawhorses in the middle of the room
rested a coffin of unvarnished white oak. The lid was
on the floor, but Jacob was too short to see into the
coffin.

"Mother," Gamble said, over his shoulder. "Who
is in the casket?"

She put a finger to her lips to shush him. She was
dressed all in black, but her veil was pulled up to
reveal her face. Her eyes glittered in the darkness.

He turned back. Gradually, he became aware of
other figures in the dark corners of the room, human
figures in frayed black robes but with the beaks of
buzzards for faces. Fighting the fear rising in his
chest, he asked:

"What are those things?"

"This is a wake," she said.

"But those are monsters."

"I told you not to look, Jacob" she said, shaking
her head sadly. "I told you not to look."

"Who's in the coffin?"

His mother was suddenly at the table, shuffling
a deck of cards. The leather-bound family Bible
was open in front of her. The breeze blew stronger,
riffling the thin pages of the Bible and scattering
most of the cards on the floor. She dealt what she

*had left in her hand, one at a time, placing them
under the edge of the Bible. She clasped a hand to
her mouth.*

*"What is it?" he asked. "What will happen in the
future?"*

"All things," she said.

*He knew he must look inside the coffin. He took
two steps forward, and the bird creatures began
hissing and shaking their heads.*

*"Don't, Jacob. Stay here with me until morning.
Come to bed and I will keep you warm."*

"I'm not cold."

He took another step forward.

*Buzzard heads were cocked and beaks were snap-
ping, confused, threatening. He was close enough
now that he could nearly peer over the side of the
coffin. He could hear curious wet clicking sounds
coming from inside.*

"Father?"

"Don't look, Jacob," his mother called.

He took one more step and looked into the coffin.

*It was a mass of things—land crabs—swarming
over a corpse. The stench of rotten flesh was over-
powering, but Jacob forced himself to look closer.
The crabs had stripped most of the flesh from the
face of the dead man, revealing a grinning skull.
One eye socket was empty. An eyeball dangled from
the other socket, but it was soon plucked by a vora-
cious claw.*

"Is it father?" he asked.

*"Of course not," she said. "Your father had no
death watch, no funeral. You have already looked
once—you had better look again."*

Jacob looked back.

The skeletal hands were crossed over the stomach, and in one hand was a revolver—a cap-and-ball revolver with a brass frame, the Manhattan.

Jacob backed away, shivering.

"How do I die?"

"Like all men," his mother said. "With a final breath, a last look, a dying thought. All men are finite, Jacob. Each has a limited number of heartbeats. It is a kindness that the number is a mystery, least the knowledge drive them mad."

"But you know," he said.

"Yes," she said, inspecting the cards. "The dead know."

"Tell me."

"Ask me something else."

"Did you truly love me?"

She handed him two cards—the seven and three of spades.

"You will live seventy-three years beyond the age when your father died."

"That is nonsense."

"Close your eyes, then."

"I'd be more than a hundred years old."

"You are nearly halfway there," she said.

"No, I'm seven."

There was a knocking on the cabin door.

"Tell me why my father is haunting me."

The knocking was louder.

"You said the dead know. Tell me."

"I must go," she said. "My sister has come."

* * *

Gamble woke, turned onto his back, and ran a hand over his face, which was moist with sweat. He sat up, disoriented, burning with thirst. There was just enough light coming in from the window to see that he was still in the room at the Texas House. He swung his feet to the floor, walked over to the nightstand, and poured a glass of water from the pitcher there. He drank it, then poured himself another.

There was a tap at the door.

"Sonuvabitch," he muttered.

The tap came again.

He snatched up the shotgun from where it leaned against the nightstand, crossed to the hinge side of the door, and asked who was there.

"Anise."

"Wormwood," he said. "You alone?"

"Yes."

"Just a minute."

He put the shotgun on the bed. Then he found his jeans, pulled them on, and unbolted the door. She stepped inside, and Gamble locked the door behind her.

She was wearing a robe over a chemise.

"What time is it?"

"Just after four."

His head was throbbing.

"Look," he said. "I don't think I'm your man. Your treasure hunt is either a half-baked scheme or a truly imaginative con, I don't know which—but I was drunk last night. Thanks, but no thanks."

"Shut up and listen," Anise said. "The Pinkerton man is here, at the front desk. He has roused the night manager for a room, and is asking questions."

"How do you know?"

"I had to go to the water closet down the hall, and I saw him from the landing," she said. "I know he's the Pinkerton, because he's asking a lot of questions about you."

"What kind of questions?"

"Description," he said. "Whether you had one eye or two, your hair color, your age—and how many weapons you had. Lieutenant Dunbar, is there something you haven't told us?"

"Damn Pinkerton," he said. "I didn't expect him until noon."

"He's not here to congratulate you, is he?"

Gamble was gathering up his clothes and stuffing them into the haversack.

"Do you see my other sock?"

"No," she said.

"To hell with it."

He sat on the bed and began pulling on his boots.

"You're like me, aren't you?"

"How's that?"

"Not what you appear to be."

"Act like you haven't seen me since last night, that I had plans to leave before dawn, but that I didn't say where I was going," he said.

Anise reached into the pocket of her robe and pulled out a sheaf of bills.

"Here's the five hundred," she said, putting it in his hand. "The other half when we get to the treasure cave by the twentieth."

"How do you know I'm not going out that window and jump down to the sidewalk and you'll never see me again?"

"Because we have a deal," she said. "Because you weren't that drunk. Because you want to see the treasure cave with me, even though I scare the hell out of you."

"All right," Gamble said. "But only because I'm out of ideas. Don't be in a hurry in the morning. Talk to the Pinkerton, be polite, but don't mention the gold coin."

"Do I really look that stupid?"

"When you get a chance, get yourselves to the depot across town and take the first westbound train. Change trains at Santa Fe. Go south. I'll meet you in Engle at noon the day after tomorrow."

"Engle," she said. "Day after tomorrow."

He folded the map Weathers had given him and put it in the haversack. Then he threw the haversack over his shoulder, picked up the shotgun from the bed, and started for the window.

"Haven't you forgotten something?"

"I don't think so."

She walked over, took his free hand, and guided it beneath her robe. Then she kissed him, her tongue darting into this mouth, her body pressing against his.

NINETEEN

Just before dawn, Jaeger slipped the pass key he had gotten from the night manager into the lock, slowly turned the key until the latch clicked, then swung open the door as quietly as possible. Then, revolver in hand, he sprang into the room.

Seeing the empty bed, he holstered the gun.

"Damn you," he muttered.

He walked around the room. He glanced out the window, paused at the half-full glass of water, then knelt down and looked under the bed. He stretched a hand out and retrieved a red-and-gray wool sock.

"Where is your other sock now, Jakob Gamble?" he asked.

"Who is Jacob Gamble?"

Anise was leaning in the doorway. She was dressed in a flowing green dress, a green veil covering her face.

"Ah," Jaeger said. "Excuse me. It is an old German expression, a name invoked to frighten children, much like the American boogeyman."

"And this Teutonic boogeyman wears just one sock?"

"That's why he steals socks," Jaeger said.

"And what is your excuse?"

"Pardon me, miss. I forget myself," Jaeger said, stuffing the stock into his pocket. "I am Max Jaeger, a Pinkerton man."

"I am Anise Weathers."

He came forward, took her gloved hand, and kissed it.

"I thought you might be."

"The veil."

"Because you were described to me as a beautiful young woman," Jaeger said. "I have been anxious to meet you and your uncle, and this hero soldier—this Lieutenant Dunbar—but it appears he has already vacated his room."

"I'm not surprised," Anise said. "We dined with him last night and he mentioned pressing business and much travel."

"Did he say where this business was taking him?"

"Sadly, no," Anise said. "The lieutenant seemed an intensely private individual, and it would have appeared rude to ask, don't you think?"

"Of course," Jaeger said. "But I am pleased that we early risers have found one another. It is a habit hard to break, no? May I invite you and your uncle to share breakfast with me? I am anxious to hear your account of the attempted train robbery."

TWENTY

Jacob Gamble stepped down from the passenger train onto the station platform at Engle, the haversack slung over his shoulder and the Model 97 balanced in his left hand. Even through the smoke-colored glass, the glare made him squint—the town, like the landscape itself, was twenty-three shades of white, all baking in the midday sun. On the eastern horizon were the San Andres Mountains, adding a bit of mauve to the scene.

As Gamble walked past the Santa Fe depot toward the town's main street, the station agent peered at him from the bay window. Gamble looked in his direction and tugged the brim of his hat, but the agent returned no greeting.

"There's trouble," Gamble said.

Gamble watched his shadow pumping on the hard ground in front of him as he walked toward the town's main street. He stopped to allow a herd of cattle to cross, heading for the pens near the railway tracks.

"Where you boys from?" Gamble asked one of the cowboys.

"Texas, yee-haw!" the rider, a boy of twenty, said while using his coiled lasso to nudge the cattle in the right direction. "But these fat beeves are from the Tularosa Valley. Where you from, mister?"

"Missouri."

"Missouri!" the cowboy said. "You're a long ways from home."

"I'll allow that I am," Gamble said.

As the dust from the cattle settled, he scanned the row of storefronts. Nearly all were rock, with wooden fronts. Some had been built when the town was founded, nearing thirty years ago, and Gamble thought they hadn't seen an ounce of paint since.

The most weather-beaten of the structures was the Conquistador Saloon. A hand-lettered board outside promised a cold beer and a ham sandwich for two bits.

Gamble opened the screen door and stepped inside. The place was empty, except for the bartender.

"Howdy."

"Howdy yourself," Gamble said.

"What's your pleasure?" The bartender was about thirty-five, had a pressed white shirt, and his blond hair and beard were neatly trimmed.

"The special," Gamble said, walking up to the bar.

"I have to warn you, the beer's not that cold," the man said. "We haven't had fresh ice in a week—the icehouse is just kind of a soggy mess. So, the special is warm beer and a ham sandwich."

"Forget the beer," Gamble said. "How fresh is the ham?"

"I'd eat it."

"All right, bring me a ham sandwich. What else do you have to drink?"

"We have whiskey."

"No whiskey, it's ten o'clock in the morning."

"Um, how about some water?"

"All right," Gamble said. "A ham sandwich and a glass of water. No, make that a pitcher."

"That I can do," the bartender said. "My name's Dave, by the way. What brings you to Engle? You're not a cowboy. That uniform looks to me like you might have seen some action in Cuba."

"I get that a lot."

"Just passing the time."

Gamble took a silver dollar from his pocket and placed it on the bar.

"No offense," he said. "I'm just a naturally private sort of person. I'd like things to remain that way."

"Absolutely," the bartender said.

Gamble left the bar and found a table by the front window. He leaned the shotgun against the wall, put the haversack on the floor, and sat down in the straight-backed chair farthest from the door. The bartender brought the pitcher of water and a glass, and Gamble drank slowly, looking through the dusty glass at the street.

Then he took the map from the haversack, unfolded it, and spread it out on the table. The map was hand drawn, in ink. The *Jornada* was a solid line snaking from top to bottom, and to the west of that was a wavy line that indicated the Rio Grande River. Near the river was a childish-looking drawing of an elephant. From the elephant, a dotted line ran to the southwest, into some triangles that indicated mountains. There were a cluster of ovals with wavy lines rising from them, *Hot Springs,* and not far from that a jagged peak with a hole near the top labeled, *Eye of the Needle.* Beyond that was a drawing of a house with a T-shaped window where the door should be. There was no scale or other indication of how far it was between any of the locations.

"Terrific," Gamble muttered, folding up the map.

The bartender brought the sandwich.

As he ate, Gamble thought about heading back to the Oklahoma Panhandle—and to Agnes. He had nearly five hundred dollars in his pocket. That would last a couple of years in No Man's Land, perhaps more, as long as nobody showed up with a writ for his arrest. But even if nobody came for him it would be a mean life, a scarecrow life.

"You look like you're carrying the weight of the world."

"I just shoulder my share," Gamble said, thinking he may have to reach for the shotgun. But the man standing near the table was unarmed and wore the dusty clothes of a working man. He was about thirty and had keen eyes that seemed to drink the world in.

"Sit down," Gamble said.

The man sat down. The bartender brought another glass.

"Thanks, Dave."

"You bet, Gene."

"You from these parts?" Gamble asked, as he poured the water.

"I wasn't born here, if that's what you're asking," the man said. "But been here for a spell now. Born in Nebraska, came here by way of Kansas, with my folks."

"You a cowboy?"

"Punched some cows on the Bar Cross," he said. "Pretty fair stone mason. Helped build the road from here to Tularosa. Don't know what I am, now. Leaving for New York soon."

"For God's sake, why?"

"Getting married," Gene said. "Wonderful girl. But she doesn't love this country like I do. Maybe I'll come back some day. Maybe not. *Quién sabe?*"

"Lonely will drive a man to do strange things."

Gene smiled.

"You don't speak like a working man," Gamble said.

"I've had just enough learning to ruin an honest man," Gene said. "And it's made me want to write. Ever know anybody who made their living writing? Me, neither. But I want to write, to capture the way this country looks and feels and how men talk when they think nobody's listening."

Gamble shook his head.

"That's a tall order," he said. "Maybe you should warm up on dime novels first. You can think of fifty ways to describe the same gunfight, can't you?"

Gene laughed.

"None of the cowboys I know have ever fired their guns in anger," he said. "You remind me, stranger, of somebody I met a few years back—a man who showed up at my ranch, going by the name of Hawkins, always looking over his shoulder. He liked it here, said he wanted to come back with his wife and baby boy."

"So what was his real name?"

"I think he was Bill Doolin, escaped from the federal jail at Guthrie. When he left here, he rode back to Oklahoma Territory—straight to his death."

"Heard about that," Gamble said.

"You have the same look about the eyes."

"Are you saying that—"

"Not saying a thing, friend. We mind our own business here in the Tularosa basin, not that of our neighbor, as long as it doesn't pinch us anywhere tender. And Mister Hawkins was a friend of mine, so the only tender place it pinches me is that he's gone."

Gamble nodded.

"Tell me about the country to the south and west of here."

"It's extra special rough."

"It couldn't be anything less," Gamble said. "Also, does an elephant mean anything to you? As in a place name or a geographic feature or—"

"Yes," Gene said. "There's Elephant Butte, about twelve miles from here on the Rio Grande. Named for a huge outcropping that's in the shape of an elephant. There a ferry across the Rio Grande there—one of the only places to cross, in fact, for many miles."

"That's it," Gamble said. "I'm obliged."

"You must be planning some silver prospecting, if you're asking about crossing the Rio Grande at Elephant Butte," Gene said. "Good luck. I tried my hand at prospecting, but went bust. The story of me and money is a sad one."

"Not everybody can be a Hearst."

"Or wants to be."

Gamble laughed.

"It's about time for me to get moving, Gene. I have supplies to gather."

"Go to Walton's, across the street. Tell them I sent you. They'll give you a fair deal. Make sure you buy some warm clothes—it's hotter than hell now, but it gets cold at night, especially when you get above six thousand feet."

Gamble nodded.

"Really think Bill Doolin hid out on your spread?"

"I do."

"So you think his mistake was in going back to Oklahoma Territory?"

"No," Gene said. "I think his mistake was in taking up bank robbery as a profession."

TWENTY-ONE

That night, Gamble bedded down outside of town, on a little flat spot with a juniper tree. He lay on his back beneath a blanket and a rubber tarp, a few yards from the lingering embers of a fire he had made for frying bacon and boiling coffee for his supper.

Lightning flickered in the San Andres, and thunder shook the Tularosa basin. The rain started slowly, in big drops that splattered into the white sand and made the dying fire hiss and gush smoke. Then it began to rain in earnest.

Gamble sat up, holding the rubber tarp over his head.

Laughter came from the other side of the fire, where the ghost of his father sat on a rock, a bony finger pointing at him.

"Sonuvabitch," Gamble muttered.

The skeletal jaw opened and closed.

"What do you want?" Gamble asked. *"Speak, I charge thee, speak!"*

The ghost gathered its crutch and stood, but remained silent.

"Not even for Shakespeare?"

Lightning arced overhead and the ground trembled. While the bolt flashed, the ghost became invisible, but took form again with the darkness.

"I am becoming weary of this madness," Gamble said. "It has become monotonous. For some reason, I had thought insanity would involve more variety. I am ashamed to have a father that has made such a dull shade."

The ghost shook with fury.

"Speak, damn you!"

The ghost lurched forward, the crutch knocking sparks from the fire. Gamble immediately regretted having cursed the thing, even if it was a thing of his own imagination.

It drew close to him.

Pausing less then a foot away, the ghost leaned down and peered into Gamble's face. The rain beat upon the stony white cranium and pooled in the eye sockets. The jaw dropped and rested limply upon the breast of the ragged butternut jacket.

Gamble threw off the tarp and blanket and stood.

"It has been thirty-seven years since I last laid eyes on the living you," Gamble said. "What offense have I committed that has summoned you from the grave? What commandment did I break that has interrupted your slumber? It cannot be murder, for I have killed since I was but little more than a child. It cannot be adultery, for I have long made fornication a science. Stealing? Ha! I have made my living by theft. Armed robbery is a specialty. About the only thing I will not do is bear false witness or deny

God although the old bastard makes me mad enough to spit!"

Lightning struck the juniper tree. The blast knocked Gamble to the ground, unconscious, and sent a geyser of sparks into the air. When he came around, it had stopped raining. The ghost was gone.

TWENTY-TWO

"What kinds of things did he buy?"

Jaeger had his notebook out and had assumed his most stern Pinkerton look, the one which was intended to convey serious business. Old Man Walton sat in a rocker on the porch of his general store, gently stroking a cat that was asleep in his lap.

"Why did you say you were looking for this fellow?"

"I didn't say."

Jaeger's impatience was growing. After receiving the telegram two days ago from the Santa Fe agent that Gamble had gotten off the train at the Engle depot, Jaeger had hitched a series of rides on three different railways to cross New Mexico Territory from the northeast corner down to the southwest. He had been canvassing the storefronts, trying to pick up Gamble's trail.

"What kind of law did you say you were?" the old man asked.

"I'm a Pinkerton operative," Jaeger said, his voice rising.

"Shush," the old man said. "You'll wake up Killer."
But the cat seemed far from disturbed.

"What did the subject buy?"

"The first time or the next time?"

"He was here twice?"

"It's what I said, weren't it?" the old man asked.
"Boy, you sure are dumb for a detective. Can't imaging how you fellers ever caught Jesse James. Oh,
that's right, you didn't—it were the coward Robert
Ford that done him in."

"That was long before my time," Jaeger said.
"What did he buy the first time?"

"Blanket, gutta-percha tarpaulin, skillet."

"Anything else?"

"Don't recall."

"Don't you keep a record of sales or—"

"Now why the hell would I want to do that?"
Walton asked. "Somebody comes in to buy stuff, I
cipher it out on a sheet of brown paper that I wrap
the truck in. That way they know I didn't cheat
them. I know I didn't cheat them, so why should I
copy it out for myself?"

"How do you know if you've made a profit?"

"If there's money left over at the end of the month
to buy coffee and beans, I've made a profit. Don't
nobody need more than coffee and beans, and
maybe a twist of tobacco. Of course, some people
smoke. You chew or smoke?"

"I avoid tobacco," Jaeger said. "It's a filthy habit."

"Killer don't think so."

"What Killer may or may not think is immaterial,"
Jaeger said. "Tell me about the second time he came
back. Was it the same day or the next?"

"The next. But he weren't alone."

"Describe his companions."

"In addition to the tall thin soldier we've been talkin' about, there was an English-sounding feller, and a wicked hellcat of a girl with some kind of Musselman veil over her face. She was trouble, wasn't she, Killer?"

The old man scratched the cat beneath the chin and the cat roused briefly and shook its head, annoyed.

"Sorry, Princess Killer. I'll let you sleep."

"What kind of name is that for a common cat?" Jaeger asked. "It doesn't even make sense."

"My damned cat," the old man said. "I can name it what I damn well please. It looked like Princess Killer to me. Any more of your smart Dutch lip, and you'll just have to do some real detective work instead of asking old men questions."

"Ja, sorry. Tell me the things they bought."

"They made my month, I tell you," Walton said. "They outfitted themselves real good—clothes for all three, and more cook stuff—pans and cups and a coffeepot—and more bedrolls and rope and so forth."

"Rope?"

"Lot of it," Walton said. "Three, four hundred feet."

"Did it seem they were going prospecting?"

"Nah, they didn't buy those kinds of tools—no picks or hammers or chisels. Nobody prospects anymore, not since the price of silver went bust in ninety-three. It was more like they were going to do some climbing. Had the impression they were headed for the mountains, because of the clothes they bought. Generally, you don't buy flannel this time of year unless you're going to gain a few thousand feet in altitude."

"But they did not say where they were going?"

"No," Walton said. "I asked 'em, friendly-like, but they was a closemouthed bunch. Oh, I nearly forget. They also bought five boxes of Robin Hood smokeless shotgun shells in twelve gauge."

"Yes, I understand," Jaeger said, writing furiously. "They couldn't have carried this much, they must have—"

"—had animals, yeah. Three horses and a couple of pack mules. They loaded it all in front of the store before they took off."

"Which direction did they go?"

"Out of town."

"Yes, but which direction?"

"Couldn't tell you," Walton said. "Didn't linger to see them off."

Jaeger closed the notebook.

"Thank you," he said. "You've been of some help. Good day."

"That's it?" the old man asked. "All I get is a fare-thee-well?"

Jaeger paused.

"What is it you want, then?"

"That information must be worth at least five dollars to the mighty Pinkerton detective agency."

"We are not in the habit of paying citizens for helping us bring criminals to justice."

"Hear that, Killer? Then if these strange-looking folks come back, we just might not tell old high-and-mighty Pinkerton operative here about it. In fact, we just might tell these desperadoes that the Pinkertons was looking for them."

"All right," Jaeger said.

He handed the old man a five-dollar bill.

"I'll need a receipt for that," Jaeger said.

The old man laughed so loudly that it woke the cat, which jumped down and ran beneath the porch.

"If you don't remember where they went, do you remember where they came from?"

"Don't know about the other two," Walton said, "but the soldier feller the first day walked over from the Conquistador yonder."

Jaeger tipped his bowler and crossed the street.

"What's your pleasure?" Dave the bartender asked.

"A bit of a chat," Jaeger said.

"Hell, there's no business. I ain't got nothing better to do. What you want to talk about?"

"There was a tall man in a Rough Rider uniform here two days ago. Remember him?"

"Sure. He had ice water and a ham sandwich."

"Good, good," Jaeger said. "Did you see him again?"

"Nope, that was the only time."

"How about an Englishman and a young woman with a veil over her face?"

"I would have liked to have seen that," the bartender said. "Heard they were in town yesterday, but I didn't get to lay eyes on them myself. Somebody told me they were over at the livery, buying animals."

"All right," Jaeger said. "This one time the subject

was here, did he say anything to you about what he was doing in town or where he was going?"

"He was pretty tight-lipped with me," the bartender said. "But Mister Rhodes, one of the regulars, came in here and they struck up a peculiar conversation."

"Peculiar how?"

The notebook came out of Jaeger's pocket.

"Well, I didn't understand half of it," the bartender said. "The soldier fellow had this shotgun that looked like a cannon with him and he had a map all spread out on the table, but he put it up when Mister Rhodes sat down. They talked about this and that, and about poor old Bill Doolin—"

"William Doolin? The Oklahoma Territory outlaw?"

"He's the one," the bartender said. "They mentioned Guthrie, up in Oklahoma Territory. Then the soldier asked Mister Rhodes about the elephant."

"What do you mean, the elephant?"

"Elephant Butte, southwest of here. That's where the ferry is that crosses the Rio Grande. Guess the soldier fellow was headed that way."

TWENTY-THREE

The ferry crossing across the Rio Grande was at a broad shallow spot on the riverbank, where the twenty-five-foot wooden ferry was winched up and the gate dropped onto the gravel. To the northeast loomed the massive banded formation named Elephant Butte.

"I'll be damned," Jacob Gamble said, standing on the gravel bank of the river and gazing at the rock. "It does look like an elephant, sort of, with its trunk unfurled on the ground in front of it."

"Did you think I'd lie?" Anise asked.

"Not about that," Gamble said.

The ferryman walked over and hooked his thumbs beneath the suspenders of his faded denim overalls. He was an old man with a long face that had been turned to leather by the sun and was framed by wild white hair. Beneath the overalls was a tattered and dirty red flannel long-sleeved undershirt. He was chewing tobacco and, before he spoke, he spit a brown glob into the river.

"What's wrong with her face?" The ferryman asked.

"Old wound," Gamble said.

"All of you crossing together?"

"Yes," Lord Weathers said. "What's the fare?"

"Twenty dollars."

"That sounds like rather much."

Gamble shook his head.

"Just because this fellow has a British accent doesn't make him the queen of England," Gamble said. "And even if he was rich, that's no excuse for gouging him on the fare. Your board there says twenty-five cents for men, twenty cents for animals, and fifteen cents for women and children."

"Why are women cheapest?" Anise asked.

"Pretend it's chivalrous," Gamble told her, then turned back to the ferryman. "According to your posted rates, that's a buck sixty. That seems a little high to me, but we'll pay it. In fact, we'll pay you three dollars if you'll keep your mouth shut and not tell anybody we crossed here."

The old man looked from one to the other.

"If you keep your mouth shut," Gamble said, "there's another three bucks in it for you when we come back this way in maybe a week."

"Deal," the ferryman said, and spat tobacco into the water.

Weathers reached into his pocket and handed over three silver dollars, which the ferryman took with his left hand and dropped into the breast pocket of the overalls. Then he dropped the gate on the ferry.

He helped Anise step up onto the ferry with his right hand.

"You others can load the animals," he said roughly.

"You can take all of us?"

"We'll find out, won't we?"

Gamble led his horse, a big dappled gray, onto the ferry, and the two pack mules followed. Then Weathers brought his horse, a chestnut, and Anise's strawberry roan. Although Weathers had urged his niece to purchase a sidesaddle, she would hear none of it—where they were going, she said, she would have to ride like a man.

After all were aboard, the ferryman raised the gate and began winching the ferry across the river, the water piling against the upstream side.

When they were nearly halfway across, Gamble began unbuttoning his uniform.

"What are you doing?" Anise asked.

"Getting rid of it," he said as he stripped the jacket off, revealing his bare torso. "I'm damned tired of it, and tired of people asking about what it was like in Cuba. Figure this is a good place to retire it. When old Joe Shelby and his Iron Brigade crossed the Rio Grande on their way to old Mexico after the war, he sank his battle flag in the river. That was a ways from here, but it's the same river. Seems like a good time to do the same with this."

He held the jacket out over the water, then dropped it. The khaki floated on the green water for a few moments as it was swept downstream, then slipped under, giving a final flash of yellow from one of the cuffs.

"Remember the Maine," Anise said. "And to hell with Spain."

"To hell with William Randolph Hearst," Gamble said. "It was his war, not ours. Free Cuba was just a slogan, like they use to sell soap or tonic. In this case, it was used to sell newspapers."

Then something splattered into the water a few feet away.

"What was that?" Anise asked, just as the report from the rifle reached them.

"Get down," Gamble said, pushing her toward the gate.

"Who the hell is shooting at us?" the ferryman asked.

"Don't know," Gamble said, pulling Weathers down next to his niece. "You two stay put."

He glanced over the gate and saw a man standing on the gravel bank, a black horse near him, working the lever on a Marlin rifle.

"Can't you return fire?" Weathers asked.

"Not with a shotgun," Gamble said. "Too damned far."

Another round took a bite out of the top of the gate.

"He's not a bad shot," Gamble said. "You two get flat."

Gamble ran to the ferryman and began helping pull the long wooden lever that ratcheted the craft across on the heavy rope that stretched from bank to bank.

"Do you have a rifle?" Gamble asked between pulls.

"Yeah," he said. "Back on the other bank. For all I know, the sonuvabitch is trying to kill me with my own—"

Then a slug struck the ferryman in the back. He took a few steps away from the winch, arched his back, and twisted his left hand behind him like he was trying to reach a hard place to scratch, and shook his right hand at Gamble.

"I want my three dollars when you come back."

The he fell over the side into the water.

The horses were nervous, shuffling about, and the shifting weight made the ferry scud against the current with a hollow, booming sound.

"Weathers," Gamble called, still winching. Water was bursting over the upstream side. "Calm these animals or we're all going under."

As Weathers ran in a half-crouch to the horses, another slug bored a hole in the deck next to his left boot. Gamble worked the lever furiously, his heart pounding, sweat pouring down his body. A round creased his shoulder, causing a trickle of blood down his back.

"Sonuvabitch," Gamble said. "Next time I go treasure hunting, remind me to bring a long gun."

Anise ran back and helped him winch.

"What are you doing?" Gamble asked.

"My part," she said. "We're almost there."

A slug skipped past over the water.

"He's losing the range," Gamble said.

A few feet from the bank, Weathers dropped the far gate and led the horses toward the water. As they passed, Gamble slipped the Model 97 from the saddle scabbard of the dappled gray.

"Take the mules," Gamble told Anise.

"What are you doing?" she asked.

"Making sure the sonuvabitch can't cross after us," Gamble said.

As soon as Anise had lead the last mule into the shallow water and up the bank, Gamble aimed point-blank at the two-inch thick rope and fired. The buck shot frayed the rope. He fired three more times, destroying the winch mechanism and finally severing the rope. As the rope went slack the ferry pulled away from the bank, spun, and began drifting downstream.

Gamble jumped in the water.

It was over his head.

His boots touched the bottom and he pushed off hard. He broke the surface, clutching the shotgun in his left hand, clawing at the water with the other. The smoke-colored glasses had been knocked away and lost in the river. He kicked as hard as he could, but he couldn't keep his nose above water. Gasping, he inhaled some of the green stuff, and it was like somebody had hit him in the chest with a baseball bat. As the water closed over his head, he felt a hand grasp his wrist and pull him forward. Then he felt the gravel bottom beneath his boots, and soon he was wading up to the shore, Anise's arm around him.

He threw the shotgun aside and dropped to his hands and knees, coughing up a cupful of the river.

"Come on," Anise said, picking up the shotgun by the leather strap. Her wet blue skirt was plastered to her legs and her veil was gone. "That maniac is still lobbing lead our way, hoping for a lucky shot. Let's not oblige him."

Gamble got to his feet and they climbed the bank.

Weathers was waiting with the animals just on the other side of a sheltering ridge. There was the terrible screeching sound of tortured wood downstream, and they looked back in time to see the ferry flip and break apart.

TWENTY-FOUR

Jacob Gamble found a gray bib shirt in one of the packs and put it on. Then he fished the leather eye patch from the pocket of his wet jeans and tugged it over his head.

"That's better," Anise called as she tucked her jeans into the tops of her boots. "I never liked those damned glasses anyway. Never could see what you were thinking."

"Maybe that was the idea," Gamble muttered.

"Do you think we should build a fire?" Weathers asked, handing Gamble the slouch hat they had retrieved from a bend in the river. "Dry your clothes, perhaps?"

"Let's put some miles between us and the Rio Grande before we make camp," Gamble said. "Safer that way."

"But what about the ferryman?" Weathers asked. "We should make some kind of account. Surely he has a family, and they will want to know how he died. The authorities would be interested, I'm sure, in tracking down that maniac with the rifle."

"That maniac seemed pretty determined to kill us," Anise said, rolling up the sleeves of her light blue cotton shirt. "If we stop to do the right thing, there's no telling how long we'll be held up answering questions. The days are passing, Uncle. We only have six left. And don't forget, that maniac is still roaming the other side of the river. I agree with Lieutenant Dunbar, we're safer if we press on."

"Don't call me lieutenant," Gamble said, unpinning the cavalry insignia from the hat and tossing it in the brush. "That part of my life is over."

"Then how would you like us to refer to you?" Weathers asked.

"Jacob," Gamble said, putting the slouch hat on.

"Really?" Anise asked.

"That's the name my mother gave me," Gamble said.

"How strange," Anise said.

"What do you mean?" Gamble had broken down the Model 97 and was wiping the barrel and receiver dry. "It is a common name."

"The Pinkerton detective," Anise said. "Back in Amarillo, when I caught him snooping around your room after you left, was talking to himself and mentioned a name—Jacob Gamble. He said it was a name that German parents use to scare their children. Does the name mean anything to you?"

Gamble shrugged. He was pulling a cloth patch on the end of a string through the barrel.

"As I said, it's common as dirt."

"Yes," Anise said. "It is a popular name. But for it to be spoken in the room you'd just left . . ."

"Sounds like a curse to me," Weathers said. "You

know, that Pinkerton chap may have simply been doing some hard cursing in German and not wanting to explain the full meaning to you, my dear."

Gamble reassembled the shotgun.

"This Pinkerton," Gamble said. "He was German?"

"Why, yes," Weathers said. "What was his name? Oh, I know it means 'hunter' in English. Anise, do you recall?"

"Jaeger," Anise said. "Max Jaeger, but everybody called him Dutch. Know him?"

"Wouldn't say that," Gamble said, stuffing the magazine with dry shells.

"Ever meet him?"

"Once," Gamble said. "In Guthrie."

"He must not have remembered the meeting," Weathers said. "At least, he didn't mention it. Surprising, considering the interest he showed in you at Amarillo. Seemed very disappointed that you had already gone. Was asking all sorts of questions— including if we had a photo of you."

"What did you tell him?"

"Very little," Anise said. "Just as you wished."

Gamble nodded.

"Jacob, is there something we should know about you and this Pinkerton?" Anise asked. "Could it have been Jaeger on the other side of the river trying to kill us."

Gamble was silent.

"He has no reason to trail you?" she pressed.

"I can't imagine it was Dutch Jaeger on the other side of the river, throwing lead all by himself," he said. "That's not Pinkerton style. When they're ready to come after somebody, they never come alone."

Gamble slid the shotgun into the saddle scabbard, then put his boot in the left stirrup and swung up into the saddle of the dappled gray.

"We'd better move," he said.

TWENTY-FIVE

Jaeger swung down from the saddle of the black horse and onto the gravel of the riverbank. He had ridden downstream, scouting a place to cross, when he spied the body of the ferryman. The body had washed up on the lip of a sandbar, feet-first, and the man's face was turned to the water, his wild white hair swaying with the current.

Jaeger walked out onto the sandbar, grasped the body by one shoeless foot, and dragged it out of the water. Then he grabbed a shoulder strap of the man's overalls and turned the body over. The ferryman's eyes were wide and milky in his blue face. His hands were locked, the palms open.

"What a shame," Jaeger said, removing the folding Kodak from his pocket. "These criminals have no regard for human life. This madman Gamble has killed the ferryman."

He opened the bellows and adjusted the exposure for the cloud-filled sky.

"Gamble has kidnapped Lord Weathers and his pretty niece. He will kill them, too, after raping the girl. But an alert Pinkerton operative will chase Gamble down, and the criminal will die in a desperate shootout with the brave detective, no?"

He leaned down and framed the dead man's face in the viewfinder. Then he tripped the shutter.

TWENTY-SIX

They began to climb out of the basin, leaving the scrub and rocks and white sand behind. Anise was in the lead, on the strawberry roan, followed by Weathers on the chestnut. Jacob Gamble trailed behind, glancing behind him every so often, but seeing nothing.

They were driving deep into the foothills of the Black Range, at the top of which was the Continental Divide. Had they gone a little north, they would have been on the road to the silver mining camp of Chloride, which boomed the decade before, but which had gone bust with the Panic of 1893; a little south, and they would have made the silver capital of Kingston, once the largest city in New Mexico Territory but now all but a ghost town.

In an hour they stopped and passed around a canteen. When Weathers excused himself to take a necessary walk in the brush, Gamble asked Anise if they were going in the right direction.

"Yes," Anise said.

"You're sure? It's been—"

"I know how long it's been," she said. "And yes, I'm sure. I recognize all of this country. We're headed for the Eye of the Needle, and we should make it by day after tomorrow. From there, we're not far from the cave."

"And I get my other five hundred dollars."

"Yes, if we make it in time."

Gamble capped the canteen.

"So what happens at dawn on the twentieth?"

Anise smiled.

"It's the summer solstice, right? The longest day of the year," Gamble said. "So, is it some kind of astronomical timing of light and shadow? A golden beam pointing the way to the treasure cave? Celestial fireworks? I've known a lot of treasure witches in my day, old folks who use willow switches and whatnot to look for gold, and they were all wild for this astronomical rubbish. There's a Rider Haggard novel that uses this trick, I believe. Having lived in England for the past twelve years, I think you should be familiar with it."

"Do you doubt me, Jacob?"

"I'm from Missouri."

"What do you mean by that?"

"It means I must see to believe."

"Ah," Anise said. "My uncle can tell you that I do not read novels, or newspapers, for that matter. The affairs of others—imagined or otherwise—do not interest me."

"What does interest you, Miss Weathers?"

"Fortune," she said.

"Your guardian seems to be well off," Gamble said. "Neither of you seem to want for anything. You have an ample reserve of cash from which to buy supplies and hired guns. Why risk your neck out here in the wilderness? Don't you have enough of what you want?"

"Nobody ever has enough," Anise said. "Whether it's love, money, or power, it just creates an appetite for more. Don't you find that's true, Jacob?"

"You're asking the wrong man," Gamble said.

"Are you claiming you've never had love?"

"Not that lasted."

"Money?"

"Would I be here?"

"Ah, but power. Don't you thirst for more?"

"Hearst has power," Gamble said. "I'm just another piece on the chessboard. A pawn."

"Oh, you're no pawn," Anise said. "A knight, perhaps. What destructive masculine power you possess. How does that make you feel?"

"Anybody can pull a trigger," Gamble said.

"That's like Da Vinci saying anybody can wield a brush," Anise said. "You are an artist, Jacob Dunbar—the artist of the terrible."

"Sure. Whatever you say."

Anise laughed. Her auburn hair fell over her eyes, and she brushed it away with the back of her hand.

"I am glad you are no longer staring at my chin," she said. "It is almost as annoying as staring at my chest. But not quite."

Weathers came back.

"We should have bought some iron for you and your niece when we were back at Engle," Gamble said, looking at the trail behind them.

"That's what we hired you for," Weathers said. "I am a pretty fair shot when it comes to grouse, but not men. Besides, how were you to know we'd run into trouble?"

"I always run into trouble."

TWENTY-SEVEN

They camped that night beside a stream that fell clear and cold from the high mountains, and although Jacob Gamble cautioned against building a fire, Weathers insisted.

"Can't make tea without a fire," he said.

"Makes us easy to spot."

"Still worried about your maniac?" Weathers asked. "I'm sure we've left him far behind on the other side of the Rio Grande. Besides, why on earth would he want to follow us?"

"I can think of a reason," Anise said. She was sitting beside the fire, her legs drawn up beneath her, watching Gamble as he fed the flames with some deadwood he had gathered.

"And what reason is that?" Weathers asked.

"We're after treasure," she said.

"But nobody knows that, my dear."

"Oh, we haven't told anyone," she said. "But I'm sure they could smell it, just the same. People know. Isn't that right, Jacob Dunbar?"

"Sometimes," he said. "People know."

In the distance, a mountain lion screamed.

"Good Lord," Weathers said. "Was that a cat?"

"Yes," Anise said. "A big one."

Gamble took a pot and walked down to the stream. He knelt and dipped it full of water, then walked back and placed it over the fire.

"You'll have tea soon," he said. "Then I think we should smother this fire and have a cold supper. We have bread and cheese. That will do me."

"If you think so," Weathers said.

"It's best," Gamble said. "This is the kind of country that attracts folks who don't live by any rules."

"Would that include you?" Anise asked.

"I have rules," he said. "You just haven't been watching."

After they had eaten, Weathers excused himself and went to his bedroll, saying the day's excitement had done him in. Gamble and Anise remained by the ashes of the fire, talking in low tones.

"Perhaps I shouldn't have led him here," she said. "I forget that he is nearing sixty-five. To me, he has always been the same."

"Hope I get around as well as he does when I'm sixty-five," Gamble said. "But that isn't as far off as it once was."

"We all get older, at the same rate, a day at a time," Anise said. "Time is a very democratic thief. What I would not have given to have the years since my rescue back. Oh, do not give me that look. I am not being unkind. Never was there a more grateful niece. But civilization is the cruelest of man's inventions. Oh, how even a silk collar does chafe. I might as well have been in a zoo because of all of the stares I have gotten."

"How is it that you have an English uncle?"

"A family weakness," she said. "My father, Udall Weathers—my uncle's brother—was the previous Lord Weathers. It's a manorial title, connected to a damp old house on the outskirts of London. With too much money and too little sense, my father developed a taste for elephant hunting and made several trips to Africa in the late sixties. After he had slaughtered all of the big game the dark continent had to offer, he became interested in killing bison, so he brought his express rifle to America and shot them by the hundreds from a Union Pacific railway train. When he tired of that, he went to Omaha where he spent some of his nights with the prostitutes in the Burnt District and his days sleeping at the Hotel Fontenelle. My mother was a sixteen-year-old chambermaid at the hotel, a daughter of Irish immigrants, Catholic of course, and in every way unsuited, so of course my father married her. I was born nine months later, in April 1870."

"Of course," Gamble said.

"My sister came two years after that. My father remained in America, got involved in one failed scheme after another, and through a series of misadventures got himself and his wife killed on the banks of the Rio Colorado long after the Mohaves were assumed to be pacified, leaving their daughters to be taken captive. You know the rest about being traded to the Apaches."

"I know what you have told me."

"It is strange," Anise said, "but when I try to

recall my father's face, the sound of his voice, I cannot. My mother remains vivid in my memory. But not my father. When I look at him in the old portraits and photographs, I am staring at a stranger. Does your father still live?"

"I lost my father when I was a boy," Gamble said. "It was during the war, in Missouri. My father had joined up with old Joe Porter to beat the Yankees but was wounded and captured damned quick. He and some others were put into jail at Palmyra, in Marion County, and were scheduled for execution as punishment for the disappearance and presumed murder of a Yankee informer by the name of Andy Allsman."

"So he helped kill this informer?"

"My father didn't have anything to do with it," Gamble said. "Nobody knows who did. But the Yankee provost marshal, a devil by the name of Strachan, ordered my father and nine others shot by a firing squad to teach the rebels a lesson. My mother and I walked to Palmyra and she convinced the provost to release my father. He gave the order, but it was too late."

"Why was it too late?"

"By the time he gave the order, my father was dead of his wounds. Shot in the leg. Bled to death."

"And how did she convince this Strachan?"

"How do you think?"

Anise nodded.

"I would have done the same."

Gamble stared at her.

"It was a little more complicated than that."

"I'm sure it was," Anise said. "But I would have done the same."

"What was your mother's name?"

"Eliza Gamble."

The name seemed to hang in the air between them.

"So, you *are* the bogeyman who scares good little German boys and girls. Is Dunbar a complete fabrication?"

"My mother's maiden name," Gamble said. "I used it when I joined the Rough Riders to get out of Oklahoma Territory."

"And why did you have to flee the territory?"

"Because there was bad blood between us."

"How bad?"

"I killed two of Jaeger's cousins in self-defense," Gamble said. "Of course, they had a warrant for my arrest from Kansas, where I killed the brother-in-law of the governor. But the sonuvabitch deserved killing. And then I escaped from federal custody at Guthrie."

"Impressive record," she said. "But you might have shared this with my uncle and me before hiring on."

"Perhaps you misunderstand the theory behind a fugitive assuming an alias," Gamble said.

"And the train robber?"

"In on it," Gamble said. "I was the third man, and things went a bit sour when one of my partners killed the express messenger, killed the other partner, and tried to kill me before I beat him to it. I had nearly gotten away with the payroll when the conductor and your uncle hailed me as a hero."

"I need a drink."

Anise went to the packs, found the bottle of whiskey,

and came back with a pair of tin cups. She uncorked the bottle and poured three fingers in each.

"This was supposed to be for snakebite or some other emergency."

"I'd say this qualifies," Anise said. "Cheers."

Gamble took a sip. Anise took a deep swallow and wiped her mouth with the back of her hand.

"I know, not very ladylike," she said. "But I'm not much of a lady. Problem is, your story doesn't bother me all that much. What I'm most concerned about now is how badly this Dutch Jaeger wants your hide, and how it's going to interfere with us getting the Confederate gold out of that cave. How bad do you think he wants you, Jacob?"

"It is a passion," Gamble said. "Now that he has picked up my trail, after a year of thinking that maybe I was dead or otherwise gone for good, there will be no stopping him short of killing him. That I'm happy to do, but he is one tough sonuvabitch. And ruthless."

She drank the rest of her whiskey, then took Gamble's cup.

"You think he's out there."

"Sure of it," Gamble said. "Oh, he had to find another crossing, and that would have cost him half a day. But he can travel faster than we can."

"What are we going to do?"

"I don't know," Gamble said. "But I'll tell you what I'm going to do. I'll leave camp, go in some other direction. He'll follow me and leave the both of you alone. You can make it the rest of the way, Anise. You're plenty tough. Like my mother."

"You say that like it's a bad thing."

"You'd have to have known her," he said. "I'll gather my things."

"You don't have to go yet."

"Best if I start directly."

"This is the last time I'll see you?"

"Probably," he said. "I'll never shake the damned Pinkertons. If Jaeger doesn't succeed in killing me now, he'll go back to the nearest railway depot and telegraph the news that I'm alive and in the territory. I'll make a run for old Mexico, if I can, but odds are I'm going to end up full of holes on a picture postcard."

She began to unbutton her shirt.

"Your uncle."

"He sleeps like the dead."

She threw the shirt to one side.

"Let me break those damned rules I hate so much," she said. "Fuck me, Jacob Gamble, and remind me what if feels like to be alive. I know you want to from the way you look at me. Don't fight it, just do what you want with me. Then you get to walk away. That's what men want, isn't it?"

He jumped on top of her, his hands on her shoulders, pinning her to the ground. She lifted her head and kissed him hard enough to draw blood.

TWENTY-EIGHT

Jacob Gamble had found a rocky point overlooking the valley where Anise and her uncle slept. It was cold that morning, and he put on the mackinaw he had bought in Engle. As soon as it was light enough to see, he began leaving easy sign as he rode the dappled gray across a meadow, through every patch of soft ground he could find, and then up a volcanic slope of hard rock where the horse left no prints.

He rode over to a pile of breakdown forty yards away and tied the gray to a dead and twisted juniper tree on the back side. It was a good place for an ambush. The rocks made a natural fortress, and if Jaeger followed the trail to the volcanic shale, he would be close enough to be blown out of the saddle by a load of buckshot from the Model 97.

Gamble placed the shotgun on the top of a flat rock, placed a box of Robin Hood shells beside it, and began to fill the pockets of the Mackinaw with ammunition. Then he settled down with his back against a rock and waited. The air smelled of pine and rain.

About seven o'clock he saw, far across the valley, Anise and her uncle riding away, each leading a pack mule. He watched as they made their way up to high ground in the southwest, and then disappeared behind a stand of cedars.

At eight o'clock he saw a lone rider on a black horse approaching from the east, at an easy but determined pace, following the path the trio had taken to the campground before. The rider disappeared behind the trees, then emerged five minutes later, following the path that Gamble had taken across the meadow and up the volcanic slope to his outcropping. Even from a quarter of a mile away, Gamble recognized the brown bowler hat.

"Good," Gamble said. "Come on, you ruthless sonuvabitch."

Then, halfway across the meadow, the rider stopped. He could see the bowler swivel first to the left, and then to the right. "What are you doing?" Gamble asked. "Come on, don't you see the tracks?"

Then it seemed as if the rider stared straight up the slope to the pile of rocks where Gamble was hidden. He slowly turned the horse, riding away to the southwest.

Gamble uttered florid curses.

"Now, what?" he asked. "You're going after *them?*"

Gamble took the shotgun and slipped it into the scabbard, untied the gray, and swung up into the saddle. He started down the northeastern side of the slope, out of view of the rider.

Then he stopped.

"But why would he go after them?" he asked,

patting the horse's neck. "He can't know about the gold. Whatever the reasons, it can't be good."

Gamble turned the horse, crossed the slope, and made for the southwest. He caught up with the rider an hour later. The man on the black horse had just entered a slot canyon, too narrow for two horsemen to pass inside and too confined for the man's lever-action rifle to give him much advantage.

Gamble pulled the shotgun from the scabbard and held it at the ready as he used his knees to urge the dappled gray into the canyon. Ahead, he could hear the sound of rushing water. He passed some shoulder-height petroglyphs on the canyon wall, brick red in color, circles and spirals, elk that looked like dogs, and a flute-playing medicine man with an antler headdress and an exaggerated phallus.

"You're right," he told the glyph.

He urged the gray ahead, the hoofbeats hidden by the sound of the water. He leaned first one way and then the next as he rode through a serpentine section of the canyon, then rounded a turn and found Jaeger standing beside his horse, reaching beneath its belly to tighten the cinch strap. Gamble had the drop on Jaeger, but if he fired, he would gut-shoot the horse as well.

"Hello, Dutch."

Jaeger reached for the Marlin lever-action rifle in the saddle scabbard, but the commotion had made his horse skittish, and the animal turned away from Jaeger. Seeing a couple of feet open up between Jaeger and the animal, Gamble fired, but his own horse was moving sideways now—and he missed. The report of the Model 97 rang the slot canyon like a bell and ricocheting buckshot zinged and whirred away.

"Remember this sound?" Gamble asked as he cycled another round into the chamber, *ch-chink!* "Kind of makes you want to wet yourself, doesn't it?"

"Jakob Gamble," Jaeger said. "Still hanging on to your scarecrow life, I see."

"Put your hands up."

"Why?"

"Just put 'em up, Dutch."

Jaeger raised his hands.

"Where's that nasty little pistol of yours?"

"In the saddle bag."

Jaeger was stepping backward, toward his horse.

"Stop it right there," Gamble said.

"To make it easier for you to kill me?"

Jaeger's back was now against his horse's shoulder.

"Stay away from that saddle Marlin and keep your hands where I can see them," Gamble said. He had the shotgun trained on Jaeger, and the reins held in his right hand, beneath the pump, but the dappled gray was getting even more anxious. The horse began to shuffle and throw its head.

"Easy," Gamble said, trying to calm the animal.

Then the gray rocked and wheeled, turning Gamble the wrong way in the passage. Gamble swung the shotgun around, attempting to keep Jaeger covered, but Jaeger had ducked beneath the belly of his horse, snatched the Marlin from the scabbard on the other side of the saddle, and was now running at top speed down the narrow canyon.

Gamble slipped down from the saddle, but couldn't get a shot because the black horse was in the way. Jaeger half-turned and snapped off a quick shot behind him with the Marlin, missing Gamble but hitting his own horse in the neck.

The horse screamed and bolted into the canyon wall, shaking rocks loose from above, then fell, blood gushing from the wound to stain the canyon wall. The animal fell and drunkenly tried to get up, its hooves flailing, eyes wild.

"Damn it," Gamble said.

He shouldered the Model 97 and sent a round of buckshot into the horse's skull. He searched Jaeger's saddlebags, but found no revolver.

He led the dappled gray over the carcass of the dead horse and down the slot canyon. High along one wall, he noticed a pair of metal pipes bolted to rock, then crossing over and disappearing out of sight.

"What the devil?"

One pipe was about eighteen inches in diameter, and the other was smaller, the thickness of a tin can. Both were stained with rust, but appeared to be still in service, because the joints were damp and water beaded on the underside of each.

He exited the canyon, past a thirty-foot waterfall that filled a pool at the base of the cliff. Above, he could see the pipes snaking down from the upper pool and heading into the canyon. Gamble guessed the water was for a mining camp far down the slope, or perhaps to run the machinery at one of the old silver mills.

The horse lowered its head and drank. Gamble glanced around, to make sure Jaeger wasn't lying in ambush. Then he knelt by the pool, cupped some water in his left hand, and drank it. The water was snowmelt, cold and flat.

Then he noticed a reflection on the surface of the water, or a vision, he did not know which, of someone standing behind him. It was an Apache warrior of indeterminate age, carrying a Springfield carbine, wearing a faded pink shirt, buckskin leggings, a red paisley headband, and a blue scarf gathered with a silver concho.

"Don't you know?" Gamble asked the reflection. "You've all been pacified."

The image did not move.

"You ghostly types are not much for conversation, are you?" Gamble asked the reflection. "Well, when you see my father, tell him that I appreciate the favor of his company, but that I wish he could be a little more direct about whatever it is that he wants to get across to me. Unless his goal is just to haunt me, Jacob Marley fashion, and in that case, he has succeeded."

Then Gamble rose, mounted his horse, and rode off, not bothering to look behind him.

TWENTY-NINE

"Jacob!" Anise cried as Jacob Gamble walked into the firelight, leading the dappled gray. "You nearly frightened me to death. I heard somebody approaching. Why didn't you call out—and why have you returned?"

"Yes, old man—why?" Weathers asked.

Uncle and niece were sitting together on a log, drinking tea from enameled cups.

"I didn't want to announce my presence, just in case you two weren't alone," Gamble said, lifting a stirrup onto the horn and beginning to unsaddle the horse.

"Why wouldn't we be alone?" Anise asked.

"The maniac was Jaeger, and after we separated this morning, he followed the both of you, not me," he said. "I met up with him in a little canyon a few miles back, and we traded shots, but he got away. He's on foot, though—his horse was killed in the fight."

"Are you all right?"

"No holes in me, if that's what you mean," Gamble

said, lifting the saddle from the back of the horse and placing it on the ground.

"We're glad of that," Anise said. "And glad to see you, of course. But I don't understand. If Dutch Jaeger is after you, why would he follow us instead?"

"That's what I asked myself. I didn't like any of the answers."

"Here, let me do that," Weathers said, gently taking hold of the gray's bridle. "I've cared for horses all of my life—as every good English gentleman should—and at least I can make myself of some use now."

"Obliged," Gamble said. "Although you shouldn't be tending after me so kindly, considering I have brought so much trouble to the both of you."

"It's not your fault," Weathers said.

"I'm afraid it is," Gamble said. "All of it."

"What do you mean?"

"We will discuss it later, Uncle," Anise said. "Jacob is tired and undoubtedly hungry and we should feed him first."

"Quite so," Weathers said.

"Come sit," Anise said.

Gamble eased himself down to the ground with his back against the log and the shotgun beside him. He was glad for the mackinaw, because it was getting colder the higher they went. Anise dipped him a plate of beans from the pot, then apologized for not having coffee.

"I'll drink anything, as long as it's hot."

"Tea, then," she said. "How do you like it?"

"I don't know. The last time I can remember

having tea was back in Missouri, with my mother. We would drink sassafras tea as a remedy."

"Did you like the taste?"

"Yes," he said. "It was like root beer. Of course, I put a lot of sugar in it when I was a boy."

"Sugar, then," Anise said.

He ate the beans and then cupped the tea in his hands and stared at the dying fire.

"So Dutch Jaeger escaped your terrible gift," Anise said.

"Yes."

"How?"

"Because I should have killed him and his horse in the same shot when I had the chance, but I hesitated because of the horse," Gamble said. "I ended up having to shoot the horse anyway, after Jaeger hit it with a stray shot."

"The bastard," Anise said.

"The first time I met him, he told me he had the necessary quality to become a Pinkerton operative, that he was a ruthless sonuvabitch. And he has proved it at every opportunity since."

"Now what?"

"I take you back," Gamble said. "See you safely on the train at Engle, then I fend for myself, like I always have."

"But what about the fortune?" she asked.

"No amount of gold is worth dying for," Gamble said.

"I won't hear of it."

"Jaeger has a Marlin and probably a revolver and we are three people and have only a shotgun," Gamble said. "He's got the firepower and he has the range. All he has to do is find the campfire, lurk in the dark for the right moment, and kill us off one by one."

"We're only one day away."

"Yeah, but dead is a long time."

"I'm not going back," Anise said. "I've waited thirteen years for this and I will not be denied. Don't gulp the tea, sip it. It's not coffee."

"Right," Gamble said.

Weathers came and sat down near them.

"What's the fuss about?"

"Your lieutenant wants us to turn back," Anise said.

"Because of the maniac, yes," Weathers said. "And you, of course, want to press on. I understand both of your points of view completely. But in this case, as the ranking member of the family and as the lieutenant's employer, I rather think it is I who should make the decision."

"Of course," Anise said.

"We are continuing," Weathers said. "We are nearing the last chapter of the book. How cruel it would be to terminate the story now! We would be pleased if you would accompany us, Lieutenant, but you are under no obligation. Consider yourself a free agent."

"Thank you," Gamble said.

"Also, you have earned the five hundred dollar bonus that was promised should you get us safely to our destination by the twentieth of June. We are two days ahead of that schedule, so you have earned that bonus."

"As a free agent," Gamble said. "I respectfully decline."

"You are certain?"

"I am," Gamble said. "Also, you should know that my name is not Dunbar—it is Gamble, Jacob Gamble. While I did serve with the Rough Riders, I am also an outlaw with a very long career. When we met on the train, I was there to help rob it."

"Of course you're an outlaw," Weathers said. "Do you think I'm really such an old fool to believe that you weren't? When you're in the market for a gun-slinger, you don't hire the aspirant with the spot-less record. You hire the one that has had some experience in that line of work."

"Oh, my," Anise said.

"All of the great English heroes have been out-laws, from Robin Hood to Henry Morgan," Weath-ers said. "Even our late Victorian hero, the explorer Captain Sir Richard Burton, was a scoundrel."

"Now, Uncle."

"Oh, your father would have told you the same, because he knew Burton—and undoubtedly picked up some of his worst habits from the man. I can only thank God that Udall never fathered a child during his many forays into native cultures   miscegenation is the most heinous of sins."

"Uncle!"

"All right," Gamble said. "But I insist we dose the fire now and sleep in shifts."

"I will take the first watch," Weathers said.

"Then you have custody of the shotgun," Gamble said, handing over the Model 97.

"It is heavy," Weathers said. "And quite unlike the doubles I am used to."

"It works a little differently," Gamble said. "There's already a round in the chamber. You have to pull the hammer all the way back to full cock before it will fire. It's on half cock now, which is safest—that way it doesn't discharge if the gun is dropped or the hammer gets bumped. Once fired, to chamber a new round, you pull the pump back like this and throw it forward again. The magazine holds five rounds."

Weathers nodded.

"Wake me when you judge it to be midnight," Gamble said.

That night, he dreamed again of Missouri. Again, he was a boy. But this dream was not something woven of fear and regret, but instead was a memory made real.

It was an evening in the early spring—late March, perhaps, but not yet April. The war was still years off. His father had come in from the fields. They had eaten together as a family at the small table in a corner of the cabin, and even his mother seemed content.

His father scooted his chair back from the table, packed his cob pipe with tobacco, and held a match to the bowl. He blew out the match and smiled through the smoke.

"What did you learn today, Jacob?"

"We drilled on Reverse Oval Capitals," Jacob said. "Forever."

"*It is difficult to write properly without the Reverse Oval Capitals,*" his father said. "*I am quite mad about them myself, and endeavor to use them frequently.*"

"*John, don't tease the boy,*" his mother called.

"*I'm not teasing,*" his father said. "*There is nothing so beautiful as good penmanship. What else did you study today? History? Math?*"

"*We discussed the traitor, Senator Benton.*"

"*Traitor?*" his father cried. "*Why, Old Bullion was no traitor. He called for a return to hard money and to hell with the banks and paper money printed by the bushel basket. There is no substitute for gold. You remember that.*"

"*Mister Everett said Benton had betrayed Missouri by declaring against slavery and that he was glad the old man was dead and could do no more harm.*"

"*Old Bullion was a Democrat, first and last,*" his father said. "*He was right to oppose the peculiar institution—as I do. Just don't tell the preacher Larkin Skaggs those sentiments, or we'll be run out of the Baptist Church.*"

"*No more politics,*" Eliza Gamble called. "*The boy already gets in enough fights.*"

"*All right,*" his father said, reaching for the old fiddle that was hanging from a peg driven into the rough-hewn wall. "*A music lesson, then. Son, there are some that say this is the devil's box—an instrument for damnation—but I say otherwise. It can praise God as well as any human voice, perhaps better. Here, son. Take it. Tell me what you feel.*"

Jacob took the fiddle. It was light, much lighter than

he expected, considering the amount of sound his father could coax from it. He ran his thumb over the strings and the body of the fiddle thrummed with life.

"Try the bow," his father said.

Jacob took the bow in his left hand.

"No, use your right," his father said.

Jacob switched hands, put the fiddle in the crook of his arm as he had seen his father do, and awkwardly drew the horsehair over the strings near the bridge. A most terrible cry emanated from the fiddle, as if it were being tortured.

His father laughed.

"It gets easier," his father said. "Hold the bow loosely in your hand, as if it were a feather. Yes, that's it. Now, draw it lightly over the strings, keeping the speed steady."

Jacob tried again, but the result was hardly better than the first time.

"I can't do it," he said.

"You will, in time," his father said. "Just as you now effortlessly make those Reverse Oval Capitals, you will be able to do this."

His father took the fiddle and the bow, put it in the crook of his right arm, held the bow poised for a moment over the instrument, and then began an old Irish ballad. The music was at once beautiful and sad and when his father had played the last note, the mood lingered.

"It has a voice," Jacob said.

"Yes, it does," his father replied. "It is my voice, the things that I feel, and the fiddle can say things for which there are no words. Without it, I am less than myself. With it—and you, and your mother—

I am whole. We speak the language of men. This, the language of angels."

Jacob nodded.

"When I am gone—and we all go away some day, every one of us—then this fiddle will be yours, and so, too, will be the language of both men and angels."

"Yes."

"Where is the fiddle, Jacob?"

Gamble woke. He sat up. The fiddle—of course, it was the fiddle, left behind in Kansas.

THIRTY

The scrubby plateau was layered in mist and surrounded by rugged red-walled cliffs, and scattered about were scalding pools of water that sometimes surged, bubbled, and spat. As the dappled gray stepped carefully along the edge of the pool, Jacob Gamble leaned over and stared at the unquiet water. The animal was made uneasy by the steam rising from the surface, and the phenomena seemed a bit unnerving to Gamble as well.

"Boilings," Gamble said. "Didn't know there were any within five hundred miles."

"What do you suppose heats the water?" Weathers asked.

"Some kind of volcanic action would be the rational explanation," Gamble said, turning in the saddle. "But as spooky as this place is, it wouldn't surprise me if it turned out to be the fires of hell itself."

"I find the landscape rather placid," Anise said.

"Peaceful can also be spooky," Gamble said. "You

die up here, and nobody but the wolves might find your body for the next hundred years."

"Perhaps," Anise said. "But what a place to spend eternity."

They continued riding. The day wore on and the mist disappeared and they gained another thousand feet in elevation and the ground became even more rocky. Above them was a chimneylike spire of red rock that looked as if it had been built by a very drunk bricklayer. At the top of the spire was a jagged opening.

"Eye of the Needle?" Gamble asked.

"Yes," Anise said. "We're close, now."

"What do you suppose our elevation is?" Weathers asked.

"Six or seven thousand feet, I reckon," Gamble said. "But I could be wrong—this is not my kind of country. Back in Missouri, any rock over a couple of thousand feet is called a mountain."

"Do you miss it?" Anise asked.

"Like I miss my mother."

"Think you'll ever see it again?"

"There's about the same chance of me seeing Missouri again as there is of me ever seeing her," Gamble said. "I came to the West because I became just a bit too notorious to remain home. Don't think I can return until I'm good and dead."

By mid-afternoon they had come to a massive rock cliff, banded in black and red, as sheer and formidable as the wall of an ancient castle. Near the top of the cliff, fifty feet above them, was a weathered oval void in the rock, and set beneath the overhanging arch was an edifice built of many thousands of flat, bricklike stones. A T-shaped window was set in the middle of the structure, and it was flanked on each side by four square windows, adding to the castlelike appearance.

"It is even more magnificent than you described, my dear," Weathers said enthusiastically, his head cocked back, his hands crossed over the saddle horn. "Have you ever seen anything like it, Mister Gamble?"

"Once," Gamble said. "In Arizona Territory, but on a smaller scale. That place had critters in it."

"Bears and mountain lions are common," Anise said, dismounting from the strawberry roan. "You have to be careful not to get cornered in a cave or a narrow place."

"Not the kind of critters I meant," Gamble said. "So, the treasure cave is up there? In the pueblo?"

"Some distance behind that big one, yes," Anise said. "This is the corner property of a city that stretches down both sides of a narrow canyon on the other side."

"The Apache lived here?"

"No," Anise said. "This is considered the ancestral homeland, but the Apache never inhabited these dwellings. The tribe has only been in this area for a few hundred years, and these buildings are far older. Geronimo said that no human being ever slept up there, that this is where the gods lived during their time on earth."

"What's this place called?"

"Doesn't have a name, at least not in English," Anise said.

"And how do we get up there?"

"See those holes drilled into the cliff? There used to be a catwalk that led up there to that window shaped like the letter 'T,'" she said. "We're going to chop some wood, jam it in those holes, and string a rope to the top."

"Afraid it was something like that," Gamble said. "You should have found somebody younger for this."

Gamble thrust a pine stake as thick as his forearm into the hole in the cliff wall a foot above his head, placed the toe of his left boot into a hole at his knee level, and raised himself up. He was more than halfway to the cliff dwelling.

"You're going too fast," Anise said.

"I'm going fast because I'm scared," Gamble said, pausing to adjust the coil of rope over his shoulder. "If I go any slower, I'm going to freeze and they'll have to peel me off this cliff come next spring."

"Don't think about how far up you are."

"That helps me not to think about it, thanks."

He reached overhead and stabbed another hole, found another foothold with his toe, and placed his weight on his left foot. Then his foot slid out of the hole and he was left dangling from the stake, his boots skittering on the cliff.

"Sorry," Gamble called, finding another foothold.

"For God's sake, can't you tie that rope off to something?" Weathers called.

"There's nothing to tie it to, at least not yet," Gamble said, then grunted as he pulled himself up. "If I dash my brains out on the rocks below, will you do humanity a favor and just leave my body there, as a warning to others?"

"You have a peculiar sense of humor," Anise said.

"Everything about me is peculiar," Gamble said. "My sense of humor is simply extra peculiar."

Ten minutes later, he heaved himself up into the T-shaped window and sat for a moment, panting. His face was slick with sweat and his pulse was drumming in his ears.

"Throw the rope," Anise called.

"Let me tie it off first," he said, looking over the interior. There were stairways going off each side, off kilter, and the back wall was open, allowing a view of the canyon behind, with pueblos dotting the cliff wherever there was an arch or protruding ledge.

"Gods, hell," Gamble said. "They look like wasp nests."

He tied the end of the rope to a beam protruding from an inside wall, then tested it with his weight. Satisfied it would hold, he walked over to the T-shaped window, uncoiling the rope as he went.

"Ready?" he called.

"I've been ready," Anise said.

He tossed the rope.

"Got it," she said.

In two minutes, she was standing beside Gamble, gazing out of the T-shaped window to the east. The valley stretched beneath them, trees and rocks and the occasional glint of water. Standing like a sentinel on the not-too-distant horizon was the Eye of the Needle.

"It's just as I remembered it," she said. "My God,

but I have waited a long time to be here. But it was worth it. It was worth it, don't you think?"

"I don't know," Gamble said. "We haven't found the treasure yet. Ask me later."

"Of course," Anise said. "How foolish of me."

She waved at her uncle. He removed his hat and used it to wave back. The shotgun was slung over his shoulder.

"Now, we have to wait?" Gamble asked. "Until dawn."

"No," Anise said, a trace of sadness in her voice. "We don't have to wait. We can get on with it."

"But the solstice?" he asked. "Celestial fireworks?"

"No reason to wait," she said. "There's no light show, no finger of God to point the way, no celestial event to be witnessed through the needle. It will be just another dawn. No fireworks."

Gamble stared at her.

"You almost had me believing in it," he said. "But why all the nonsense? Why would you make up such a thing?"

"I never said there would be fireworks. I just said we had to be here by the solstice, that's all. And we're here, that's what counts."

"But—"

Anise pressed a slender finger to her lips.

"You were hired to get us here and you did, gun-slinger," she said. "The answer to the whys and wherefores were never part of the deal."

"I'll be damned," Gamble said. "Again."

"You've been done no harm."

"I was lied to."

"No, you lied to yourself."

"And your uncle?" Gamble asked. "Does he know about the solstice surprise? That there *isn't* one?"

"Lower your voice," she said. "Do not speak of my uncle. There are things you do not understand."

"A damned many things, apparently."

She put her hands on her hips.

"You have not been a paragon of truth yourself."

"I'm an outlaw, remember? Outlaw. People expect me to lie."

"You think I have lied about the gold?"

"Almost certainly," he said.

She crossed her arms.

"All right," she said. "We shall see."

She leaned out over the cliff.

"Uncle," she called. "We are going to do some scouting. Will you be all right?"

"Of course," he said. "Reconnoiter the old place and tell me what you find. But you have to wait until the morning for the treasure cave, is that right?"

She hesitated.

"Yes, Uncle," she said. "That's right. It will be revealed at first light."

"Splendid," Weathers said.

Anise glanced at her feet.

"He is an inveterate reader of Rider Haggard," she said. "The notion has made him happy. Tomorrow, he thinks the sun will shine through the Eye of the Needle and reveal a treasure door in the cliff face, guarded by skeletons and rattlesnakes."

"And how do you intend to handle tomorrow?"

"I don't know," she said. "But no matter what I do, it will break the old man's heart. But I can't think of that now. Just shut up about it, will you. Follow me."

She led Gamble up the right-hand staircase, across a narrow ledge, and into a larger room. As they walked across the dirt floor, Gamble paused to pick up a corncob. It was so old and dessicated that it weighed almost nothing.

"Gods, huh?" he asked. "Last time I checked, the gods didn't eat corn on the cob."

"Not your gods, perhaps," she said.

Gamble crushed the cob in his fingers.

She exited a doorway, went down another flight of stone steps, and followed a path that terminated at the opening to a natural cave. On either side of the entrance were badly weathered petroglyphs. The carvings depicted skeletal figures and coiled rattlesnakes.

Gamble laughed.

"They're as real as anything else in this world."

"Right," Gamble said. Then he tried to duck into the cave, but she grabbed his sleeve.

"You can't," she said. "Not yet."

"Why not?"

"The sacred words," she said. "Turn away."

"What?"

"You heard me. Turn away."

Gamble turned his back while Anise knelt. He heard her scraping the ground with a pebble, and then heard her whisper something that sounded like no human language he had ever heard before. Then she stood and told him it was all right.

"Go on," she said.

He ducked into the cave and saw nothing but

darkness. He fumbled in his pocket for his matches, found one, and struck it against the rock wall. The match flared and he could see the cave was large, about the size of his entire boyhood cabin in Missouri, and there were objects piled against the walls.

He went to the wall and began to slowly walk, holding the match. There were swords black with rust, a dented breastplate and a battered helmet to match, a heavy Spanish bit, reed arrows with obsidian points, a flintlock rifle with half the stock missing, stone clubs, a Walker Colt with a badly rusted cylinder, a Springfield rifle with a burst barrel, and rotting bundles of sticks and bone whose meaning Gamble could only guess.

"What do you see?"

"History," Gamble said.

The match burned down to his fingers and he dropped it.

"It's a war museum," she said. "Apache culture is based on war. This is their British Museum, their Library of Congress. Every campaign, every victory, every loss. These were not raids, which are a trifling matter to acquire property. These are tokens of war, meant to take the enemy's life—and his soul."

Gamble lit another match.

"Why don't you come in?"

"No," she said. "I . . . I cannot. Not yet."

He went on around the wall, looking at more rifles and spears and tattered guidons, and then he came to a strongbox. He knelt down, holding the match close to the lid, and read the stenciled inscription: *Territory of Arizona, CSA*. The lock was broken and he flung back the lid. A mound of coins gleamed a dull gold color in the match light.

He grabbed a handful of coins from the top. They were heavy, and with the same designs as the one Anise had shown him at the restaurant in Amarillo.

"I don't believe it," he said.

"You've found the strongbox," she said.

The flame bit his fingers and he dropped the match. He shoved the coins in his pocket and made for the shaft of light behind him. He emerged from the cave, pulled one of the coins out, and examined it in the sunlight. They were dull, with a green patina.

"What the hell?" he asked. "Are these tarnished?"

"Gold bullion doesn't tarnish."

"That's what I thought."

Gamble took out his pocketknife, opened the blade, and gouged across Seated Liberty on the face of the coin. It was a silvery gray color beneath.

"Lead."

"Plated with an alloy of copper and who knows what," Anise said. "They shine up pretty good, though. You could almost believe it's the real thing when you've been drinking and wishing. My uncle was mostly wishing. Believed me when I told him I'd had it tested."

"Oh, hell," Gamble said,

"I told you the Apaches used them sometimes to cast bullets," she said. "And you don't think wise old Geronimo would have shot golden bullets at the horse soldiers, do you?"

He threw the coin as far into the canyon as he could.

"The North counterfeited Confederate paper money

by the boatload," Anise said. "It helped win the war for them. The Apaches got the strongbox when they slaughtered a Yankee detail early in sixty-two. This was obviously an attempt to hoodwink somebody into thinking the Confederacy had actually minted some gold, but the rhymes and reasons behind it are as dead as the Yankee soldiers the Apaches killed."

Gamble laughed.

"Well, it worked," he said. "It hoodwinked me."

Anise smiled.

"Why?" Gamble asked. "Why the fairy tale? The solstice, the gold, none of it makes any sense. Are you particularly cruel or simply insane?"

"Neither, I hope," she said. "Listen to me, Jacob. When I was found thirteen years ago—"

Gamble slapped her, hard.

"Enough lies."

She touched the corner of her mouth and looked at the blood on her fingertips.

"Good," she said. "Blood is good. It's real."

A rifle shot rang out from somewhere below.

THIRTY-ONE

There were five more shots by the time Jacob Gamble had run to the T-shaped window and looked down. Weathers was at the base of the cliff, the Model 97 to his shoulder, pointing it at Jaeger, who was facing him, thirty yards away.

Jaeger was holding the lever-action Marlin at hip level.

"Kill him," Gamble shouted.

"I'm trying," Weathers said. He was jerking the shotgun's trigger, but nothing was happening.

"Pull the hammer back," Gamble said. "All the way."

Weathers lowered the shotgun a bit and pulled the hammer back with his thumb. It locked into place with a soft click. But before he could bring the gun back to his shoulder, Jaeger fired, and the bullet hit the old man in the thigh. Weathers fell to one knee, firing the Model 97 toward the sky as he went down. The barrel of the shotgun wavered as he struggled to hold it in his right hand. His left hand was pressed against his thigh, which was bright with blood.

"What's happening?" Anise asked, running up behind Gamble. "On, no. Uncle!"

"Get down," Gamble said.

"Hello up there," Jaeger called, waving. "You are not armed, are you? I should think you would be sending blue beans my way if you were."

"Leave the old man alone, Dutch," Gamble said.

"He still has a very big gun in his hand," Jaeger said. "I may have to kill him in self-defense. Or would that be murder, just as you murdered my cousins. Which is it, Lieutenant Dunbar?"

"Hell, you killed one of them yourself."

"*Ja,* scarecrow, this is true. But it was necessary."

"You wanted me, now you've got me. Let the girl and her uncle go."

"But I have all three of you," Jaeger said. "It is a rather convenient number, considering I once had three cousins. But no more, not for a while now."

"He has shattered my thigh bone," Weathers said, as if he were remarking on the weather. "Hit an artery as well, judging from the color and quantity of the blood. Strange, but I thought there would be more pain. That comes later, I suppose."

"Ah, what a shame," Jaeger said. "You are bleeding to death. You might ask the outlaw about what to expect. He very nearly bled to death, before a doctor in Guthrie saved him. But there are no doctors here."

The shotgun barrel wavered.

"Quite right, I suppose."

"Work the pump," Gamble called.

Weathers shifted the gun in his right hand, but kept his left pressed against his thigh.

"Use both hands," Gamble said. "Pump it."

"No, he'll kill him," Anise whispered.

"He'll kill him anyway," Gamble said.

Weathers looked up at the T-shaped window and smiled. He lifted his left hand from his leg, but became unbalanced and fell on his back.

Jaeger laughed.

"I'm going down there," Anise said, brushing past Gamble toward the rope. "We can put a tourniquet—"

"No," Gamble said, gripping her forearm. "He'll just kill you, too."

Weathers began crawling toward the cliff face, fifteen feet away. He pulled the shotgun along with him.

"Oh, how rude of me," Jaeger said. "You are probably wondering what the shooting before was all about, because there is only one hole in your uncle. Observe! I have killed all of your horses and mules except for one animal, the gray. That, I am saving for myself. The rest are gone. I may have some horse steak for my dinner tonight."

"You egg-sucking bastard," Gamble called.

"Careful," Jaeger said, pointing the rifle at the old man. "You wouldn't want me to finish him off prematurely, would you?"

Dragging the Model 97 behind him, Weathers had crawled to within a yard of the base of the cliff.

"This is rather interesting," Jaeger said. "What is the old fool up to? Let us see how this plays out."

"What do we do?" Anise whispered.

"Clear out," Gamble said. "Hop from apartment to apartment down the canyon. Run as far and as fast as you can and then hide."

"No," she said. "I will not leave him."

"Then we might all die here."

"Kill him," Anise called, "and you'll not get the gold."

"Oh, not that again!" Jaeger said. "Always with the gold. Jakob Gamble tried to use the same trick on me in Oklahoma Territory, and it did not work on me then. It will not work now."

Weathers had made it to the cliff.

"So, that is what you've been looking for?" Jaeger asked.

"That's right," Gamble said, digging in his pocket for the other coins. He held one up. "Look at this, Dutch—there's a whole strongbox full of the stuff somewhere up here. Let the old man die, and you'll never find it."

"You hold rubbish."

Weathers pulled the shotgun into his lap.

"That's right," Jaeger said. "Brace yourself against the rock and you might have enough leverage to work the action. Yes, this game is more interesting than shooting horses, don't you think?"

Gamble tossed the coin down. It landed between Jaeger and Weathers.

"Ah, you are trying to draw me in closer to the old man so he has a better chance of hitting me," Jaeger said. "That's cheating, Jacob Gamble."

"I'm lousy at baseball, Gamble said. "But here's another, and one more." He threw the first one behind Jaeger, and the next nearly at his feet. "Take a look at any of those and then you tell me they're trash."

Still keeping the rifle leveled, Jaeger stepped forward and snatched the nearest coin from the ground. While Jaeger's eyes were on the coin, Weathers found the end of the rope and passed it beneath the sling of the Model 97.

"This coin is very odd," Jaeger said. "It is also green."

Weathers tried knotting the rope, but his fingers seemed too thick for his hands.

"Get down," Gamble said, shoving Anise hard to the floor.

"What's this business?" Jaeger said, frowning at the rope in Weather's lap. "Stop that."

"You are a Teutonic egg-sucking cur," Weathers wheezed, struggling to finish the knot. "Anise, my dear, upon your return you should write a letter of complaint to Pinkerton headquarters in Chicago, and file a copy with the British consulate. They must learn that they cannot treat her majesty's subjects in such fashion."

Jaeger raised the rifle to his shoulder and fired a round into the old man's chest. Still, the old man pulled the knot tight.

"Haul away, lieutenant," Weathers said weakly.

Gamble began bringing up the rope as fast as he could. The shotgun bumped against the pine stakes and scraped on the rock wall. Jaeger fired, and Gamble ducked as the slug knocked a chunk of rock out of the T-shaped window. Jaeger levered another round and fired again, and this time the bullet whistled past Gamble's ear.

"Hard to shoot uphill, ain't it, Dutch?"

Jaeger worked the lever on the Marlin, drew a bead on Gamble's chest, and pulled the trigger. The hammer fell on an empty chamber. He had exhausted his magazine.

"Schiesse!"

The shotgun was nearly at the top.

He dropped the Marlin and clawed for the Reichsrevolver in its holster. He got it free at about the same time that Gamble was grabbing the barrel of the shotgun, and by the time Jaeger had the revolver extended in his hand, Gamble was pumping a round into the chamber of the shotgun.

Jaeger began running forward as he pulled the double-action trigger twice and the 10.6mm slugs pockmarked the cliff face below the T-window. Gamble leaned far out from the window and fired, but that angle was bad and the buckshot splattered the ground behind Jaeger.

"Ha, you missed!" Jaeger shouted, flattening his body against the rock. He was beneath a slight bulge, which prevented Gamble from seeing him.

"So did you, Dutch."

Gamble glanced over at Weathers. He was leaning to one side.

"My uncle?" Anise asked.

"Dead," Gamble said. "I'm sorry."

She nodded.

"But the old boy did good," Gamble said. "He got us the shotgun. We've got a chance, now. He gave us that."

"He showed no fear."

"None," Gamble said. "Damn few of the soldiers I knew remained as calm under fire as he did. You should be proud."

She closed her eyes and rested her forehead on his back.

"Scarecrow!" Jaeger called. "We find ourselves

in a dilemma, no? A regular Mexican standoff. If I move out from beneath this ledge, you have a clear shot. If you climb down the rope, I've got the drop on you. What to do?"

Gamble racked another round into the chamber. The ejected shell bounced on the stone of the window ledge, then fell to the ground.

"See who has the most nerve, I reckon."

THIRTY-TWO

Jacob Gamble sat in the T-shaped window, his legs dangling over the edge, the shotgun across his lap. Gamble had been watching the bottom of the cliff for hours, waiting for Jaeger to show himself. The sun was slipping toward the Continental Divide, abandoning the valley to shadow, and a light wind was rustling the spruce and pine. Not far off, a wolf howled, and was answered by a wolf chorus.

Anise came up behind him and placed a hand on his shoulder.

"We're going to have to do something and quick," Gamble said. "In a couple of hours, it will be too dark to keep watch. I don't like the thought of the sonuvabitch roaming around loose in the dark. I also don't like the thought of those wolves getting close to your uncle's body."

"There's the rifle Jaeger dropped," Anise said. "One of us could get it while the other covers from up here."

"No good," Gamble said. "The Marlin's dry."

"We could wait him out from up here," Anise

said. "He can't scale the cliff without us knowing it. It would take him days to walk around to the other side, even if he knew the path."

Gamble shook his head.

"We've got Jaeger cornered," he said. "He can't surprise us. I'm reluctant to give up that advantage. Also, he's armed with a handgun, which places him at a disadvantage—if he's off a foot one way or the other, he's likely to miss altogether. If I'm off by the same, the buckshot is still likely to kill him."

Anise nodded.

"The problem is how to get down the cliff and keep the shotgun trained on Jaeger's rat hole at the same time," Gamble said. "I really need both hands to aim, fire, and pump the shotgun."

"One of us could lower the other down."

"No, you don't have the strength in your arms and shoulders," Gamble said. "You'd drop me on my head."

"I wasn't talking about me lowering you down," she said. "I was thinking the other way around."

Gamble hesitated.

"You can handle a hundred and fifteen pounds of woman, can't you?"

He eyed her coldly.

"What troubles me is whether you can handle eight pounds of shotgun. If you miss, Jaeger will kill you and take the Model 97, too."

"Then tie the shotgun to the rope," Anise said.

"Have you ever fired a gun before?"

"No," Anise said.

"Then what do you think the odds are that you'll hit a bull's-eye with your first shot, dangling at the end of a rope, against an experienced killer?"

"Long."

"It would take more than beating long odds," Gamble said. "It would take nothing less than a miracle, and I'm not sure either of us are candidates for a favor of that magnitude."

"Depends."

"On what?"

"Which gods you pray to."

"You scare me," Gamble said. "You know that, right?"

Anise smiled.

Gamble was holding the shotgun by the grip, his finger curled over the trigger guard. He extended his left arm, trying to keep the shotgun level. His wrist weakened and the barrel dipped, and he had to use his right hand to steady it.

"If only I had another hand," Gamble said. "But maybe . . ."

"What?"

He began removing the sling from the barrel swivel.

"If I can strap the stock of the shotgun to my forearm, that will keep the strain off my wrist and allow me to point and fire it while using my other hand to hold onto the rope," he said.

"But you won't be able to work the pump."

"I'll only have one shot," he said. "At least, until my feet are on the ground and I can use my other hand. But I'm betting I can kill the kraut-eating sonuvabitch before he can kill me. Here, help me strap this cannon to my arm."

With the sling still attached to the swivel at the shoulder stock, Anise began wrapping the loose end around and around as Gamble held the gun tight against the inside of his forearm.

"Tighter," Gamble said.

She tightened the strap, then drew it around several more times, working toward the grip.

"Now, tie it off."

She knotted the end over the back of his hand.

"Good," Gamble said, shaking his arm and seeing that the gun didn't loosen. Wrapping the rope around his right arm, he eased himself out over the lip. Then, he looked back.

"You know—"

"Yes, I know, if he kills you then I'm to throw myself off the cliff and dash my brains out on the rocks below so I don't suffer a fate worse than death. I've heard it all before."

"That's not what I was about to say."

"What, then?"

"Forget it," Gamble said.

"Tell me."

"The moment's gone."

"Were you going to tell me you love me?"

"Not on your life," Gamble said. "I was about to say that it is strange, the first time I killed a man—and began my career in crime—I was standing atop a considerable rock in Taney County, Missouri. Now, my life and my wicked career may end on yet another rock."

"Yes, and you'll likely ascend bodily to heaven from this same rock. What a saint. If you're not going to declare love or at least passion, will you please get on with it?"

"Gladly."

He began easing himself down, from one pine stake to another, the rope slithering over his right arm, using his right hand like a vise, keeping his left arm pointing at Jaeger's hiding place. He could feel the rope biting into his flesh, and soon blood was flowing down his arm and dripping from his elbow. Halfway down, his right arm began to cramp, but he pushed the pain to the back of his mind and concentrated on pointing the shotgun.

"Where are you?" Gamble whispered. "I know you're still there, Dutch—I can feel you. Just give me the chance, and I'll send you where I sent your cousins."

The lower he got, the more he could see beneath the overhang where Jaeger had hid. When his boots were still twenty feet above the ground, Gamble heard an odd scuffling sound, and he knew that Jaeger was sliding back against the wall to keep from being seen.

Then the scuffling stopped, and Gamble knew Jaeger was getting ready to spring. Gamble pushed off the wall with his feet and released his hold on the rope. As he fell, he saw Jaeger lunging forward, the revolver extended in his hand.

His finger jerked the trigger at about the same time that the revolver began to bark. The shotgun boomed and the recoil traveled up his wrist and elbow like a mule kick. Then he hit the ground, his legs folded beneath him, and the shotgun hit the ground and then the barrel slapped back and struck him on the left side of his face.

The world was turned on its side, his ears were ringing, there was blood in his eye, and as if from far away he could hear the pop of the revolver in Jaeger's hand.

Gamble stood and staggered a few steps back, dragging the shotgun still clutched by the leather strap held tightly in his left hand, trying to make the world stop spinning long enough to get a bearing on Jaeger. Then he saw him, the Reichsrevolver held in a white-knuckled grip, advancing in halting steps.

Gamble lifted the shotgun and grasped the pump with his right hand. He tried pulling the mechanism back, but it only moved about an inch and then jammed. Looking down, he saw that the slide was bent and that the stock had been shattered by a round from the revolver.

"Ja, you cannot make that awful sound now!"

The revolver was held in Jaeger's right hand, but his left clutched his stomach. As he took another jagged step, a sausage of bluish-pink intestine peeked from beneath his hand.

"Part of you is oozing out there, Dutch."

The barrel of the Reichsrevolver was less than a foot from Gamble's head. He could see Jaeger's finger tighten on the trigger.

"Ficken sie!"

The hammer snapped on a spent cartridge.

Jaeger cursed and snapped the gun twice more.

"Well," Gamble said. "Who's all out of blue beans now?"

"Damn you, scarecrow."

Jaeger sat heavily on the ground. He looked in disgust at the revolver, then flung it away. Gamble shook off the leather strap and dropped the broken shotgun on the ground. He felt his wrist with his other hand.

"I think it's broken," he said.

There was a howl.

"The wolves," Jaeger said. "Coming closer now."

"Probably smell the fresh blood."

"Tell me," Jaeger said. "Is it . . . how bad is it?"

"Bad," Gamble said. "The worst."

Jaeger nodded.

"You're hit," he said.

"Where?" Gamble asked, looking at his torso.

"Side," Jaeger said. "Under your arm."

"Ah," Gamble said, probing with his fingers. The bullet had dug a furrow across his ribs. "If it hadn't hit the stock, it probably would have killed me."

"Shame," Jaeger said.

"Jacob," Anise said, releasing the rope and dropping the last foot to the ground. "Are you all right?"

"I'm in one piece."

Anise looked at Jaeger and winced.

"What do we do?"

"Leave him for the wolves."

Jaeger laughed.

"We can't," Anise said.

"He would us."

She picked up the shotgun from the ground.

"It's broken."

"I know," she said, turned the gun around and getting a grip on the barrel as if it were the oldest of weapons, a club. Then she swung the gun as hard as she could, driving the receiver into the side of Jaeger's head. He slumped and then gave a kind of gasp. She swung the gun twice more, caving in the top of his skull.

She wiped a fleck of blood from her brow with the back of her hand.

"Feel better?" Gamble asked.

"It was necessary," she said.

She threw the broken gun aside. It clattered impotently on the rocks. Then she turned to look at Gamble.

"You're shot," she said.

"Grazed, anyway," he said. "Wrist is broken. And my head hurts."

"You look like hell," she said.

"That's all right, you don't have to thank me."

"You nearly got yourself killed."

"The important word in that sentence is nearly," Gamble said. "Any gunfight that you can walk away from is a good one. And I could walk, if I wanted to."

A trickle of blood ran into Gamble's eye. He blinked hard and tugged up the collar of his shirt to wipe it away.

"Let's get out of here," Gamble said. "You can ride the gray and I'll lead him. We'll have to send somebody back after your uncle."

"Don't be crazy," she said. "It's almost dark. We'd break our necks. And you don't look like you're in any shape to go anywhere, not just yet. We have to wait until morning. I'll get some things from the mules and we'll set up camp here against the cliff."

"I don't like sleeping near dead people."

"Be a man, would you?"

"Right," Gamble said, easing himself to the ground. He lay on his back and looked up at the deepening blue sky. In the east, a new moon was rising over the needle.

Anise knelt beside Jaeger's body.

"What the hell are you doing?"

"Searching his pockets," she said. "For useful things."

"Look for aspirin."

She pulled out the notebook, flipped through the pages, then tossed it aside. She found the stack of photographs and did the same. There was a half-full box of ammunition for the Marlin rifle, which she put aside. Then she found the folding camera.

"Hello," she said.

"What is it?" Gamble asked.

"A Kodak."

She looked over at Gamble.

"You're going to look like death in the morning."

"Yeah, this goose egg is already swelling something fierce," Gamble said, feeling the bruise over his left temple with his fingers. "I'm going to be as blind as Oedipus in the morning."

"Think about what I just said."

"You think . . ."

"Yes," Anise said. "It is finally time to have your photo taken."

THIRTY-THREE

"Stop fidgeting," Anise said.

Jacob Gamble was on the ground, his head propped on a pillow-sized rock, the broken shotgun placed across his chest. His left eye was swollen shut and blood was crusted from his temple to the side of his neck.

"Get on with it," Gamble said.

She held the unfolded pocket camera in one hand, placed her other hand on her hip, and shook her head.

"Something's not quite right. Hold still."

She leaned down and looped a finger beneath the strap of the eye patch, then lifted it off. The milky, unseeing eye made Gamble seem quite dead.

"There," she said. "Now, hold your breath."

Gamble heard the shutter click.

"Now all we have to do is slip this back in Jaeger's pocket and dump his body where somebody will find it," she said. "If we leave it here, it may be years."

"I know the place," Gamble said, moving the shotgun aside and sitting up. "There's a slot canyon down below the boilings. It has a couple of water pipes running through it. Seemed like they were still carrying water. Somebody has to come check on those pipes every so often."

"Especially if we put a hole in one of them," Anise said.

"Where's the sun?"

"It's about eight o'clock. Can't you see at all?"

"No," Gamble said. "If you could bring me some water, perhaps I could get the swelling down."

She came back, knelt beside him, and handed him a kerchief and a canteen. He wet the cloth and pressed it against his eye. She placed the eye patch in his other hand.

"Jacob," she said. "You're going to have to go it alone back down to the *Jornada.*"

"Go on."

"I'm going to Mexico," she said.

"That's insane."

"Thirteen years ago, I wasn't freed at Geronimo's camp," she said. "It was when my captivity began. Do you remember me speaking of a warrior named Massai? He is my husband. I was no slave. The Apaches are my people."

"Then your people are at Fort Sill with old Geronimo. They keep him and about three hundred of the tribe on exhibit, like in a zoo, but let the old man out once in a blue moon to tour with the Wild West shows. That's where your Massai would be."

"No," she said. "Massai is here. He came this morning, just as he has on every summer solstice since my capture, to a place we both knew well."

"Let me guess," Gamble said. "Tall fellow, paisley

headband, Springfield carbine? Saw him at the waterfall at the head of the slot canyon. Or rather, saw his reflection. Reckoned he was a ghost."

"No ghost," Anise said. "After my capture, I was made to feel ashamed. I told the truth to the soldiers, over and over, begged them to let me go back, but I was slapped—and worse. Nobody wanted to hear my story. They told me to keep still, that I was a disgrace to white civilization, that it would have been better had I died. Once my uncle claimed me and took me back, I had learned to keep my mouth shut. It took me years to gain my courage, and then to fashion a story that would compel him to bring me back."

"And the Mohaves?"

"I wasn't captured," she said. "My father sold me to the tribe after my mother abandoned the family. The tattoos are coming of age tattoos, not a branding reserved for slaves. Later, I was traded to the Apaches, but gladly because Massai claimed me from the very first."

"Your sister?"

"I have no idea where Olive is now," she said. "She went off with my father, so whatever fate claimed him probably took her as well. I told my uncle they were both dead so he wouldn't look for them. After so many years passed without word, I assumed my lie had become truth."

"Where's Massai been since 1886?"

"Mexico, mostly," Anise said. "He was always the best of the warriors, nobody could ever catch him, and he knows this country better than any living man. Nobody is looking for Apaches now, anyway. We aim to live in peace."

"Whenever I hear somebody say that, I know heads are going to get busted," Gamble said. "I'd like to talk to this Massai, because I think you are out of your wicked little mind. Ask him to come over here."

Anise laughed.

"He will not come near you," she said. "He says you have the sacred 'enemies-against' power, like Geronimo, but that you are crazy like all white men and that you use the power badly because your heart is wounded. He wishes that someday your heart will heal, but that you have followed the black path for so many years that you don't know any other way to walk."

Anise paused.

"He does have a request, however. He would like to take the broken shotgun and place it in the war cave."

"Sure," Gamble said. "Why not? That should confuse the hell out of somebody, someday."

"Good," Anise said. "We are taking the Marlin with us, but will leave you the Springfield, a handful of shells, and some food and water. We need the horse, but will place Jaeger beneath the water pipes in the narrow canyon before we go."

"What about the body of your uncle?"

"Buried," Anise said. "A Christian prayer was said."

"Funny," Gamble said. "I didn't hear the lightning."

Anise stood.

"You'll be able to see well enough to begin walking out in a day, maybe less," she said. "You'll have the carbine, if you need it, but I think the wolves will leave you alone—they've gorged themselves on the horses and mules. Oh, and you have a thousand dollars in the pocket of your mackinaw. Thought you deserved that bonus after all."

"So, that's it?" Gamble asked. "You walk away I don't know if there's really a Massai or where you're really headed or whether anything you've said is true?"

"You'll have the Springfield," she said. "I couldn't conjure that, now could I?"

She leaned down and he could feel her hair brushing his chest and her breath on his face. Then she kissed him, and for a moment he could taste the absinthe from the hotel bar at Amarillo.

"Farewell, Jacob Gamble," she said.

THIRTY-FOUR

Jacob Gamble sat in the doorway of the empty soddie, watching the sun as it sank toward the western horizon. He had been there, unmoving, for most of the day, the old Springfield resting against his knee. His left hand, up to his forearm, was bound and splinted.

His horse, dragging its reins, was chewing at some weeds it had pulled down from the soddie's roof.

Gamble did not rouse until the bone wagon creaked to a stop in front of him. The bone hauler jumped down from the box. He wore an old straw hat tightly over his head.

"Don't I know you?" the bone hauler shouted.

"We met, once," Gamble said.

"That's right, near Dodge."

"Sure," Gamble said. "Near Dodge."

"Any bones around here?"

"Haven't spotted any," Gamble said.

"Damn," the bone hauler said.

"There used to be a girl live here," Gamble said.

"Her name was Agnes. She lived here for a long time. Do you know what happened to her?"

"Agnes?" the bone hauler asked. "Hell, yes. She took off."

"When?

"About the end of June."

"Where'd she go?"

"Took off with some outlaw. Horse thief. Let's see, what was his name? Phillips. Kid Phillips. Escaped from jail with Bill Doolin a while back. Know him?"

"No."

Gamble stood.

"What do you want for that rifle?" the bone hauler asked.

"The Springfield? It's not worth much."

"I ain't got much."

"You still cutting on yourself with that knife?"

"Sometimes," the bone hauler said guiltily.

"I think I'll hold onto the rifle," Gamble said. "I might need it. But here, I have something else for you."

Gamble held out fifty dollars.

"Go back to Dodge," he said. "Clean up. See a doctor."

The bone hauler sneered.

"Ah, you keep your money," he said, climbing back into the wagon. "The bone market will come back. It has to. Things keep dying, don't they?"

1900

THIRTY-FIVE

The man wearing the smoke-colored glasses walked into the hardware store from Oklahoma Avenue, carrying a package under his arm he had just picked up from the express office at the Santa Fe depot. He walked up to the gun counter and placed the package on top of the glass case.

Andrew Farquharson threw aside the *Police Gazette* and looked at the shipping label on the package. It had a return address of Woodward, Oklahoma Territory.

"Who do you know in Woodward?"

"My attorney," the man in the glasses said. He was about fifty, and thin, with a full salt-and-pepper beard. The brim of his black Stetson and the shoulders of his equally dark coat were peppered with road dust.

"What have you been reading about in that newspaper?"

"The World's Fair at Paris," the boy said. "It opens April fifteenth—that's next week. They say they have motion pictures that talk."

"What do you mean, talk?"

"With sound," the boy said enthusiastically. "Like Vitagraphs, but where you can hear people talk and sing and hear them play music. Can you imagine?"

"No," he said.

The man glanced over at the stack of nickel postcards by the cash register. He reached over and picked one up. The photo was of what looked like a very dead man, his head propped on a rock, a broken shotgun across his chest. One eye was swollen shut and the other was milky and lifeless,

"That's the outlaw Jacob Gamble," the boy said. "Gruesome, ain't it? He was killed by a Pinkerton in New Mexico after escaping from the federal jail here. But he got the Pinkerton, too, so they're both dead."

"You seem to know a lot about it."

"Oh, there's more to the story," the boy said. "There was a big shootout here in the street and Gamble came in here and got the shotgun he used. It was a Model 97. He left his old converted cap-and-ball pistol behind. Told me to keep it for him. Wanna see?"

"Love to."

Andrew reached beneath the counter and brought out the Manhattan. He placed it on top of the glass.

"Do you mind?"

"Go ahead, Mister."

The man picked up the gun with his left hand, thumbed open the loading gate, and examined the cylinder.

"It's been converted to center fire."

"Yeah," the boy said. "I forget to tell you about

that. When Gamble escaped from the federal jail, down on Second and Noble, he came here and got the same shotgun he used to kill the Jaeger cousins. I wasn't here, but he asked old man Morris—that's my dad's partner—to tell me to keep it and have it changed over to center fire, so he could find cartridges for it. Said he'd be back for it, sooner or later. Guess he was wrong."

"Guess so," the man said.

"I think it's the same shotgun in the picture, but it's hard to tell. Nobody ever found it, anyway—or the body, neither. Just the picture in the Pinkerton detective's camera."

The man put the Manhattan back on the counter and scratched his beard.

"Say, I have a notion to own that gun. How much would you take for it?"

"Oh, it's not for sale," the boy said. "It's what you call a . . . well, it's sort of a museum piece."

"I understand," the man said. "How about a hundred dollars?"

"Why, no," the boy said. "I couldn't."

"A hundred and fifty."

"Dang it," the boy said. "That's a lot of money, but—"

"Two hundred."

"I'll throw in a box of shells," Andrew Farquarson said. "It shoots pretty fair for an old gun."

"Some do."

The man took a roll of bills from his pocket and peeled off ten twenties and placed them on the counter.

"Thanks," the boy said. "What brand of ammo you want?"

"Robin Hood."

"Sure," he said.

The boy placed the box of cartridges on the counter and the man slipped them into the pocket of his black coat, along with the old revolver.

"I'll have one of these, too," the man said, taking a postcard.

"Take it," the boy said. "They printed 'em by the thousands."

The man picked up his package.

"I reckon we're settled up."

Andrew Farquharson stared at him.

"Yeah," he said. "I guess so. Who did you say was your attorney in Woodward?"

"Temple Houston," the man said, and thumped the package. "He sent me this fiddle that he picked up from a pawnshop up in Kansas."

The boy nodded.

"What's wrong?" the man asked. "You look like you've seen a ghost."

"Gamble was called the fiddling outlaw," the boy said slowly. "And Temple Houston was his attorney."

"Ah, the world is full of strangeness," the man said. "But I'm no ghost. I'm as real as rock. All the same, if that telephone rings . . ."

"Yes, sir?"

"Don't answer it."

The man touched the brim of his hat, turned, and walked out onto Oklahoma Avenue without looking back.

Turn the page for an exciting preview of

SAVAGE GUNS

A Cotton Pickens Western

by William W. Johnstone
with J. A. Johnstone

On Sale October 2010
Wherever Pinnacle Books Are Sold

CHAPTER ONE

I was mindin' my daily business in the two-holer when I got rudely interrupted. Now I like a little privacy, but this morning I got me a bullet instead. There I was, peacefully studying the female undies in the Montgomery Ward catalog, when this here slug slams through the door and exits through the rear, above my head.

"Hey!" I yelled, but no one said nothing.

"You out there. Don't you try nothing. This here's the law talking. I'm coming after you."

But I sure didn't know who or what was in the yard behind Belle's roomin' house. I thought maybe a horse was snorting or pawing clay, but I couldn't be sure of it. I wanted to see what was what, but the half-moon that let in fresh air was high up above me, and I had my business to look after just then. You can't do nothing in the middle of business.

I don't know about you, but I wear my hat when I'm in the two-holer, just on general principles. A man should wear a hat in the crapper. That's my motto. It was a peaceful enough morning in the town of Doubtful, in Puma County, Wyoming, where I was sheriff, more or less. So that riled me some, that bullet that slapped through there knocking my good 5X gray felt beaver Stetson topper, which teetered on the other hole but did not drop. If it had dropped down there, I'd a been plumb peeved.

I thought for a moment I oughta follow that hat through the hole and get my bare bottom down there in the perfumed vault, but that was plum sickening, and besides, how could I slide a hundred fifty pounds of rank male through that little round hole? I don't need no more smell than I've already got. When I pull my boots off, people head for the doors holding their noses. It just wouldn't work. If someone was gonna kill me, they held all the aces.

The truth of it was that I wasn't finished with my business, and all I could do was sit there and finish up my private duties, and rip a page out of the Monkey Ward catalog, and get it over with. Like the rest of us who used the two-holer behind Belle's boardinghouse, I was inclined to study ladies' corsets and bloomers and garters for entertainment, saving the wipe-off for the pages brimming with one-bottom plows, buggy whips, and bedpans. Them others in Belle's boardinghouse, they felt like I did, and no female undie pages ever got torn out of the catalog. That sure beat corncobs, I'll tell you.

"Sheriff, you come outa there with your hands up and your pants down," someone yelled. I thought maybe I knew the feller doin' all that yelling but it was hard to tell, sitting there with pages of chemises and petticoats on my lap.

"Hold your horses," I said. "I ain't done, and the

longer it takes, the better for you, because I'm likely
to bust out of here with lead flying in all directions."

That fetched me a nasty laugh, and I knew that
laugh, and I thought maybe I was in more of a jam
than I'd imagined.

But no more bullets came sailing through, and I
finished up, and ripped out a page of men's union
suits, and another page of hay rakes and spades, and
got it over with. I wasn't gonna bust out of there
with my pants down, no matter what, so I stood, got
myself arranged and buttoned up, drew out my service revolver, and with a violent shove, threw myself
out the door and dodged to the left just to avoid any
incoming lead.

It sure didn't do me no good. As my mama used
to tell me, don't do nothing foolish.

Sure enough, there before me were eight, nine
ratty-assed cowboys on horses, all of the lot waving
black revolvers in my direction, just in case I got notions. And also a dude with a buckboard, holding
some reins.

"I shoulda known," I said to the boss, who was the
man I figgered it was.

"I told you to come out with your pants down, and
you didn't. That's a hanging offense," the man said.
"You do what I say, and when I say it."

"My pants is staying put, damn it," I replied.

I knew the joker, all right. I'd put his renegade boy
in my jail a few months earlier, and now the punk
was peering at the blue skies through iron bars. This
feller on a shiny red horse waving a nickel-plated
Smith and Wesson at me was none other than Admiral Bragg. And the boy I was boardin' in my lockup,

he was King Bragg, and his sister, she was Queen Bragg. Mighty strange names bloomed in that family, but who was I to howl? I sure didn't ask to have Cotton hung on me, and Pickens neither, but that how I got stuck, and there wasn't nothing I could do about it except maybe move to Argentina or Bulgaria.

Them names weren't titles, neither. Bragg's ma and pa, they stuck him with the name of Admiral. If he'd of been in the navy he might have ended up Admiral Admiral Bragg. But the family stuck to its notions, and old Bragg, he named one child King and the other child Queen. It was King Bragg that got himself into big trouble, perforating a few fellers with his six-gun, so I caught him and he would soon pay for his killin' spree. I think the family was all cheaters. Name a boy Admiral, and the boy's got a head start, even if he ain't even close to being an admiral. Name a girl Queen, and she's got the world bowin' and scrapin' even if she ain't one.

I was a little nervous, standing there in front of King's pa with seven or eight Bragg cowboys pointing their artillery at my chest. Makes a man cautious, I'd say.

"Drop the pea-shooter, sheriff," Admiral Bragg ordered.

I thought maybe to lift it up and blow him away, which would have been my last earthly deed. It sure was temptin' and my old pa, he might've approved even as he lowered the coffin. Nothing like goin' out in style.

But there was about a thousand grains of lead pointing straight at me, and I chickened out, and set

her down real slow, itching to pull a trick or two on
these rannies. I sure was mad at myself for not spitting a few lead pills before I got turned into Swiss
cheese. It just put me out of sorts, but I figured at
least I was alive to get my revenge another day. So
I set her down slow.

"Now you get into the buckboard, Sheriff," said
Admiral Bragg. "We're taking you for a little ride."

I got in, sat next to the old fart who held the reins.
I knew the feller, old and daft, with a left-crick in his
neck that some said was from a botched hanging.
He spat, which I took for a welcome, so I settled in
beside him. There was still about a thousand grains
of lead aimed at me, so I sat there and smiled at
these gents.

The old feller slapped rein over the croup of the
dray, and we clopped away from there, heading
down the two-rut road out of Doubtful in the general
direction of the Bragg ranch. I sort of had a hunch
what this was about and it wasn't too comfortable
thinkin' about it.

Bragg was one of the biggest stockmen around
Doubtful, and had a spread up in the hills north of
town that just didn't quit, and took a week with a
couple of spare Sundays to ride across. He called it
the Anchor Ranch, and it sure did anchor a lot of
turf. He controlled as much public land as anyone in
the West, and had an army of gunslicks to pin it all
down, given that it wasn't his turf but belonged to
Uncle Sam.

I guess that wasn't so bad; he raised a lot of beef
and his men kept the saloons going in Doubtful.
Admiral was a tough bird, all right, but I didn't have

no occasion to throw him into the iron-barred cage in the sheriff office, so I pretty much ignored him and he ignored me until now.

I sort of didn't like the way this buckboard was surrounded by his gunslicks and we was headin' out of town, me a little bit against my will. But the bores of all them pieces aimed my way kept me from doing much complainin' about all that.

Old Admiral, perched on that shiny red horse, he ignored me, so I didn't have a notion what this was all about or how it would end. Or maybe I did. All this here stuff had to do with that scummy son of his, King Bragg, who grew up twisted and bad, and got himself into big trouble. From the moment King was big enough to wave a Colt six-gun around, he was doing it, shooting songbirds and bumblebees and gophers and snakes. It must have been a trial for old Admiral to keep that boy in cartridges, because that's about all that King did. He got mighty fine at it, too, and could shoot better and faster than anyone, myself included. He could put a bullet through the edge of the ace of spades and cut that card in two.

Well, that kid, soon as he was big enough to ride into town on his own, without his ma or pa, was bent on showing the good citizens of Doubtful who was who. It wasn't lost on that boy that his pa was the biggest rancher in those parts, and maybe the biggest cattleman in the Territory, if not the whole bloomin' West.

He also was fast. Throw a bottle or a can or a silver dollar into the skies, and King would perforate it, or pretty near sign his name with bullet holes

in a tomato can. I had to chase the kid out of a few
saloons because he was only fifteen or so, and he
didn't take kindly to it, but that was all the trouble I
had, until the day he turned eighteen.

He come into Doubtful that day, few months ago,
on his shiny black stallion, wearing a brace of
double-action Colts, a birthday gift from his old
man. I didn't pay no attention, but maybe I should
have. I was busy with all that paperwork the Territory wants all the time, full of words I never heard
tell of. I don't lay any claim to being more than
fifth-grade schooled, so sometimes I got to get
someone who's got more smarts to tell me what's
what. But I make up for it by being friendly and en-
forcing the law pretty good.

Anyway, King Bragg tied his horse up on saloon
row and wandered into the Last Chance wearing his
new artillery. I wasn't aware of it, or I'd of kicked
his ass out. He's too young to hoist a few shots of
redeye, and I'd of turned the brat over my knee and
paddled his butt for pretendin' to be all growed up.

Well, next I knew, there was a ruckus, a bunch of
shots to be exact, and I pop out of my office and
hustle over to saloon row. There's a mess of shouting from the Last Chance, so I hurry over there and
it was plain awful. There were three dead cowboys
sprawled on the sawdust, leakin' blood. A few
fellers were trying to stanch the flow some, but it
was hopeless, and that threesome finished up their
dying while I watched, and then people were just
staring at one another. King Glad was sitting in the
sawdust, his emptied revolver in his hand. The
barkeep, he was starin' over the bar, and them

cowboys in there, they were staring at the dead
ones, and there's me, law and order, staring at the
whole lot, wondering who did what to who, and
why. It wasn't a very fine moment.

Well, I asked them cowboys a few questions and
then pinched the kid, brought him in and locked
him up, and got him tried by Judge Nippers, who
told the jury the kid was guilty as hell, and sentenced him to hang by the neck until dead. And
Doubtful, Wyoming, was going to see a hanging in
just two weeks. In fact, I'd just hired Lemuel Clegg
and his boys to build me a gallows and charge it
to Puma County. Meanwhile, the Bragg family
lawyer was screechin' and hollerin', but it didn't
do no good. That punk killer, King Bragg, was
going to swing in a few days and there was nothing
I could do about it. Me, I'm all for justice, and with
all them dead cowboys lying around, I'm thinkin'
it ought to be sooner, but all that was up to Judge
Nippers.

I sorta thought maybe this was connected to that,
but I don't take no credit for smart thinking. Whatever the case, I was being transported by a rattling
old buckboard out of town by some pretty mean-
lookin' fellers with a lot of .45 caliber barrels
poking straight at me, so I didn't feel none too comfortable.

"What's this here all about, Admiral?" I asked.

But that wax-haired, comb-bearded blue-eyed
snake wasn't talking. He was just leading this here
procession out of Doubtful, with me in the middle.
I sure was getting curious. But I didn't have to wait

too long. About two miles out of Doubtful, right where a bunch of cottonwoods crowded the creek, they were steering toward a big old tree, with a mighty thick limb pokin' straight out, and hanging from that limb was a noose.

CHAPTER TWO

I sure didn't like the looks of that noose. That thing was just danglin' there, swaying in the breeze. That rope, it was thick as a hawser, and coiled around the way them hangmen do it. Like someone done it that had done it a few times and knew what to do.

Them cowboys and gunslicks was uncommon quiet as we rode toward that big cottonwood, which was in spring leaf and real pretty for May. But I wasn't paying attention to that. All I was seein' was that damned noose waiting there for some neck. I was starting to have a notion of whose neck it was waiting for, and that didn't sit well with my belly, and I sure wasn't a happy sheriff, I'll tell you.

It got worse. That old goat driving the buckboard headed straight to that noose, and when it was plain dangling in my face, he whoaed the nag and there it was, that big hemp noose right there in front of me. None of them slicks was saying a word, and none of them had put away their artillery, neither. I knew a few of them. There was Big Nose George, and Alvin Ream, and Smiley Thistlethwaite, and Spitting Sam. They didn't think twice about putting a little lead into anything alive. You had to wonder why Bragg kept those bozos around. Times were peaceful enough, at least until now.

"Admiral, this ain't a good idea," I said.

He laughed softly. You ever hear a man laugh like that, like he was enjoying my fate? Well, it's not something a person forgets, a laugh like that.

"I'm the law, Admiral, and you'd better think twice."

I was thinkin' maybe I'd go down fighting, but before I could think longer, that old boy beside me wrapped his knobby old arm around me, and one of them slicks grabbed my hands, yanked them behind me, and wrapped them in thong until my arms were trussed up tighter than a fat lady's corset. Me, I'm not even thirty and had a lot of juice in me still, and I wrestled with them fellers but it was like kicking a cast-iron stove. They knew what they was up to, and had me cold.

I began thinking that them spring leaves coming out on the cottonwood would be about the last pretty thing I'd ever see. I don't rightly know why I kept that sheriff job but I had. I sorta liked the fun of it, and I was never one to dodge a little trouble. I kinda thought one of my deputies might be hunting for me now, but I was just being foolish. Them fellers slept late and played cribbage or euchre half the night in the jailhouse.

I didn't need any explanations. Admiral Bragg, he was getting even with me. Hang that boy, hang me. There wasn't no point in asking a bunch of questions, and no point in trying to talk him out of it. The hard, belly-grabbing truth was that this thing was gonna happen and there wasn't no way I could jabber and slobber my way out of it.

But I wasn't dwelling on it. I was eyeing the bright blue sky, and hearing some red-winged blackbirds making a racket down on the creek, and feeling good mountain air filling my lungs, and thinkin' of my ma and pa, and how they brought me into the world and raised me up.

I writhed some, but there was a passel of them around me in the buckboard, and strong hands pinning me while one of them slicks pulled off my 5X gray beaver hat and dropped that big, scratchy noose right over my neck. It was the first time I ever felt a noose and it wasn't a very good feeling. It was just a big, cold, scratchy twisted rope, and now it rested on my shoulders, and one of them slicks tugged it pretty tight, and tipped it off to the side a little so as to break my neck.

So I was standin' there in that buckboard with a noose drawn tight on my young neck, and all trussed up and they all backed off and left me standing there, my knees knockin' and waiting for the final, entire, no-return end. I wondered if Admiral Bragg was gonna preach at me some, tell me this was his brand of justice, or whatnot, but he didn't. He just nodded.

That old knobby-armed geezer, he settled down in the wooden seat of the buckboard, me standing in the bed, and then he let loose with his whip, smacked the dray right across the croup, and away it went, jerking me plumb off my pins as the wagon got yanked out from under me. Then I tumbled past the wagon and started down, feelin' that hemp yank hard at my neck and jerk my head back, and then I felt myself topple to the ground, and couldn't figure what happened. I wasn't dead yet. Maybe this was just the last gasp. I bunged myself up some, hitting that dirt so hard, and landing on a cottonwood root, too, so that I was really hurtin' and that noose was as tight as a necktie at a funeral, and pretty quick I was starin' up at the sky and seein' lots of blue, and the pale green of them cottonwood leaves.

"Now you know what a hanging is," Admiral said.

That was the dumbest thing ever got said to me.

They rolled me over and cut that thong that had me tied up like some beef basting on a spit. I felt some blood return to my wrists and hands, and I flexed my fingers, discovering they was alive, all ten or eleven, or whatever I got. And they loosened that scratchy hemp and pulled that thing loose and tossed it aside. One of them slicks even slapped my 5X gray beaver Stetson down on my head. And then they let me stand up, even if my legs was trembling like a virgin in a cathouse.

I couldn't think of nothing to do, so I slugged Admiral, one gut-punch and a roundhouse to his jaw, and he staggered back as my boot landed on his shin.

That might not have been too smart, but it sure was satisfying. He let out a yelp and in about two seconds half of them slicks was pulling me off and holding me down. I figured they'd just string me up for certain, and make no mistakes this time, but

Admiral, he got up, dusted off his hat, wiped some blood off his lip, and smiled.

This sure was getting strange.

All them slicks let go of me, and I was of a mind to arrest the bunch for manhandling a lawman, but the odds weren't good. I never got a handle on arithmetic, and took long division over a few times, but I know bad odds when I see them.

Admiral Bragg, he spat a little more blood, and nodded.

That old knobby-armed geezer, he fetched that hemp rope and brought her over to me, but he wasn't showing me the noose end. I was more familiar with that end that I even wanted to be. No, he showed me the other end, which had been razored across, clean as can be, save for one little strand that sort of wobbled in the morning breeze. I hated that strand; it pretty near did me.

They'd cut that rope for this event, and I sure wondered why. This whole deal was to scare the bejabbers out of me, and it sure as hell did.

"King won't be so lucky," Admiral Bragg said.

"No, but neither was them three he killed."

"He didn't kill them."

"I saw them three lying in the sawdust. Every last one a cowboy with the T-Bar Ranch."

"And you jumped to conclusions."

"There was the barkeep and two others, saying King Bragg done it, and they testified in court to it."

"You've got two weeks to prove that he didn't do it. Next time, the rope won't be cut."

"You tellin' me to undo justice?"

"I'm telling you, my boy didn't do it, and you're going to spring him."

"That boy's guilty as hell, and he's gonna pay for it."

Admiral Bragg, he sort of scowled. "I'm not going to argue with you. If you're too dumb to see it, then you'll hang."

Me, I just stared at the man. There was no talkin' to him.

"Get in the wagon, or walk," Bragg said. "I'm done talking."

I favored the ride. I still was a little weak on my pins. So I got aboard, next to the geezer, and the buckboard rattled back to town, surrounded by Bragg and his gunslicks and cowboys. They took me straight to Belle's rooming house and I got out, and they rode off.

The morning was still young, and I'd already been hanged and told I'd be hanged again.

It sure was a tough start on a nice spring day.

I looked at them cottonwoods around town and saw that they were budding out. The town of Doubtful was about as quiet as little towns get. I didn't feel like doing nothing except go lie down, but instead, I made myself hike to Courthouse Square, where the sheriff's office was, along with the local lockup.

Bragg made me mad, tellin' me I was too dumb to see what was what.

It sure was a peaceful spring morning. Doubtful was doing its usual trade. There was a few ranch wagons parked at George Waller's emporium, and a few saddle horses tied to hitch rails. A playful little spring breeze, with an edge of cold on it, seemed to coil through town. It sure was nicer than the hot summers that sometimes roasted northern Wyoming. I was uncommonly glad to be alive, even if my knees wobbled a little. I smiled at folks and they smiled at me.

I got over to the courthouse which baked in the sun, and made my way into the sheriff's office. Sure enough, my undersheriff, Rusty, was parked there, his boots up on a desk.

"Where you been?" he asked.

"Getting myself hanged," I said.

Dusty, he smiles crookedly. "That's rich," he said.

I didn't argue. Dusty wouldn't believe it even if I swore to it on a stack of King James Bibles.

"You fed the prisoner?"

"Yeah, I picked up some flapjacks at Ma Ginger's. He complained some, but I suppose someone with two weeks on his string got a right to."

"What did he complain about?"

"The flapjacks wasn't cooked through, all dough."

"He's probably right," I said. "Ma Ginger gets it wrong most of the time."

"Serves him right," Dusty said.

"You empty his bucket?"

"You sure stick it to me, don't ya?"

"Somebody's got to do it. I'll do it."

Dusty smiled. "Knew you would if you got pushed into it."

I grabbed the big iron key off the peg and hung my gunbelt on the same peg. It wasn't bright to go back there armed. King Bragg was the only prisoner we had at the moment, but I wasn't one to take chances. I opened up on the gloomy jail, lit only by a small barred window at the end of the front corridor. Three cells opened onto the corridor. King was kept in the farthest one.

He was lyin' on his bunk, which was a metal shelf with a blanket on it. The Puma County lockup wasn't no comfort palace. King's bucket stank.

"You want to push that through the food gate there?" I asked.

"Maybe I should just throw it in your face."

"I imagine you could do that."

He sprang off the metal bunk, grabbed the bucket, and eased it through the porthole, no trouble.

"I'll be back. I want to talk," I said.

"Sure, ease your conscience, hanging an innocent man."

I ignored him. He'd been saying that from the moment I nabbed him out at Anchor Ranch. I took his stinking bucket out to the crapper behind the jail, emptied it, pumped some well water into it and tossed that, and brought it back. It still stank; even the metal stinks after a while, and that's how it is in a jailhouse.

I opened the food gate and passed it through.

"Tell me again what happened," I said.

"Why bother?"

"Because your old man hanged me this morning. And it set me to wondering."

King Bragg wheezed, and then cackled. I sure didn't like him. He was a muscular punk, young and full of beans, deep-set eyes that seemed to mock. He was born to privilege, and he wore it in his manners, his face, his attitude, and his smirk.

"You don't look hanged," he said, getting smirky.

I sort of wanted to pulverize his smart-ass lips, but I didn't.

"Guess I'm lying to you about being hanged," I said. "So, go ahead and lie back. Start at the beginning."

The beginning was the middle of February, when King Bragg rode into Doubtful for some serious boozing, and alighted at saloon row, five drinkin' parlors side by side on the east end of town, catering to the cowboys, ranchers, and wanderers coming in on the pike heading toward Laramie.

"You parked that black horse in front of the Last Chance and wandered in," I said, trying to get him started.

"No, I went to the Stockman and then the Sampling Room, and then the Last Chance. Only I don't remember any of that. Last I knew, I took a sip of redeye at the Last Chance, Sammy the barkeep handed it to me, and I don't remember anything else. I couldn't even remember my own name when I came to."

CHAPTER THREE

There's some folks you just don't like. It don't matter how they treat you. It don't matter if they tip their hat to you. If you don't like 'em, that's it. There's no sense gnawing on it. There was no sense dodging my dislike for King Bragg. I don't know where it come from. Maybe it was the way he kept himself groomed. Most fellers, they got two weeks to live, they don't care how they look. But King Bragg, he trimmed up his beard each morning, washed himself right smart, and even washed his duds and hung them to dry. That sure was a puzzle. The young man was keeping up appearances and it didn't make no sense. Not with the hourglass dribbling sand.

Now he stood quietly on the other side of them iron bars, telling me the same story I'd heard twenty times, and it didn't make any more sense now than the first time he spun it. It was just another yarn, maybe concocted with a little help from that lawyer, and it was his official alibi. Actually, it was more a crock than an alibi.

What King Bragg kept sayin' was that he had dozed through the killings, and when he woke up, he was holding his revolver and every shell had been fired. So he'd gotten awake after his siesta and got told he'd killed three men. And that was all he knew.

Well, that was a crock if ever I heard one.

"Maybe you got yourself liquored up real good, got crazy, picked a fight with them T-Bar cowboys, spilled a lot of blood, and got yourself charged with some killings."

That was the official version, the one that had convicted King Bragg of a triple murder. The one that was gonna pop his neck in a few days.

He stared. "I have nothing more to say about it," he said.

"Well I got nothing more to ask you," I said.

"Why are you asking? I've been sentenced, I'm going to hang. Why do you care?"

"Your pa, he asked me to look into it."

"Admiral Bragg doesn't ask anyone for anything. He orders."

"Well, now that's the truth. He sort of ordered me to."

"What did he say?"

"He didn't. He just hauled me out of Belle's crapper and hanged me."

"Now let me get this straight. My father—hanged you?"

"Noose and drop and all."

"I don't suppose you want to explain."

"It sure wasn't the way to make friends with the sheriff, boy."

"You calling me boy? You're hardly older than I am."

"I got the badge. I get to call old men boy if I feel like it."

"So my father, he hanged you?"

"Complete and total. And when I'm done here, I'll going to haul his ass to this here jail and throw away the key."

King Bragg laughed. "Good luck, pal."

He headed over to his sheet metal bunk, flopped down on it, and drew up that raggedy blanket. Me, I was satisfied. That feller wasn't gonna weasel out of a hanging with that cock and bull story. As for me, I was ready to hang him whether I liked him or not, because that was justice. A man shoots three fellers for no good reason, and he pays the price. I'd just have to deal with Admiral Bragg one way or the other. Now I'd talked with the boy to check his story and nothing had changed.

I didn't much like the thought of pulling the lever, but it would be my job to do it. They made me sheriff, and now I was stuck with it. I could quit and let someone else pull the lever that would drop King Bragg from this life. But I figure if a man's gonna be a man, he's got to do the hard things and not run away. So when the time comes, I'll pull the lever and watch King drop. Still, it sure made me wonder whether I wanted to be a lawman. It was more fun being young and getting into trouble. I was still young, but this wasn't the kind of trouble I was itching for. My ma used to warn me I had the trouble itch. If there was trouble somewhere, I'd be in the middle of it. Pa, he just said, keep your head down. Heads is what get shot.

I thought I'd ask a few more questions, just to satisfy myself that King Bragg done it, and his ole man was being pigheaded, more than usual. Admiral Bragg was born pigheaded, and some time it would do him in.

This sheriff business wasn't really up my alley. It would take someone with more upstairs than I ever had to ask the right questions. I could shoot fast and true, but that didn't mean my thinkin' was all that fast. There was a feller I wanted to jabber with about all this, the barkeep over to the Last Chance Saloon, Sammy Upward. That was his sworn-out legal monicker. Upward. It sure beat Downward.

The Last Chance was actually the first bar you hit coming into town, or the last one if you were ridin' out. That made it a little wilder than them other watering places. The rannies riding in, they headed for the first oasis they could find. It didn't matter none that it charged a nickel more for redeye, fifteen cents instead of a dime, and two cents more, twelve in all, for a glass of Kessler's ale. It didn't matter none that some of them other joints had serving girls, some of them almost not bad lookin', if you didn't look too close. And it didn't matter none that the other joints were safer, because the managers made customers hang up their gunbelts before they could get themselves served. No, the Last Chance was famous for rowdy, for rough, and for mean, and that's why young studs like King Bragg, he headed there itching for some kind of trouble to find him.

It wasn't yet noon, but maybe Upward would be

polishin' the spittoons or something so I rattled the double door, found it unlocked, and found Upward sleeping on the bar. He lay there like a dead fish, but finally come around.

"We ain't open yet, Sheriff," he said.

"I ain't ordering a drink. I'm here for a visit."

"Visits cost same as a drink. Fifteen cents."

He hadn't yet stirred, and was peerin' up at me from atop the bar. That bar was sorta narrow, and he could fall off onto the brass rail in front, or off the back, where he usually worked, and where he had easy access to his sawed-off Greener.

"We're gonna visit, and maybe some day I'll buy one," I said.

"Someone get shot?"

"Not recently."

"I could arrange it if you get bored. If I say the word, someone usually gets shot in this here drinkin' parlor."

He peered up at me. He needed to trim the stubble on his chin, and maybe put on a new shirt, and maybe trade in that grimy bartender's apron for something that looked halfway washed.

"Tell me again what you told the court," I said.

"How many times we been through that, Sheriff? I'm tired of talking about it to people got wax in their ears."

"All right, pour me one."

"I knew you'd see it my way, Cotton."

The keep slid off the bar, examined a glass in the dim light, decided it wasn't no dirtier than the rest, and poured some redeye in. The cheapskate poured about half a shot. I dug around in my britches for a dime and handed it to him.

"I owe you a nickel," I said. "Start with King Bragg coming in that night."

He didn't mind, or pretended he didn't.

"Oh, he come in here, and he was already loaded up. I could see by how he weaved when he walked."

"Why'd you serve him?"

"I make my living by quarters and dimes and nickels, damn you, and I'd serve a stumbling drunk if he had the right change. Hell, I'd even serve you, Cotton, even if it made my belly crawl. Just lay the change down, and I'll take it, and that's the whole story."

"You sure are touchy. How come?"

"I'll be just as touchy as I feel like, and I'm tired of telling you the story over and over. I ain't gonna tell it to you no more. You heard it, you've tried to pick it apart and you can't. Now finish up and get out. I don't want you in this place. It's bad for business."

Upward was polishin' the bar so hard it was pulling the varnish off.

But I wasn't quitting. "What did King Bragg say to them T-Bar cowboys?"

"He said—oh, go to hell."

"That what he said?"

"No, that's what I'm telling you. I'm done yakking."

"How many T-Bar cowboys was in here?"

"I don't know. Just a few."

"Was Crayfish with the boys?"

"I don't remember. You want another drink? Fifteen cents on the barrelhead."

The man I was talkin' about owned the T-Bar, a few other ranches, and wanted Admiral Bragg's outfit, too, just so he could piss on any tree in the county and call it his. His name was Crayfish Ruble. I don't know about that Crayfish part, but since I got Cotton hung on me, I don't ask no one about their first names. Not Crayfish, not Admiral. Crayfish Ruble had a southern name but I'd heard he was from Wisconsin, and who knows how he got a name like that. He come west with some coin in his jeans and bought a little spread, and then began muscling out the small-time settlers and farmers, paying about ten cents on the dollar, and pretty soon he was the biggest outfit in Puma County, and the T-Bar kept Doubtful going. Without the T-Bar, Doubtful would be a ghost town, and no one would know Puma County from New York City.

I sorta liked Crayfish. He was honest in his crookedness. Ask Crayfish what he wanted from life, and he'd not mince any words. He wanted all of Puma County, as well as Sage County next door, and Bighorn County up above, and half the legislature of Wyoming, along with the judges and the tax assessor. I asked him, and that's what he told me. I also asked him what else he wanted, and he said he wanted half a dozen wives, or a good cathouse would do in a pinch, and his own railroad car and a mountain lion for a house pet. He got no children, so there ain't nothing he wants but land and cows and judges and women. You sorta had to like Catfish. He was a plain-speaker, and he sure beat Admiral Bragg for entertainment. Catfish tried to buy out Admiral, but Admiral, he filed a claim on every waterhole and

creek in all the country, and that led to bad blood
and they've been threatening to shoot the balls off
each other ever since. There's no tellin' what gets
into people, but I take it personal. I gotta keep order
in this here Puma County, and I know from experience that when a few males got strange handles,
like Admiral and Crayfish, or Cotton, there's trouble a-percolatin' and no way of escaping it. The
feller with the worst handle usually wins, and I've
always figured Admiral is a worse name than Crayfish, and even worse than Cotton, though I'm not
very happy with what got hung on me.

Well, I was gonna go talk to Crayfish again, for sure.

"Sammy, I think I asked you a question. Was
Crayfish Ruble in here when the shooting started?"

Upward just polished the bar, like he didn't hear me.

"Who pays your wages, Sammy?"

I knew who. It was Crayfish. He owned the Last
Chance, but didn't want no one to know it, so the
name on the papers was Rosie, but she didn't have a
dime more than she could make on her back, and
someone put up a wad to buy this place, and it was
Crayfish."

"I get my pay from Rosie," he said.

I leaned across the bar and grabbed a handful of
apron and pulled him tight. I seen his hands clawing
for that Greener under the bar, so I just tugged him
tighter.

"Don't," I said.

"Who owns this joint?"

"Never did figure that out," he replied.

"You're a card, Upward. I think I'm going to look
a lot closer at this here triple murder. Somebody

shot three of Ruble's hands, and maybe it was King Bragg, just like the court says it was, but maybe it was someone else; you know who and ain't saying. And I'm poking around a little more until I got a better handle on it. This ain't makin' me happy."

Upward, he didn't like that none.